Praise for
THE GHOST TREE

"...ristina Henry's riff on classic small-town horror is full of
...d and dark magic, with themes that resonate heavily in
...ty-first century America. Henry's storytelling is her own
... of witchcraft."
—Christopher Golden,
New York Times bestselling author of *Ararat* and *Red Hands*

"...enry is able to keep all the strands of her spider's web
...oven together in a neat and concise way. . . . The end result
... a complex, interesting story that maintains suspense and
...trigue page after page after page."
—Sadie Hartmann, *Cemetery Dance*

Praise for
LOOKING GLASS

"M...erizing. . . . These somber, occasionally disturbing
no...s offer a mature take on the children's story but balance
the ...rors of the City with hope."
—*Publishers Weekly*

"Fans will delight in discovering the unknown family
backgrounds and future fate of Alice and her wild and
bloody Hatcher."
—*Booklist* (starred review)

Praise for
THE GIRL IN RED

"An engrossing page-turner that will delight anyone who loves running through thought experiments about the apocalypse."
—Paste

"With *The Girl in Red*, Christina Henry once again proves that retellings don't necessarily lack originality." —*Kirkus Reviews*

Praise for
THE MERMAID

"Beautifully written and daringly conceived, *The Mermaid* is a fabulous story. . . . Henry's spare, muscular prose is a delight."
—Louisa Morgan, author of *A Secret History of Witches*

"There is a current of longing that runs through *The Mermaid*: longing for the sea, for truth, for love. It is irresistible and will sweep you away." —Ellen Herrick, author of *The Sparrow Sisters*

"A captivating tale of an intriguing young woman who finds herself in the world of the greatest showman, P. T. Barnum. Original and magical, this is a novel to dive into and savor."
—Hazel Gaynor, *New York Times* bestselling author of
The Cottingley Secret

Praise for
LOST BOY

"Christina Henry shakes the fairy dust off a legend; this Peter Pan will give you chills."

—Genevieve Valentine, author of *Persona*

"Never wanting to grow up, never wanting anyone else to grow up, doesn't look like such an innocent and charming ambition anymore. . . . *Lost Boy* is a riveting story on its own, but it gets extra force from its questioning of what we used to take for granted. Heroes and villains: It seems we got them the wrong way round."   —*The Wall Street Journal*

"Multiple twists keep the reader guessing, and the fluid writing is enthralling. . . . Henry immerses the reader in Neverland and genuinely shocks. . . . This is a fine addition to the shelves of any fan of children's classics and their modern subversions."

—*Publishers Weekly* (starred review)

"This wild, unrelenting tale, full to the brim with the freedom and violence of young boys who never want to grow up, will appeal to fans of dark fantasy."   —Booklist

"Turns Neverland into a claustrophobic world where time is disturbingly nebulous and identity is chillingly manipulated. . . . A deeply impactful, imaginative and haunting story of loyalty, disillusionment and self-discovery."

—RT Book Reviews (top pick)

Praise for
ALICE

"I loved falling down the rabbit hole with this dark, gritty tale. A unique spin on a classic and one wild ride!"

—Gena Showalter, *New York Times* bestselling author of
The Darkest Promise

"*Alice* takes the darker elements of Lewis Carroll's original, amplifies Tim Burton's cinematic reimagining of the story and adds a layer of grotesquery from [Henry's] own alarmingly fecund imagination to produce a novel that reads like a Jacobean revenge drama crossed with a slasher movie."

—*The Guardian* (UK)

"A psychotic journey through the bowels of magic and madness. I, for one, thoroughly enjoyed the ride."

—Brom, author of *The Child Thief*

"A horrifying fantasy that will have you reexamining your love for this childhood favorite."

—RT Book Reviews (top pick)

Praise for
RED QUEEN

"Henry takes the best elements from Carroll's iconic world and mixes them with dark fantasy elements. . . . [Her] writing is so seamless you won't be able to stop reading."

—Pop Culture Uncovered

"Alice's ongoing struggle is to distinguish reality from illusion, and Henry excels in mingling the two for the reader as well as her characters. The darkness in this book is that of fairy tales, owing more to Grimm's matter-of-fact violence than to the underworld of the first book."

—*Publishers Weekly* (starred review)

CHRISTINA
HENRY

HORSEMAN

TITAN BOOKS

Horseman
Hardback edition ISBN: 9781789095975
Waterstones edition ISBN: 9781789099959
Export edition ISBN: 9781789098488
Trade paperback edition: 9781789098471
E-book edition ISBN: 9781789095982

Published by Titan Books
A division of Titan Publishing Group Ltd.
144 Southwark Street, London SE1 0UP.
www.titanbooks.com

First Titan edition: September 2021
This paperback edition: September 2022
10 9 8 7 6 5 4 3 2 1

A CIP catalogue record for this title is available from the British Library.

Printed and bound in Great Britain by CPI Group Ltd.

For all the butterflies

PART ONE

A drowsy, dreamy influence seems to hang over the land, and to pervade the very atmosphere . . . Certain it is, the place still continues under the sway of some bewitching power, that holds a spell over the minds of the good people, causing them to walk in a continual reverie. They are given to all kinds of marvellous beliefs; are subject to trances and visions; and frequently see strange sights, and hear music and voices in the air.

—WASHINGTON IRVING,
The Legend of Sleepy Hollow

1

Of course I knew about the Horseman, no matter how much Katrina tried to keep it from me. If ever anyone brought up the subject within my hearing, Katrina would shush that person immediately, her eyes slanting in my direction as if to say, "Don't speak of it in front of the child."

I found out everything I wanted to know about the Horseman anyway, because children always hear and see more than adults think they do. Besides, the story of the Headless Horseman was a favorite in Sleepy Hollow, one that had been told and retold almost since the village was established. It was practically nothing to ask Sander to tell me about it. I already knew the part about the Horseman looking for a head because he didn't have one. Then Sander told me all about the schoolmaster who looked like a crane and how he tried to court Katrina and how one night the Horseman took the schoolmaster away, never to be seen again.

I always thought of my grandparents as Katrina and Brom though they were my grandmother and grandfather, because the legend of the Horseman and the crane and Katrina and Brom were part of the fabric of the Hollow, something woven into our hearts and minds. I never called them by their names, of course—Brom wouldn't have minded, but Katrina would have been very annoyed had I referred to her as anything except "Oma."

Whenever someone mentioned the Horseman, Brom would get a funny glint in his eye and sometimes chuckle to himself, and this made Katrina even more annoyed about the subject. I always had the feeling that Brom knew more about the Horseman than he was letting on. Later I discovered that, like so many things, this was both true and not true.

On the day that Cristoffel van den Berg was found in the woods without his head, Sander and I were playing Sleepy Hollow Boys by the creek. This was a game that we played often. It would have been better if there were a large group but no one ever wanted to play with us.

"All right, I'll be Brom Bones chasing the pig and you be Markus Baas and climb that tree when the pig gets close," I said, pointing to a maple with low branches that Sander could easily reach.

He was still shorter than me, a fact that never failed to irritate him. We were both fourteen and he thought that he should have started shooting up like some of the other boys in the Hollow.

"Why are you always Brom Bones?" Sander asked,

scrunching up his face. "I'm always the one getting chased up a tree or having ale dumped on my head."

"He's *my* opa," I said. "Why shouldn't I play him?"

Sander kicked a rock off the bank and it tumbled into the stream, startling a small frog lurking just under the surface.

"It's boring if I never get to be the hero," Sander said.

I realized that he *was* always the one getting kicked around (because my opa could be a bit of a bully—I knew this even though I loved him more than anyone in the world—and our games were always about young Brom Bones and his gang). Since Sander was my only friend and I didn't want to lose him, I decided to let him have his way—at least just this once. However, it was important that I maintain the upper hand ("a Van Brunt never bows his head for anyone," as Brom always said), so I made a show of great reluctance.

"Well, I suppose," I said. "But it's a lot harder, you know. You have to run very fast and laugh at the same time and also pretend that you're chasing a pig and you have to make the pig noises properly. And you have to laugh like my opa—that great big laugh that he has. Can you *really* do all that?"

Sander's blue eyes lit up. "I can, I really can!"

"All right," I said, making a great show of not believing him. "I'll stand over here and you go a little ways in that direction and then come back, driving the pig."

Sander obediently trotted in the direction of the village and turned around, puffing himself up so that he appeared larger.

Sander ran toward me, laughing as loud as he could. It was all right but he didn't really sound like my opa. Nobody sounded like Brom, if truth be told. Brom's laugh was a rumble of thunder that rolled closer and closer until it broke over you.

"Don't forget to make the pig noises, too," I said.

"Stop worrying about what I'm doing," he said. "You're supposed to be Markus Baas walking along without a clue, carrying all the meat for dinner in a basket for Arabella Visser."

I turned my back on Sander and pretended to be carrying a basket, a simpering look on my face even though Sander couldn't see my expression. Men courting women always looked like sheep to me, their dignity drifting away as they bowed and scraped. Markus Baas looked like a sheep anyway, with his broad blank face and no chin to speak of. Whenever he saw Brom he'd frown and try to look fierce. Brom always laughed at him, though, because Brom laughed at everything, and the idea of Markus Baas being fierce was too silly to contemplate.

Sander began to snort, but since his voice wasn't too deep he didn't really sound like a pig—more like a small dog whining in the parlor.

I turned around, ready to tell Sander off and demonstrate proper pig-snorting noises. That's when I heard them.

Horses. Several of them, by the sound of it, and hurrying in our direction.

Sander obviously hadn't heard them yet, for he was still galloping toward me, waving his arms before him and making his bad pig noises.

"Stop!" I said, holding my hands up.

He halted, looking dejected. "I wasn't that bad, Ben."

"That's not it," I said, indicating he should come closer. "Listen."

"Horses," he said. "Moving fast."

"I wonder where they're going in such a hurry," I said. "Come on. Let's get down onto the bank so they won't see us from the trail."

"Why?" Sander asked.

"So that they don't see us, like I said."

"But why don't we want them to see us?"

"Because," I said, impatiently waving at Sander to follow my lead. "If they see us they might tell us off for being in the woods. You know most of the villagers think the woods are haunted."

"That's stupid," Sander said. "We're out here all the time and we've never found anything haunted."

"Exactly," I said, though that wasn't precisely true. I had heard something, once, and sometimes I felt someone watching us while we played. The watching someone never felt menacing, though.

"Though the Horseman lives in the forest, he doesn't live anywhere near here," Sander continued. "And of course there are witches and goblins, even though we've never seen them."

"Yes, yes," I said. "But not here, right? We're perfectly safe here. So just get down on the bank unless you want our game ruined by some spoiling adult telling us off."

I told Sander that we were hiding because we didn't want to get in trouble, but really I wanted to know where the riders were going in such a hurry. I'd never find out if they caught sight of us. Adults had an annoying tendency to tell children to stay out of their business.

We hunkered into the place where the bank sloped down toward the stream. I had to keep my legs tucked up under me or else my shoes would end up in the water, and Katrina would twist my ear if I came home with wet socks.

The stream where we liked to play ran roughly along the same path as the main track through the woods. The track was mostly used by hunters, and even on horseback they never went past a certain point where the trees got very thick. Beyond that place was the home of the witches and the goblins and the Horseman, so no one dared go farther. I knew that wherever the riders were headed couldn't be much beyond a mile past where Sander and I peeked over the top of the bank.

A few moments after we slipped into place, the group of horses galloped past. There were about half a dozen men— among them, to my great surprise, Brom. Brom had so many

duties around the farm that he generally left the daily business
of the village to other men. Whatever was happening must be
serious to take him away during harvest time.

Not one of them glanced left or right, so they didn't notice
the tops of our heads. They didn't seem to notice anything.
They all appeared grim, especially my opa, who never looked
grim for anything.

"Let's go," I said, scrambling up over the top of the bank.
I noticed then that there was mud all down the front of my
jacket. Katrina would twist my ear for sure. "If we run we can
catch up to them."

"What for?" Sander asked. Sander was a little heavier than
me and he didn't like to run if he could help it.

"Didn't you see them?" I said. "Something's happened.
That's not a hunting party."

"So?" Sander said, looking up at the sky. "It's nearly
dinnertime. We should go back."

I could tell that now that his chance to play Brom Bones
had been ruined, he was thinking about his midday meal and
didn't give a fig for what might be happening in the woods. I,
on the other hand, was deeply curious about what might set a
party of men off in such a hurry. It wasn't as if exciting things
happened in the Hollow every day. Most days the town was
just as sleepy as its name. Despite this—or perhaps because
of it—I was always curious about everything, and Katrina
often reminded me that it wasn't a virtue.

"Let's just follow for a bit," I said. "If they go too far we can turn back."

Sander sighed. He really didn't want to go, but I was his only friend the same as he was mine.

"Fine," he said. "I'll go a short way with you. But I'm getting hungry, and if nothing interesting happens soon I'm going home."

"Very well," I said, knowing that he wouldn't go home until I did, and I didn't plan on turning around until I'd discovered what the party of horsemen was chasing.

We stayed close to the stream, keeping our ears pricked for the sounds of men or horses. Whatever the adults were about, they surely wouldn't want children nearby—it was always that way whenever anything interesting occurred—and so we'd have to keep our presence a secret.

"If you hear anyone approaching, just hide behind a tree," I said.

"I *know*," Sander said. He had mud all down the front of his jacket, too, and he hadn't noticed it yet. His mother would tell him off over it for hours. Her temper was the stuff of legends in the Hollow.

We had only walked for about fifteen minutes when we heard the horses. They were snorting and whinnying low, and their hooves clopped on the ground like they were pawing and trying to get away from their masters.

"The horses are upset," I whispered to Sander. We couldn't

see anything yet. I wondered what had bothered the animals so much.

"Shh," Sander said. "They'll hear us."

"They won't hear us over that noise," I said.

"I thought you wanted to sneak up on them so they wouldn't send us away?" he said.

I pressed my lips together and didn't respond, which was what I always did when Sander was right about something.

The trees were huddled close together, chestnut and sugar maple and ash, their leaves just starting to curl at the edges and shift from their summer green to their autumn colors. The sky was covered in a patchwork of clouds shifting over the sun, casting strange shadows. Sander and I crept side by side, our shoulders touching, staying close to the tree trunks so we could hide behind them if we saw anyone ahead. Our steps were silent from long practice at sneaking about where we were not supposed to be.

I heard the murmur of men's voices before I saw them, followed immediately by a smell that was something like a butchered deer, only worse. I covered my mouth and nose with my hand, breathing in the scent of earth instead of whatever half-rotten thing the men had discovered. My palms were covered in drying mud from the riverbank.

The men were standing on the track in a half circle, their backs to us. Brom was taller than any of them, and even though he was the oldest, his shoulders were the broadest, too.

He still wore his hair in a queue like he had when he was young, and the only way to tell he wasn't a young man were the streaks of gray in the black. I couldn't make out the other five men with their faces turned away from us—they all wore green or brown wool coats and breeches and high leather boots, the same style as twenty years before. There were miniatures and sketches of Katrina and Brom in the house from when they were younger, and while their faces had changed, their fashions had not. Many things never changed in the Hollow, and clothing was one of them.

"I want to see what they're looking at." I whispered close to Sander's ear and he batted at me like I was an annoying fly.

His nose was crumpled and he looked a little green. "I don't. It smells terrible."

"Fine," I said, annoyed. Sander was my only friend but sometimes he lacked a sense of adventure. "You stay here."

"Wait," he said in a low whisper as I crept ahead of him. "Don't go so close."

I turned back and flapped my hand at him, indicating he should stay. Then I pointed up at one of the maples nearby. It was a big one, with a broad base and long branches that protruded almost over the track. I hooked my legs around the trunk and shimmied up until I could grab a nearby branch, then quickly climbed until I could see the tops of the men's heads through the leaves. I still couldn't quite see what they were looking at, though, so I draped over one of the branches and scooted along until I had a better look.

As soon as I saw it, I wished I'd stayed on the ground with Sander.

Just beyond the circle of men was a boy—or rather, what was left of a boy. He lay on his side, like a rag doll that's been tossed in a corner by a careless child, one leg half-folded. A deep sadness welled up in me at the sight of him lying there, forgotten rubbish instead of a boy.

Something about this sight sent a shadow flitting through the back of my mind, the ghost of a thought, almost a memory. Then it disappeared before I could catch it.

He was dressed in simple homespun pants and shirt, a brown wool jacket much like my own over it. On his feet were leather moccasins, and that was how I knew it was Cristoffel van den Berg, because his family was too poor to afford shoe leather and cobbled soles, and all of the Van den Bergs wore soft hide shoes like the Lenape people. If it weren't for the moccasins I wouldn't have known him at all, because his head was missing. So were his hands.

Both the head and hands seemed to have been removed inexpertly. There were ragged bits of flesh and muscle at the wrist, and I saw a protruding bit of broken spine dangling where Cristoffel's head used to be.

I hadn't liked Cristoffel very much. He was poor, and Katrina always said we should be compassionate to those in need, but Cristoffel had been quite the bully, always looking for a chance to take out his pique on someone. He ran in a little gang with Justus Smit and a few other boys who had no personality to speak of.

Cristoffel had tried it out on me once and I'd bloodied his nose for him, which earned me a lecture from Katrina on proper behavior (I was subjected to these endlessly, so I never bothered to listen) and a clap on the shoulder from Brom, which had warmed my heart despite Katrina's shouting.

I hadn't like Cristoffel, but he didn't deserve to die. He didn't deserve to die in such an awful way. I was glad Sander couldn't see. He had a delicate stomach and he'd have given us away by getting sick on top of the group below.

There were splashes of blood all around on the track. The men didn't seem to want to get any closer to the body, though whether this was out of respect or fear I could not tell. They were murmuring softly, too softly for me to make out the words at first. All of the horses pulled on their reins except for Brom's horse, Donar, a great black stallion three hands taller than all the others. He stood still, the wide flare of his nostrils the only indication that he was troubled.

Finally Brom gave a great sigh and said, loud enough for me to hear, "We'll have to take him back to his mother."

"What are we supposed to tell her?" I recognized this voice as Sem Bakker, the town justice. His shoulders were curled forward, as if he were trying to hide from what he was seeing.

I didn't have much use for Sem Bakker, who was always too hearty when he saw me and thought it was a fine thing to pinch my cheeks and comment on how much I'd grown. He had no children of his own and clearly had no notion of how children like to be treated. I did not like to have my cheeks pinched by anyone, much less the town magistrate with his dirty fingernails.

Brom didn't have much use for Sem Bakker either, whom he considered as lacking in basic common sense, something that ought to have been a requirement to be a justice. But then most people who lived in the Hollow were farmers or tradesmen, and had no desire to meddle in affairs of the law. Not that there were so many crimes in the Hollow, really—it generally amounted to little more than breaking up fights at the tavern and sending the offending parties home to have their ears burned by their angry wives—though now and then something more serious occurred.

All in all, though, the Hollow was a peaceful place to live, and was lived in by the descendants of the same people who'd founded the village. Strangers rarely visited, and almost never stayed. The Hollow was, in many ways, like a diorama in a box—never changing and eternal.

"We'll tell his mother what we know," Brom said, and I recognized the trace of impatience in his voice. "We found him in the woods like this."

"He's got no head, Brom," Sem Bakker said. "How do we explain about the lack of head?"

"The Horseman," one of the other men said, and I recognized the gruff tones of Abbe de Jong, the butcher.

"Tch, don't start with the Horseman nonsense," Brom said. "You know it isn't real."

"*Something* killed that boy and took his head," Abbe said, pointing at the corpse. "Why couldn't it be the Horseman?"

"Could be the damned natives," said another man.

I couldn't see his face because of his hat, and couldn't pinpoint his voice, either, though I knew everybody in the Hollow just as they all knew me.

"Don't start with that nonsense, either," Brom said, and there was a hard warning in his tone that would have made any man with sense back down. Brom was friends with some of the native people who lived nearby, though no one else in the village dared. Mostly we left them alone and they left us alone, and that seemed to be the best plan for everyone.

"Why not? They lurk around in these woods, taking any animals they want—"

"The animals are wild, Smit, anyone can have them," Brom said, and now I knew who Brom was arguing with—Diederick Smit, the blacksmith.

"—and we all know they've stolen sheep—"

"There's no proof of that, and since you're not a sheep farmer, I hardly see what it has to do with you," Brom said. "I'm the only sheep farmer for miles around."

"I don't want to hear your defense of those savages," Smit

said. "The proof is right here, before our eyes. One of them killed this poor boy and took away his head and his hands for one of their pagan rituals."

"Now you listen here," Brom said, and I could see him swelling with anger, his shoulders seeming to grow broader, his fists curling. "I won't have you spreading any of that around the Hollow, you hear me? Those people have done nothing to us and you have no proof."

"You can't stop me from speaking," Smit said, and though his words were brave and his arms were nearly as muscled as Brom's, I heard a little quaver in his voice. "Just because you're the biggest landowner in the Hollow doesn't give you the right to run everyone's lives."

"If I hear one word accusing the natives of this murder I'll know who started the rumor," Brom said, stepping closer to Smit. "Just remember that."

Brom towered over the blacksmith, as he towered over every man in the Hollow. He was built on a scale almost inhuman. I saw Smit's shoulders move, as if he considered a retort and then decided better of it.

"If it's not the natives that only leaves the Horseman," De Jong said. "I know you don't like it, Brom, but it's true. And you know, too, that as soon as word gets out about the boy's circumstances, everyone else in the Hollow will think the same."

"The Horseman," Brom muttered. "Why will none of you

say what's probably true—that someone from the Hollow did it?"

"One of us?" De Jong said. "People from the Hollow don't kill children and cut off their heads."

"It's a good deal more likely than the mythical Headless Horseman." Brom didn't believe in a lot of the things people in the Hollow believed in. It wasn't the first time I'd heard him refer to someone else's ideas as nonsense.

Even though everyone in the village attended church on Sunday there was a good deal of what the pastor called "folk beliefs"—and he shared some of those beliefs himself, which was unusual for a man of God, or so Katrina told me. It was something about the Hollow itself that encouraged this, some sense that there was lingering magic in the air, or that the haunts in the far woods reached their hands out for us.

Once, a long time ago, I'd stepped off the track close to the deep part of the forest. I remembered Sander going mad with anxiety, calling for me to come back, but I only wanted to know why nobody in the Hollow went any farther than that point.

I hadn't seen any witches, or goblins, or the Horseman. But I had heard someone, someone whispering my name, and I'd felt a touch on my shoulder, something cold as the wind that came in autumn. I'd wanted to run then, to sprint terrified back to the farm, but Sander was watching, so I'd quietly turned and stepped back on the track and the cold touch moved away from me. If Brom had known about it he would have been proud of my bravery, I think—that is, if he didn't box my ears for going where I wasn't supposed to. Not that he did that very often. Katrina was the one who meted out discipline.

"If you don't think it's the Horseman then it's not someone from the Hollow," De Jong insisted. "It must have been some outsider."

"No one's reported strangers passing through," Sem Bakker said.

"That doesn't mean they haven't passed through, only that no one was aware of them," Brom said, with that tone he always saved just for Sem—the tone that said he thought the other man was an idiot. "A man could cross these woods and none of us would ever know, unless a hunter happened upon him."

Sem flushed. He knew what Brom was doing, knew full well that Brom Bones thought he was a fool. He opened his mouth, ready to argue more, but one of the other men cut him off.

"Let's just return the boy to his mother," Henrik Janssen said. He was a farmer, like Brom, and his lands bordered ours. Some quality in Henrik Janssen always made me feel uneasy around him. "There isn't much that can be done right now. If it was the Horseman, then that is part of life here, isn't it? It's the risk we take by living so close to the edge of the world."

There was a general murmur of assent. This would seem callous in other places, other villages, but in Sleepy Hollow strange things were true, and sometimes those strange things reached out their claws. It wasn't that people didn't care; it was that they accepted horror in exchange for wonder.

"The boy's father will be a problem," Sem Bakker said.

This was a sideways reference to Thijs van den Berg's habit of drinking until he'd spent all his pay and left nothing for his family. He was the most volatile man in the village when he was in that state, and if he couldn't find a man to pick a fight with in the tavern, then he'd go home and pick a fight with his wife—a fight she always lost, being small and unable to stand up to his fists.

Every woman in Sleepy Hollow pitied his wife, but they never dared show it to her. A prouder woman than Alida van den Berg didn't exist in the village. I often heard Katrina and other ladies clucking over what they ought to do to help the family, before deciding that Alida wouldn't accept their help in any case.

These conversations always left Katrina with sad eyes, and me with an unaccountable need to comfort her—unaccountable because we were at odds over every other thing.

"In the meantime, the family has a right to mourn and bury him," Janssen said.

There were nods all around the circle from everyone except Brom, who scrubbed his face with his hands, a gesture that meant he was irritated, and doubly irritated on top of it because he wasn't allowed to express that feeling.

I felt my grasp slipping and gasped before quickly recentering myself, pushing my knees into the branch to keep steady. I was worried that the men might have heard me, but at that moment Brom unbuckled his saddlebag and pulled out a blanket for Cristoffel's remains. All the men's attention was focused there, and none of them looked around at me.

Brom knelt beside Cristoffel and carefully rolled the boy's body onto the blanket before tucking the edges so that none of Cristoffel was actually visible. All that was left of him—that boy who bullied other children and who was so poor that he couldn't afford shoes—was a sad little lump wrapped in cloth. None of the other men spoke, or moved to help him, and I felt an unreasoning anger at that moment. Whatever Cristoffel's failings, he'd been a person, and only Brom was bothering to treat him like one. Every other man only thought of Cristoffel as a problem to be solved or explained.

I wondered why most of them had bothered coming along. Then I wondered why the men had rushed out to this spot in the forest to begin with. Someone else must have discovered the body and reported it—but who? I assumed it was one of the men in the party, who would have been on horseback. Why wouldn't that person have done just as Brom had and wrapped the body up to return to the Hollow? Why had that person left Cristoffel on the trail?

A few moments later Brom mounted his horse, Cristoffel's

body cradled in one arm. The other men followed suit and they slowly filed away, their horses walking at a respectfully slow pace.

Only Diederick Smit lingered, his gaze fixed on the place where Cristoffel's body had lain. He stood staring so long that it seemed like he'd fallen into a trance. Finally, he turned his horse and followed the others.

My hands were cramped from holding on to the branch for so long and my back was covered in sweat, even though I'd been very still.

"Ben!" Sander said. He spoke in a whisper, as if he were still afraid of being heard by someone. His face was a pale blotch against the fallen leaves.

"I'm coming," I said, easing backward until I reached the trunk of the tree. Then I carefully swung down, my hands clinging to the branch, and grabbed the trunk with my knees so I could shimmy down. I dusted the bark off my breeches.

"Cristoffel van den Berg was killed by the Horseman!" Sander said, his eyes the size of Katrina's teacups.

"No, he wasn't," I said, trying to summon up the same contempt that Brom had used on the other men. "Didn't you hear what they were saying? Opa said it was nonsense."

Sander gave me a doubtful look. "Just because Mynheer Van Brunt says it doesn't mean it's true. I mean, everyone in the Hollow knows about the Headless Horseman, and what else could have killed that boy? It's not as if there are people roaming around taking heads for no particular reason. Only the Horseman does that."

I would not admit to Sander that what he said made sense. It was the first thought that had occurred to me, too, when I saw Cristoffel's body without a head. But if Brom said it wasn't true, then it wasn't true.

I felt too tired to argue with Sander, though. Cristoffel was dead and I didn't know how to feel about it, much less about the way he had died. We turned toward home in silence, each of us lost in our own thoughts.

When we reached the edge of the village Sander turned away toward his home—his father was the notary and the family lived in the flat above the notary office—and I continued on away from the village proper toward our farm. I wondered if Brom was home yet. I wondered if he would tell Katrina what had happened that day.

The Van Brunt property was easily the largest in the valley, partly because Katrina's father had gifted all of the Van Tassel land to his son-in-law when Katrina married Brom, and partly because Opa was a shrewd operator who was quick to snatch up any land that might go for sale nearby. As a result it was no short walk from the woods to my home, and by the time I arrived, I was sweaty as well as dirty.

I thought to sneak around to the kitchen and go up the servants' stairs—our cook, Lotte, was my sympathetic conspirator—but before I could, the front door swung open.

Katrina stood there, her eyes snapping, and I knew that she was in a towering rage.

"Where have you been? The singing master is here for your music lesson."

Music lesson. I hated music lessons. I hated the singing master and his breath that always smelled of licorice and the way he smacked my hands with a little wooden stick whenever I accidentally hit the wrong note on the piano.

"And why are you covered in mud?" she said, scanning me up and down.

"I was in the woods with Sander, playing Sleepy Hollow Boys," I said, looking at my boots.

"How many times have I told you?" she said, coming out on the porch and grabbing my ear. "You are not a boy, Bente, you are a *girl*, and it's high time you started acting like one."

I said nothing, only glared at her. I hated it when Katrina told me this one thing, the one thing that I never wanted to hear.

I had been born a girl, and if I was a girl then that meant I could never be the leader of the Sleepy Hollow Boys, never be the person everyone in town looked up to and respected just like my grandfather Abraham Van Brunt—that man known as the one and only redoubtable Brom Bones.

2

I was far too dirty to be allowed into the parlor, and the time it would take to bathe meant that the singing master had to depart without administering my hated lesson. I heard Katrina apologizing to him as I trudged up the stairs in my bare feet, my boots and socks having been deemed far too filthy for a civilized house and whisked away to be cleaned.

Katrina's chastising had left my face red, but I still felt slightly smug that I'd managed to squirm out of my hour with the singing master. It was especially well done as I had completely forgotten that it was Tuesday and therefore hadn't planned this escape at all.

The tub was carried up the stairs by two of the scullery maids, both of whom did not seem pleased at the extra work generated by the need to go down again and fetch water simply because I could not be troubled to behave like a proper female. I ignored their filthy looks. No one was ever going to make me be a female, not even Katrina. Once I was old enough I was going to cut my hair and run away and be a man in some place where no one had ever heard of me.

Katrina came up to my room while I was soaking in the hot water. I sank down so my face was half hidden and all she could see were my eyes.

"You can keep your tart looks to yourself, Bente," Katrina said, pulling one of the chairs to the edge of the tub. She gave me that special look that she reserved just for me, the one that said she was at the end of her rope. "I know that you don't like it, but you're far too old to run around and act like a wild thing. All the other girls your age know how to sew and sing and comport themselves with decorum in public."

I lifted my head so my mouth was above the water. "I don't want to sew or sing. I want to ride and hunt and learn how to be a farmer, like Opa."

"You can't be a farmer, Bente, but you might be a farmer's wife, like me. Is that really so bad?"

Trapped in the house. Organizing the servants and the shopping, planning parties and sewing circles and good works. Always squeezed by stays that were tied too tight, always suffocated by the parlor air, never to see the sun unless I was on the arm of a man escorting me to church.

"Yes," I said, shuddering. "It sounds terrible."

I saw a flash of hurt in Katrina's eyes, and I was immediately sorry, but then a moment later she spoke, and any regret that I had disappeared.

"It's too bad that you find it terrible because you are stuck with it. You're a girl, about to become a woman, and you will by God learn how to behave like one."

"No, I won't, because I'm not a girl," I muttered, and ducked my head under the water so I couldn't hear what she said in response. That didn't work out so well for me because a moment later Katrina fished me out by my braid.

"Ow!" I cried. She wasn't tugging all that hard but I wanted her to feel bad about it all the same.

She roughly unbound my hair, muttering in Dutch all the while. She often did this, resorting to her father's language when her temper peaked. She poured water over my head using the cup next to the tub.

"Your hair is dirtier than any of the animals' hair," she muttered as she soaped my scalp. "The pigs are cleaner than you, Bente."

My hair was long and thick and curly and always got in my way so I never combed or washed it properly, only wrapped it in a braid and stuck it under a cap in hopes that people would accept me as a boy. This would have worked anywhere except the Hollow, where everyone knew me and I knew everyone else. There was no hiding yourself in a crowd in Sleepy Hollow. We were a small and insular people—which was, very likely, the reason why Katrina was always so angered by my behavior. Everyone in the village knew her grandchild was unruly and unwomanly.

Then again, things had a strange way of coming true in the Hollow. If I stayed a boy long enough then everyone else might believe it.

My mother, Fenna, had apparently been the very vision of feminine beauty—fair and blue-eyed and always comporting herself perfectly, much like Katrina. My grandmother had quite admired her daughter-in-law, and always reminded me that I did not measure up.

I'd never met my mother. She and my father, Bendix, had died when I was very young. I had no memory of them at all, though sometimes I stared at the portrait of them in the hall downstairs and imagined I remembered their faces, smiling as they bent down to me.

I sulked while Katrina scrubbed my hair and face and fingernails. The condition of my hands was almost worse than my hair—there was mud embedded beneath the nails and half of them were torn and ragged from climbing trees. I suffered in silence as Katrina supervised the washing of the rest of me, and when I was through, she dumped a bucket of water over me to rinse. It was so cold that my teeth chattered and I glared at her as she rubbed me all over with a wool cloth to dry. The wool was rough, not finely spun like the thread for clothes, and by the time she was finished all my skin was as red as a summer tomato.

Katrina stood watch as I dressed, making sure I put on my shift and dress and stockings, and then she combed out my hair and tied it at my neck with a ribbon. My hair felt heavy and itchy, the strands curling loosely all around my face and neck.

"There," she said finally, surveying her handiwork. "You look like a proper girl now. Go downstairs and practice your reading."

"I haven't had my midday meal yet," I said. My insides were twisted up with hunger. I'd been out and about for most of the day, and now that I was still, my body reminded me that it had been some time since breakfast.

For just a moment there was a flash before my eyes, the sight of Cristoffel's dead body on the trail. But I put it away in the place in my brain where I kept upsetting things. I wasn't supposed to know about Cristoffel, so I couldn't speak of it with Katrina. Better not to think about it in any case. Better to argue with my grandmother about food and lessons.

"You missed it because you were out in the woods where you don't belong, so you can just go without until supper," Katrina said. "And no sneaking into the larder, either."

I stomped out of the room so she'd know how angry I was, just in case she hadn't already divined that information from my glare. *Practice reading? Go without dinner?*

It was unfair, horribly unfair, and she'd never think of doing it if she didn't consider me a girl. If I was a boy then I would be petted and indulged and allowed to do whatever I wished and to eat all the food I wanted, because boys must grow big and strong. Girls were to be lithe and slender like willows, with delicate white hands and tiny feet. Katrina constantly cut off my food at meals, because she said I ate far too much for one of my sex, and that if I kept eating I'd be an oak tree.

I did not see that it mattered how much I ate, because nothing on this earth was going to make me any smaller. I did not have delicate hands, or tiny feet. I was rather built on the same scale as my grandfather—taller than all of the girls my age in the village, taller than most of the boys, too. My hands were big and rough and my feet seemed to grow every three months, my toes pushing through the leather of my boots. I had none of the soft fat in my cheeks that other girls did. My chin jutted forward like Brom's, with just a hint of a dimple. My torso was straight, my legs long as a colt's. I would never look like the girls in the village, and part of my resentment toward Katrina came from her stubborn belief that if I only changed my ways, I would.

"You don't make enough of yourself, Bente," she would say, eyeing me up and down in that way that made me feel like a pig for sale.

And that's just what you are, a pig to be trussed and sold to the highest bidder when the time comes—some whey-faced boy with good prospects and no spirit, someone who will expect you to be quiet and biddable.

"Never," I said to myself as I went into the parlor and threw myself into one of the chairs. "I'll never bend for any man."

There were some tedious books of poetry stacked on the table beside the chair. I picked one at random and opened it, but my mind soon drifted back to what Sander and I had seen in the woods. Who had taken Cristoffel's head and hands? Why would a person do such a cruel thing? What purpose could it serve?

I heard the door from the kitchens open and close, and then a great voice boomed through the house. "Katrina! I've returned."

"Opa," I said, and dropped the very boring poetry to one side, running into the hall.

There he was, standing at the foot of the stairs, so huge and alive that he seemed to suck all the air out of the room. He turned when he heard me, and his great wide smile broke across his face and he opened his arms wide for me.

I hurled myself into them, because even though I was big, my opa was much, much bigger and he could still hold me like a child if he wanted. He squeezed me tight and I realized then that the sight of Cristoffel's sad little body had bothered me much more than I wanted to admit.

"And how's my Ben today?" he asked, putting me down and looking me in the eye. This was one of the things I loved best about him, that he always asked me questions and seemed interested in my answers, and that he gave me the same attention he would give any adult. "What's the matter, Ben?"

Brom always knew when something was bothering me.

I didn't want the one and only Brom Bones thinking I was weak, especially since I wanted to talk to him about Cristoffel. It would take some fast talking for me to convince him that I deserved the information in the first place, because as soon as Katrina found out what happened, the topic would be forbidden. Katrina always forbade anything interesting from being discussed around me.

"I'm just a little hungry and my eyes were watering," I said. This was ridiculous and I think Brom knew it, but he was also wise enough to know that my excuse meant I didn't really want to talk about what was troubling me at the moment.

"Go and ask Lotte for some bread and butter," Brom said. "She had some for me when I came in and there's still a bit of the loaf left from yesterday."

"She's not to go begging Lotte for a snack," Katrina said, coming down the stairs. "Bente isn't allowed anything until dinner."

Brom's face had broken out in his usual grin at the sight of Katrina, but that grin faltered as she spoke. He looked from her to me and back again.

"What's all this, Katrina? Surely Ben can have a piece of bread. We aren't so poor as that."

Katrina halted a few steps above Brom, just out of reach. I had the feeling that this was calculated, because Brom had a tendency to grab her and snuggle her until she saw his way. They were quite disgustingly romantic for old people. Stopping where she did meant that she wasn't going to allow herself to be distracted by him.

"Bente missed her lesson with the singing master," Katrina said.

Brom winked at me, but made sure his head was turned so Katrina didn't see. "Come now, my love, I was never one to enjoy music lessons myself. You can't blame Ben for not wanting to be stuffed in the parlor when there's only a few good days of autumn left before winter."

This was why I loved my opa more than anyone in the world. He *understood*. But Katrina—she didn't even try to understand me. She only wanted me to fit into her idea of the world.

"She's supposed to be learning how to act like a lady, Brom! It's her duty to learn music and comportment, not to run in the woods like a wild animal. She's too old for that."

"In the woods?" Brom asked, his gaze sharpening. "Where were you playing in the woods, Ben?"

It occurred to me that I ought to prevaricate, because if Katrina found out that I'd followed the men through the woods I'd be in even more trouble than I already was. Katrina cut in fast so I didn't have to lie.

"It doesn't matter *where* in the woods," Katrina said. "She's not supposed to be there at all! Didn't you hear a word I said?"

"Ben, go in the kitchen and ask Lotte for some bread and butter," Brom said.

He gave Katrina a meaningful look, the one he always gave when he wanted to talk to her alone. She didn't catch his meaning, though, because she was too angry to see it. All she saw was Brom contradicting her instructions.

I caught his look, though, and knew what it meant—that he wanted to talk to Katrina alone about what he and the other men had found in the woods that morning.

"I just *said* she wasn't to—" Katrina began.

"Thanks, Opa!" I cut in brightly, and ran to the kitchen before Katrina could finish. If I stayed quiet and stood right by the kitchen door, I might be able to hear what they said.

There was a little passage that connected the main foyer to the kitchen, and it ran at an angle so that if someone came through the foyer door they could stand unseen by anyone in the main room of the kitchen. I heard Lotte talking idly with one of the kitchen maids, their voices soft and punctuated by the occasional trill of laughter. Good smells drifted toward me—meat simmering in herbs, freshly baked bread—and my stomach rumbled. I ignored it. It was far more important to hear what Katrina and Brom had to say than to bother about food at the moment. I pressed the door open just a crack—it swung easily in both directions so the servants could push it open when they were carrying tea trays to and from the parlor—and listened, holding my breath.

". . . thank you not to undermine my authority with the girl, Brom," Katrina was saying. "Half the reason she's an undisciplined savage is because she knows you'll always let her have her way."

"Yes, yes," Brom said in a low voice.

I couldn't see them but I imagined him rubbing his hands up and down her shoulders, like he always did when she got in a temper. It occurred to me that Brom often treated Katrina like a recalcitrant horse that just needed to be soothed down with strokes and sugar lumps.

"I can't help it. She reminds me so much of her father," Brom said.

"Yes, and look at the end he came to," Katrina said. "If he'd been more cautious and less wild . . ."

She trailed off. I frowned. What was Katrina talking about? My father, Bendix—I was named for him, so that Brom could call us both "Ben"—and my mother, Fenna, had died of the fever that had swept through Sleepy Hollow when I was just a toddler. What did my father's lack of caution have to do with it? Nobody could help catching a fever. That was in the hands of God, or so the preacher always said.

"Katrina," Brom said, and there was a chiding tone now. "How can you speak so of your own son?"

She sighed, and it was a tired and sorrowful sigh—the same sort that she always gave me.

"In any case," Brom said, before Katrina could speak, "what you mention is important to what I want to tell you. Justus Smit discovered a body in the woods this morning."

Ah, that explains it. I'd wondered why the person who'd discovered Cristoffel in the woods hadn't simply taken the body back to the Hollow. Justus Smit was about my age, and I expect that when he saw the body he'd panicked and run straight back home. He might not have even discovered Cristoffel. Since they were friends there was a good chance Justus had been with Cristoffel when . . . well, when whatever happened had happened. And we didn't know what that was.

Again I felt a tickling in the back of my brain, a sense that I was forgetting something important. But then Katrina spoke again and all of my attention focused on the conversation I wasn't supposed to hear.

"What was he doing out in the woods instead of helping his father?" Katrina asked. "I thought he was acting as Diederick's apprentice?"

"I don't know why the boy wasn't at the shop," Brom said impatiently. "I don't keep everyone's business in my head like you do, Katrina. I just know that I was coming out of the notary's when Justus sped past with a face white as a cloud, and there was blood on his hands."

"So naturally you followed him and got yourself involved. You always have to be in the middle of everything, Brom."

"I do not."

"You do, but continue."

"Well, I grasped the boy by his shoulder and asked if he

was all right, and he told me that he'd come upon the body of another boy in the woods, but he wasn't certain who it was because the head was missing. I suspect he knew but was scared to say."

Katrina gasped. "The head was missing?"

"Yes. And his hands."

There was a clapping sound, and then Katrina's voice came out muffled. She must have covered her face with her hand. "Like Bendix."

I went rigid. *Like Bendix? Like my father? What was all this? How could a man who'd died of a fever lose his head and his hands?*

"It was Cristoffel van den Berg, Katrina," Brom said.

Katrina began to weep, and I heard the rustle of clothing that meant Brom had taken her in his arms. "Oh, his poor mother. His poor, poor mother," she said, over and over.

I felt a little sorry then that I'd been so mean to her earlier. I knew it was hard for Katrina. Every time she looked at me she saw the son she'd lost, and her failure to mold me into the young lady she thought I should be. I ought to be nicer to her, but it was hard when what she wanted for me and what I wanted for myself were so different.

I gently eased the door back into place so Katrina and Brom wouldn't notice, and tiptoed around the passage. Lotte, the cook, and Eliza, one of the kitchen maids, were at the long work table peeling potatoes for supper. There were two golden rounds of bread cooling nearby. Lotte looked up when I entered.

"Ah, Master Ben! What can I do for you?" Lotte said. Lotte treated me like a boy because I'd asked her to, and because she was my friend.

"Opa sent me to have some bread and butter—he said there was some of yesterday's loaf left."

"Well, Eliza and I just finished off that bit," Lotte said, "but you can have a slice of tonight's if you like. It's still warm from the oven."

"Yes, please," I said. Even if Lotte and Eliza hadn't finished yesterday's bread Lotte would have given me some from the fresh loaf. As I've said, Lotte was my friend and confidant, and she fussed over me like I was her little duckling.

"Keep on with those potatoes, Eliza," Lotte said, as she stood to fetch the knife and butter.

Eliza flashed me a sour look. I was not Eliza's friend and confidant. In fact, Eliza, like most of the servants, quite resented me. They generally saw me as someone who created more work for them—like the scullery maids having to drag water upstairs for my bath in the middle of the day—and at the moment it seemed Eliza was going to get stuck finishing off the potatoes by herself while Lotte tended to me.

This prediction came true, as Lotte spent the next quarter of an hour buttering my bread and making a cup of tea for me and then sitting and chatting instead of peeling root vegetables.

Eliza tried her best to burn holes in me with her glare but I was impervious. Anyway, Lotte was the head cook and she wasn't obligated to peel potatoes if she didn't want. She was perfectly within her rights to delegate the task to an underservant.

I did my best to stay bright and cheerful for Lotte, but underneath my mind was churning. Katrina had said my father died the same way Cristoffel had. Quite obviously that meant my father had not died of a fever at all, but why had no one ever told me of this? It was well-nigh impossible to keep a secret of any kind in the Hollow. And if my father had died that way—more than ten years ago—then why had it happened again? Did that mean they hadn't caught the culprit last time?

Of course they didn't, fool. If they had then everyone in town would know about it, and instead of talking about the Horseman when they saw Cristoffel, they'd be talking about my father and whoever hurt him. Unless it really was the Horseman.

After a bit Lotte got up and bustled around the kitchen, attending to the evening meal, and I grabbed an apple from the larder (still ignoring Eliza's burning resentment) and slipped out the back door.

The kitchen garden was only a few steps away, the summer vegetables mostly gone. The branches of still-green herbs nodded at me as I passed.

Beyond the garden were the great fields of the Van Tassel— now Van Brunt—land. Most of the summer wheat had been harvested, the golden blanket turned into rough stalks with no heads. Soon the hay would be collected, too, and sold to those with farm animals to be used as feed over the winter.

Beyond the wheat fields was a large green plot for the sheep. Brom had decided a few years ago that he wanted to be a sheep farmer, too. Katrina had thought him absurd but Brom had prevailed and they obtained a small flock.

Brom babied those sheep. Katrina accused him of treating the sheep better than he did most people. Brom said his method would result in superior sheep, and in the end Brom was victorious—as he often was. The wool from his sheep was exceptional, and so was the meat. He soon drove every other sheep farmer in the area out of the market—no one wanted their stringy mutton any longer.

This was the sort of behavior that generally led to muttering and resentment, but Brom was so good-natured that soon all was forgiven. He helped the few other sheep farmers into other professions, lending them the money to start new ventures. Of course, all money lent was returned with interest, and so the Van Brunt coffers grew fatter and fatter. People didn't give Brom enough credit for being smart. A fair number of folk in the Hollow dismissed Brom as an oaf who'd just gotten lucky in marriage, but Brom was as shrewd as they came.

I walked toward the sheep paddock, turning the apple I held over and over in my hand. I'd been troubled enough about

Cristoffel. Then Katrina had said that he was "like Bendix," opening up several troubling possibilities. I felt like my brain was running in six different directions at once.

Katrina and Brom had always told me my parents died of fever. If that wasn't true, if Bendix had been killed like Cristoffel, then what about my mother? Had she actually died of a fever? And did anyone else know about what really happened to my father, or was it a secret that only Katrina and Brom knew?

Bendix had died more than a decade before. Did that mean that the Headless Horseman had taken his head and hands, and Cristoffel's, too? Or did it mean that there was a killer hiding among the people of the Hollow, a killer who greeted his neighbors and traded vegetables with them and sat shoulder to shoulder with them in the tavern?

I walked and thought, not really paying attention to my surroundings. I was nearly upon the sheep paddock when I noticed that the sheep were crowded close to the fence, huddled together. When I approached they didn't move away, or bleat. They were in a great trembling mass, pressed together.

Is there a wolf nearby, or a fox? The sun was setting—more time had passed since I'd come home than I'd realized—and the glare made it difficult to see. I thought there was a silhouette at the far end of the field, though, close to the ground and near the scattering of trees that separated the Van Brunt land from the next farm.

I squinted in that direction, uncertain whether I actually saw an animal there or if there was just a glare.

The dark silhouette seemed to unfold—no, unfurl, sinuous and soft—and I thought *how can an animal stand like a man?*

My breath seized inside my lungs because just for an instant I thought I saw eyes looking back at me, eyes that could not be there because no human was there, no human could possibly have eyes like that—eyes that glowed, eyes that pulled, eyes that seemed to be tugging on my soul, drawing it out through my mouth.

I turned away, gasping and choking, and the apple fell from frozen fingers. I squeezed my eyes shut tight and whispered over and over, "There's nothing there. It's just your imagination. There's nothing there. It's just your imagination."

After a few minutes the cold fear was washed away by embarrassment. What if someone had seen me acting like that? What if Brom had caught me behaving like a silly little child imagining the boogeyman?

I straightened up and forced myself to look out into the field again. There was no silhouette.

Of course there's no silhouette, you stupid little nit.

The sheep bleated and puffed, though none of them moved away from the fence. Something still had them spooked.

The sun dipped behind the trees, so the glare was gone but the shadows were longer. I climbed up on the fence and stared hard at the place where I thought I'd seen the shape of a person.

There was something on the ground there, something white.

One of the sheep died. That's what set the rest of them off.

I considered running for Brom right away, but then I decided it would be better if I had absolutely correct information to give first. After all, I wasn't afraid. I was perfectly capable of going into the field myself.

My legs trembled as I swung over the fence. I forgot for a moment that I was wearing a stupid and impractical dress and the hem got caught on a nail and ripped.

I cursed silently. Katrina would make me mend it myself, and I was terrible at sewing no matter how careful I tried to be. She didn't believe I tried to be careful at it but I did, because if my stitches were sloppy she'd only make me tear them out and start all over again.

The sheep barely moved as I passed by. Even if the animals were disturbed by the dead one in their ranks, it was strange for them to act like that. Sheep are skittish by nature, and our sheep only liked Brom. They should have scattered the moment I stepped onto the field.

I crossed the grass, pretending my heart wasn't pounding like mad. I was not going to turn around until I knew what had happened out by the copse of trees.

The wind picked up, blowing my torn skirt around my ankles, and bringing with it the dry scent of fallen leaves, mixed with the dying grass (heavily manured by the sheep) and something else. It was the ripe smell of something freshly dead, a smell like blood and waste and sadness.

I was a farm child. I'd seen plenty of dead animals in my time, animals slaughtered for dinner or that died of old age. I wasn't afraid of dead things, but something in that wind made me pause.

"Stop being a damned baby, Ben," I said, and forced my legs to move forward.

The dead sheep was very close to the trees, so close that it seemed their shadows covered the animal like a cloak. All I could make out was a white-gray blur in the grass until I was nearly on top of it.

And then I stared, and stared, because I couldn't possibly be seeing what I thought I was seeing.

The sheep's head was gone. And so were its hooves.

There was an empty cavity at the neck, a huge and gaping thing, and I could see right inside at all the pink and red slippery bits pressed together.

But the strangest thing by far was that there was hardly any blood.

There was some, of course, bits of it splashed here and there. But nothing like the amount I'd have expected to see. There should have been a pool of blood, blood that would have gushed from the neck the moment the head was removed.

And really, I thought, but my thoughts seemed like a

faraway voice coming from someone else, *it's the same as Cristoffel. There was blood splashed here and there on the track near him, but the blood wasn't anywhere near the amount it ought to be, not if his head and his hands were taken.*

I couldn't stop staring at the beheaded sheep. It was absurd, really, something funny. Why take a sheep's hooves, never mind its head? I told myself it was a comedy but I didn't feel like laughing.

This had to be some prank, or maybe a warning. I remembered the way Diederick Smit had argued with Brom in the woods, and also that it had been his son who'd found Cristoffel in the first place.

What does it mean?

I dragged my eyes from the sheep's body to the copse of trees nearby. Was the person who'd done this still hiding there, watching and waiting to see what effect their actions had on us? Was Diederick Smit or his little brat of a son (he was a brat, really, a sniveling whining boy who'd run to an adult to tell if you tapped his shoulder and he didn't like it, but would be happy to bully anyone he thought wouldn't fight back) lurking out there?

I felt suddenly furious, and stalked closer to the trees. "Hey! Diederick Smit!" I shouted. "You won't get away with this, you hear? You can't frighten a Van Brunt!"

There was no response from the woods, no rustle of a person shifting uncomfortably, no responding call. But there was someone watching. I was certain of it. I felt the press of their gaze, of their interest, their . . .

Hunger?

The feeling was so strong, so absolute. There was something out there, and it was watching me, and it was hungry.

Then I heard a word drift to me, barely a whisper.

"*Ben.*"

I ran.

3

I didn't care if it was watching. I didn't care if Brom found out I'd acted like a coward. I ran, because I wanted to live another day and I was absolutely sure that if I stayed there another moment that I wouldn't.

The sheep did not scatter as I approached, as they normally would have. They stayed pressed against the fence in one great flock.

They know, too. They know it's still out there. They're afraid that if they move they will draw its attention, that the thing hiding in the copse of trees will return for them.

I clambered over the fence, heedless of my dress, and fell gracelessly into the dirt on the other side. Somehow I managed to stand again and run toward the house.

It was darker than I'd realized now, the shadows blue and long. The kitchen door opened and warm yellow light spilled out, followed by a slender, small silhouette. Katrina. I'd never been so happy to see her.

"Bente!" she called. "Bente!"

I ran toward her, unable to respond, my voice snagged on the fear choking me.

She saw me then, and I didn't need to see her face to know she was annoyed. "Where have you been? You need to practice piano before supper . . ."

She trailed off as I came into the light and she saw the tears in my dress, the dirt on my hands and face.

"For the love of . . . You only just took a bath, Bente! Look at the state of you!"

"There was—"

"What's the point of dressing you at all?" she raged. "I ought to make you go about naked so I won't have to go to the trouble of having new clothes made. And nobody's going to drag hot water up the stairs for you again today. You'll have to wash in cold."

"But there's—"

"I told you before that you need to stop acting like a wild animal, and you turn around and do the exact thing I asked you to stop doing," Katrina said.

She reached for my ear, ready to grab and twist and drag me into the house past all the kitchen staff so that I would be humiliated. I was already much taller than her, and it only worked because I'd always allowed her to do it. She was my grandmother and she'd raised me, and I'd always thought it best not to push my rebelliousness too far.

But now I was frightened and, yes, a little angry, because she never let me speak when I wanted to, because she was always chastising me for being myself, because any fool could have seen that I was upset and she didn't care—she only cared about my torn hem and the dirt on my hands.

So when she reached for my ear I pulled away so she couldn't touch me, and her eyes widened in shock and fury.

"You little—" she began.

I cut her off. "There's a dead sheep out in the paddock and Opa needs to come right away."

"That's no excuse for—"

"Right now," I said. "I'm not going in until he comes out. Something's happened."

Some quality in my face or voice finally broke through her rage. She narrowed her eyes at me for a moment, then said, "Eliza, go and fetch the master."

Brom would no doubt be at work in his study, his jacket removed and his sleeves rolled up, hunched over sheets of parchment that detailed the various concerns of farm life. Katrina and I didn't speak while we waited for Brom. She was gazing at me speculatively, as if she'd never seen me properly before. I stared back, unwilling to be the one who broke and looked away.

I heard Brom before I saw him, heard the low rumble of his voice and the heavy tread of his steps. Everything about Brom—not just his laugh—was like an approaching thunderstorm. You heard the noise in the distance and then suddenly he was upon you.

He put his hands on Katrina's shoulders and looked curiously over her head at me. "What's the matter, my Ben?"

I felt the terror then, the terror I'd been swallowing ever since I saw the shadow bending over the dead sheep. But the servants were peering avidly at us through the door, not bothering to disguise their curiosity, and I wasn't about to show fear in front of all of them. And not in front of Katrina, either.

"Can I speak with you a moment outside? You should bring a lamp," I said, and I was very proud of the way my voice didn't tremble.

It was so important that I show Brom that I was brave, the way he was. It was so important that he didn't see me as a foolish little child.

Brom cocked his head to one side, giving me his puzzled dog look.

"The sheep are upset," I began.

Katrina broke in. "Did you get your grandfather out of the study for this nonsense? Now is not the time to be worried about the sheep's moods."

I knew she loved me, she really did—and maybe I loved her, too, somewhere deep down, squashed underneath my resentment. But sometimes she made me so angry.

Brom read my face before I said something I'd regret later. "Now, my love, let's give Ben a chance to explain."

"Opa, can you just come with me? There's something I want to show you."

Brom seemed to decide it was best for me to get clear of Katrina before a war began between us, so he said, "I'll get a lamp," and disappeared into the kitchen.

Katrina and I waited, glaring at one another, each of us ready to snap at the least provocation. I decided I wasn't going to be the one who did the provoking. I, at least, would take the high ground.

Brom returned, gave Katrina a polite, "Excuse me, my love," and slipped past her, holding the lit lamp aloft. As soon as Brom joined me, I forgot about Katrina. The only thing that mattered now was what lay in the sheep paddock beyond.

It was almost full dark now, the sky the deep blue-black of early evening. Once we were out of Katrina's earshot I explained to Brom about the strange behavior of the sheep, and the corpse I'd discovered in the field that was missing its head and hooves.

He gave me a sharp look when he heard that, a look that became sharper when I thoughtlessly said, "It's just like Cristoffel, isn't it?"

"What do you know about that?" he asked, in a tone much sterner than he usually used with me.

Before I answered, he shook his head and said, "Never mind. Katrina said you'd been playing in the woods. You weren't by any chance with that Smit boy, were you?"

"Him? Of course not." I tried to inject as much scorn as

possible into my voice when I said this, but I was a little breathless. Brom took long strides, and I had to jog to keep up.

"Good. His father is a foolish bigot and he's training his son to act in his image."

For a moment I thought I'd get away without being told off. Then he added, "We'll talk about Cristoffel and just what you were doing in the woods later."

I grimaced. Katrina was sure to find out, and then I'd be in for it. He caught my expression in the lamp's glow.

"You're not in trouble, Ben," he said, and laughed. "Whatever you did, I'd be a liar if I said I wouldn't have done the same at your age. Or worse, probably. But there's, well, there's something else afoot, and I don't like to talk about it out here where anyth— I mean, anyone can hear."

We'd reached the sheep paddock by then, and I gave Brom a curious look. I was certain he'd been about to say "anything," not "anyone."

But that's ridiculous. Brom doesn't believe in spirits and ghosts like everyone else in the Hollow.

Brom raised the lamp high and took in the huddled flock.

"Whatever is the matter, my babies?" he cooed. "Did something frighten you?"

Normally the sheep bleated happily and crowded around Brom the moment he appeared, but that didn't happen this time. One or two let out low, nervous sounds, but they didn't shift or break out of their huddle.

"Where did you say you saw the dead one, Ben?"

I pointed. "On the far side of the paddock, close to the trees."

Brom swung his legs over the fence, one and then the other. I climbed on, ready to follow, but he shook his head.

"No, you stay here, Ben."

My face flushed. I was sure he wanted me to stay because he thought I was scared, and I was annoyed because Brom didn't usually act like that.

"I'm not afraid," I said.

"I know you aren't," he said. "But whoever hurt that sheep might still be out there. I don't want any harm to come to you. I lost your father. I don't want to lose you, too."

Brom almost never talked about Bendix this way. He told happy stories, funny stories, like he was trying to implant a memory of the father I'd never known. It gave me a little pang to hear him so melancholy.

"I'll be all right," I said. I couldn't stand the idea of being left behind to wring my hands, no matter what Brom's reasoning. "Anyway, why should you go out there alone if it's dangerous? You ought to have me to look out for you. Besides, I don't think whatever killed the sheep is out there any longer."

Brom narrowed his eyes, but I couldn't read his expression.

"Why would you think that?"

"Before, when I was standing out there, I felt someone watching me. I don't feel that now."

I didn't think it necessary to mention the strange figure I'd seen, or the voice I'd heard. Brom would only say it was my imagination, or worse—he might think I was frightened. And I wasn't. I was definitely not frightened.

Brom gave me a long look. When he looked at me like that, I always had the strange feeling that he was trying to peer behind my eyes and ferret out my secret thoughts. Maybe it was only that Brom could sense when I was holding something back.

"Very well. Let's hurry then. Your oma will skin us both if supper is ruined because they waited for us."

I clambered over the fence, heard my dress tear again and winced. Katrina was going to have such a time later enumerating all of my faults—and making me fix the dress.

Brom hurried through the field and I stayed beside him. The night pressed close outside the circle of lamplight. I heard the wind in the trees and the far-off cry of a fox. I shivered. Fox calls were disturbingly human-like, and it was easy to imagine I'd actually heard the cry of a person in distress.

Maybe I had. Maybe whatever had taken Cristoffel's head, had taken the sheep's head, was still out there. Maybe it was mauling another victim as Brom and I moved through the silence, soundless ourselves except for the rasp of our breathing.

It felt slightly shameful to admit to myself that I did feel safer next to Brom. He was so strong and so fearless it was difficult *not* to feel that way.

As before, I smelled the dead sheep before I saw it. Brom's steps slowed and he wrinkled his nose.

"God almighty," Brom said. "That reeks. No wonder the sheep are keeping away."

"I don't think the smell is the reason," I said, remembering the strange eyes on the figure in the field, but Brom didn't seem to hear me.

He sucked in a hard breath, and I followed his gaze to the dead sheep revealed by the lamp.

"Oh!" I cried, and took a few steps backward.

The sheep was decomposed beyond all reason. The flesh and skin appeared to have melted away, leaving behind the skeleton and organs. The organs were moving, pulsing almost as if they were still alive. I stepped closer and then jerked my head back as I realized they were full of tiny, wriggling worms.

"How can this be?" Brom murmured.

"It wasn't like this when I found it," I said. "I found it less than half an hour ago. This couldn't have happened in that time."

"No."

I glanced at him. He stared into the trees beyond, his brows knit together.

"Opa," I said, feeling unusually tentative. I wasn't certain I wanted to say what had just occurred to me, because it was too awful to contemplate.

"Mm?" Brom said, but I could tell his attention wasn't completely on me.

"You don't think . . ." I started, gulped, tried again. "You don't think this could have happened to Cristoffel's body, do you? His, erm, skin disappearing?"

That started Brom enough to tear his attention from the trees. "Why would you think that, Ben?"

"Well, whoever hurt Cristoffel did this, too, didn't they?"

"Don't make assumptions," Brom said. "This might be a prank. In fact, I'm almost sure it is. Which means that whoever did it is still nearby, watching to see how we respond."

"A prank?" When I saw the sheep at first I'd thought someone might be playing a trick. But now that it was this melted mess in the grass, that was harder to believe. Someone had—what? Killed the first sheep so I would see a fresh kill, and then swapped it out for a rotting one while I went to fetch Brom? That was more ridiculous than the strange being with glowing eyes I'd seen. I thought that if Brom had seen that figure he wouldn't be talking about a prank.

"Opa, I don't think—"

"Shh," he said in a low voice, and handed the lamp to me. "I hear someone out there, rustling in the trees. I bet I can catch them."

"Opa, no," I said, but he was already gone.

I stood still for a moment, wondering what I should do. Should I go after him? If I did, should I bring the lamp? Brom was obviously trying to sneak up on someone, someone I was not convinced was actually present.

If there *was* an intruder though, if all this really was a prank, then Brom wouldn't thank me for getting in his way. I waited, holding the lamp, tapping my foot nervously in the damp grass. The only sound I heard was my own heart.

Th-thump th-thump th-thump

I peered into the shadows ahead, searching for any sign of Brom, waiting for his enormous silhouette to loom out of the darkness, waiting to see his sheepish grin as he confessed that the noise in the woods must have been his imagination.

Th-thump th-thump th-thump

Why was my heartbeat so loud? I couldn't possibly be that scared. Brom had only left me for a moment, and I was far too old to be scared of the dark.

Th-thump th-thump th-thump

This was ridiculous. I was Brom Bones' grandchild, and I was just as brave as any boy.

Th-thump th-thump th-thump

That's not my heart. Those are hoofbeats.

A rider, approaching fast.

Something rolled over me, a cold wind rippling through the field.

Who would be so foolish to ride so fast in the dark? You could lame a horse that way.

Th-thump th-thump th-thump

A scent drifted in that cold wind, something stronger than the scent of the decomposing sheep. It was something like the smell of the night drifting through my open window when I was half asleep, or the smell of freshly turned earth. It was something like the first whip of autumn air cutting through a perfect summer day. It was something like the cold lump in the back of my throat when I woke from a dream and didn't know where I was. It was something like the dark closing around me, squeezing too hard and too tight.

Then I saw him.

But he wasn't before me. He was in my eyes and in my ears and in my heart, making my blood run, making it gallop like he was galloping, making me long to be where he was—free and fierce under the stars.

Then the spell was gone, as fast as it had come, and I was alone in the middle of the field, trembling.

"Brom," I whispered.

Brom didn't know what was out there. Brom didn't know *he* was coming.

"Opa!" I shouted. "Opa, come back!"

I knew Brom would hurry back to me, because I didn't sound like myself. My voice was high and thin and I was not Ben the brave, Ben the one and only heir of Abraham Van Brunt. I was little Ben, scared beyond all reason.

Why didn't Brom come? My opa had to know by now that there was nobody lurking in the woods, but *he* was coming. The hoofbeats were getting louder and louder and I didn't feel them in my heart anymore.

I heard them.

Th-thump th-thump th-thump

Closer and closer.

Th-thump th-thump th-thump

"Opa! Opa!" I screamed.

I started to run toward the copse of trees. What was he doing? Why was he taking so long?

"Opa! Opa!" I heard the rush of boots in the grass and suddenly Brom was there, looming. He grabbed my shoulders to hold me in place.

"Ben, what is it? Was there somebody here? Are you hurt?"

"It's him," I choked out, then grabbed Brom's arm and tugged. "We have to leave. We have to get back to the house."

"Who, Ben? Who's here? Was it Diederick Smit?"

I pulled his sleeve but he wouldn't budge. He was looking all around now for some sign of his enemy, some sign of the man he was convinced was behind everything. I wasn't nearly strong enough to force him to move if he didn't want to move.

"Opa," I said, nearly crying in frustration. "Please, please, we need to go back to the house now. Can't you hear him?"

"Hear who? I can't hear anything, Ben, except you."

He was looking for someone to punch, someone to lay low with his enormous fists. That was how Brom Bones had always settled things when people refused to be charmed by him. But there was nobody to take a swing at, no Diederick Smit waiting for a confrontation. There was only *him*, and even Brom couldn't manage *him* with his fists.

"Listen," I said. "Listen."

Brom cocked his head to one side. The hoofbeats were closer. *He* was nearly upon us.

"I don't hear anything, Ben. This isn't like you. What on earth is the matter? Are you spooked?"

I was so desperate to get Brom back to the house that I barely noticed the slight. I wasn't the kind to get spooked, and I'd never—under normal circumstances—want Brom to think that I was. But that didn't matter now.

Brom couldn't hear the hoofbeats, but I could. There was no time to stop to wonder why. We needed to get back inside the house. I needed for Brom to be safe. I pulled on his sleeve again, and this time my fingers slipped and I stumbled, falling on my back in the grass.

The stars wheeled above me and then Brom's face was there. Brom's arms curled under me and scooped me up like I was a little child again, like I was his tiny Ben the way I used to be, before I grew into a gangly almost-adult.

As soon as Brom had me in his arms I started to shake. He pulled me close and said, "Come now, it's all right. I'm sorry I left you alone."

That made me shake even harder, because I never showed weakness like this in front of Brom.

The hoofbeats were fading now, disappearing into the

distance. *He* was going hunting somewhere else. I felt something odd then, a strange mixture of relief and disappointment.

I want to see him.

(No, you don't. Only a fool would want to see him. The Horseman takes people's heads. At least that's what they say.)

And for the third time that day I felt that there was something I knew that I'd forgotten, only this thing was different from the feeling I had before. This wasn't anything to do with Cristoffel. This was about the Horseman.

(you've already seen him)

(seen him long long ago)

But I couldn't grab the memory, and it slipped away in the face of my terror.

Brom carried me all the way back to the house, and when Katrina tried to ask questions, he told her not to fuss and that I should go straight to bed.

Katrina sent one of the maids up with me, to wash my face and braid my hair and help me into my nightdress. I submitted with unusual docility. I didn't have the energy to fight, and my brain was hardly present in any case.

The maid watched me climb into bed and pull the coverlet up to my chin. I shivered and she placed an extra blanket over me before leaving.

I stared out the window. There was a large tree that grew close to the glass, large enough that I could climb onto one of the branches and shimmy down to the ground if I wanted.

The smaller, thinner branches sometimes brushed against the panes, and I normally found it comforting. But now it sounded like a haunt trying to break into my room, something with long fingernails scraping for entry.

I rolled over and put my back to the window, shutting my eyes tight, wrapping the pillow around my head to block out the noise. I tried not to think about the night and the branches and the window and the possibility of things that belonged outside coming inside.

The events of the day soon rolled in to replace the sounds at the window. There were two things I now knew for certain that nobody else did, and I didn't know what to do about it.

First, whoever—or whatever—had killed the sheep in the field (and likely also Cristoffel) was not the Horseman. The feeling I had when I saw the silhouette by the sheep was not the same as I'd had when Brom left me alone and I heard the hoofbeats.

For a moment I thought I heard them again—*th-thump th-thump th-thump*—but it wasn't hoofbeats. It was only the pounding of my heart, speeding up as I remembered.

The hoofbeats. Brom had always insisted the Horseman was nonsense, a product of the deeply rooted superstition of Sleepy Hollow's citizens. Now I knew he was wrong. I'd always believed Brom was right about everything, but he wasn't right about this.

The Horseman was real.

4

The next morning I woke with the half-sluggish, half-overexcited feeling that came from tossing and turning most of the night. I couldn't decide if I wanted to pull the covers up and go back to sleep or jump out of bed and run in circles. After a few moments watching a small brown spider make its way across the ceiling I decided to get up. I didn't really like spiders (though I'd never tell Brom this), and the thought of spending the day in my room with even a small one was unappealing.

I dressed in my breeches and jacket, knowing Katrina would scowl at me but beyond caring at the moment. Something had shifted between us the previous day, the balance of power tilting more in my direction. She was still unquestionably queen of the household, but I'd realized I didn't have to submit to her every whim.

My pant legs seemed a little too short as I buckled my belt. I was sure they had fit better the day before. My legs sprouted overnight sometimes and I'd wake in the morning with aching muscles and a sense that I'd turned into Jack's beanstalk. Every day I was taller than the other children in the Hollow, even some that were older than me.

Katrina had only indulged my desire for boys' clothing while I was young. Brom had said, "What's the harm?" and she'd been forced to give in, because Brom hadn't been willing to argue about it. She'd probably thought that I would grow out of the impulse before it was considered indecent.

Well, I hadn't grown out of the impulse and I was never going to. I was sure of that. However, after yesterday's argument, I didn't think Katrina would be inclined to indulge me any longer. I might actually have to learn how to sew just so I could make and mend my own pants. Katrina should be pleased if I took pains at some womanly art, at least.

As I dressed I tried to work out a plan of campaign for the day. I needed to do something constructive, but I wasn't sure what that might be. Talking to Brom was at the top of the list. I needed to know more about Cristoffel—and more importantly, about my father. It meant admitting that I'd eavesdropped at the door, but I hoped Brom would overlook that. The only two people I knew of who could tell me about Bendix were Brom and Katrina, and Katrina never revealed anything to me if she could help it.

Beyond speaking to Brom, I wasn't certain. Should I try to find out more about the sheep killer? I shivered, but then I stiffened my spine. I might have broken down the day before, but I was Brom Bones' heir. I knew what to expect now, and I wouldn't be frightened again.

My mind sheared away from the Horseman. That wasn't someone I wanted to consider at the moment.

I went down to the dining room, still thinking. Brom and Katrina would surely want me to stay out of the affair, but I felt responsible, somehow, to Cristoffel. I hadn't liked him in life but I kept remembering how sad and pathetic his body had looked, tossed like litter in the forest. Someone needed to care about him. Brom would care about finding the killer, I knew. But he wouldn't be thinking of Cristoffel while he did it. He'd be thinking of the Hollow, of the other people in town, of preventing another tragedy. Now that someone (*something?*) had attacked one of our sheep as well, Brom would take the business personally.

And there's Bendix, too. Don't forget about your father.

Brom was already at breakfast, shoveling in his usual mountain of food. Covered platters were set out on the table. Katrina was conferring with Lotte about dinner. There were a few bread crumbs on Katrina's plate and nothing else. I was sure my grandmother, always concerned about retaining her girlish figure, had eaten nothing more than one slice of toast.

I sat down, feeling unusually constrained. I couldn't bring up yesterday's events in front of Katrina, who would be furious if she knew I'd been in the woods near Cristoffel's body. I certainly couldn't discuss the matter while Lotte was in the room. Katrina would consider it personal business, and we never discussed personal business in front of the servants.

Katrina glared at me as I sat down, but she didn't say anything about my attire. I attributed her restraint to Lotte's presence. Lotte gave me a small wink.

I looked down at my empty plate, my cheeks reddening. Lotte meant well. Of course she did. But that wink meant that everyone in the household knew about Brom carrying me inside the night before like a little baby. I hadn't really considered the servants. I found it troubling that people in the household might have gossiped about me with one another, might have whispered about my trembling and shaking.

Brom tapped the back of my hand. I looked up.

"It's all right, Ben," he said, and smiled.

As usual, Brom seemed to know what I was thinking and feeling. He didn't seem disgusted by my display from the previous night, either.

I lifted the covers off the platters, piling food high on my plate. My heart felt lighter than it had been since Sander and I played Sleepy Hollow Boys in the woods. That seemed an age ago instead of the previous morning.

Lotte returned to the kitchen. Katrina immediately transferred her gaze to the quantity of food on my plate. She opened her mouth and I resigned myself to an ear blistering, but Brom gave her a look I couldn't read. She subsided, her lips pressed together so tightly that they turned white.

I knew she'd only keep her feelings in check while Brom was present, so I copied my grandfather's example and shoveled food into my mouth as quickly as possible. If I was lucky I could follow Brom out when he left to do his regular rounds of the farm. Then I'd have my chance to talk to him and to escape Katrina's beady eye at the same time.

I'd only managed about half my food when Brom pushed his own empty plate away and stood.

"I'm off, my loves," he said.

"Where are you going? Can I come, too?" I asked. Lotte would let me filch something from the larder later if I was hungry. I didn't need my breakfast. It was far more important that I speak to Brom.

"Not today," he said. "I have to go into the village."

Brom and Katrina shared one of their secret looks, the ones that spoke complete conversations in a glance. Whatever Brom was about, he didn't want me knowing about it. Or at least Katrina didn't want me knowing about it. That meant it probably had something to do with Cristoffel, or maybe even Bendix. If I hurried, I could follow Brom into the village.

I shoved a few more quick bites into my mouth, nearly choking on a sausage. Even if I couldn't go with Brom, I still wanted to leave the dining room at the same time. It was not in my best interest to be the only one left in a room with Katrina.

Brom kissed Katrina goodbye, and there seemed to be an unusual tenderness between them that day. Katrina laid her hand on Brom's cheek as he pulled away and he paused, the two of them lost in each other's eyes.

Revolting, I thought. *They're so old. When will they stop acting like newlyweds?*

Though really, I supposed they weren't *that* old. Brom was only fifty-two, and Katrina fifty. Like most people in the Hollow, they'd married very young—Katrina had just turned eighteen at the time—and my own parents had done the same.

That means Katrina probably thinks you're going to get married in four years, I thought, and shuddered.

Brom finally pulled away from Katrina and clapped his hand on my shoulder. "I'll see you later, my Ben."

"I'm going out, too," I said, washing my food down with some hastily gulped tea.

"Where are you going?" they asked in unison.

It was normal for Katrina to ask, so that she could tell me not to do whatever I planned to do. But Brom was another story. He never bothered to check where I was going or who I was going with, and he never seemed to think anything I was up to was in the least troublesome. I must have really worried him, acting the way I had the day before.

"Oh, just out to find Sander," I lied.

I had zero intention of finding Sander, because though I

had no concrete plans yet, I was sure that whatever I came up with would make Sander feel uncomfortable or worried. Sander was a natural worrier, and he had a bad habit of telling his mother things that ought to stay secret between us.

"You don't understand, Ben," Sander would say. "She looks at me and it's like I *have* to tell her, like she can see the truth inside me, and if I don't let it out, she'll be even angrier."

"That's a trick," I would say back. "All mothers do that—and grandmothers, too. Katrina tries it on me all the time."

I'd learned how to withstand Katrina's stare. I was sure Sander could learn to withstand his mother, too, if he wanted. He just didn't seem to try hard enough.

Anyway, I had no inclination to tell Sander about the dead sheep or the strange silhouette in the field. Those were things for me and Brom.

(or about the Horseman)

My brain slid away from the Horseman again. I wasn't ready to think about him yet. Even when I was ready, I didn't know if I wanted to share him with Sander. Whatever had happened the night before—that was between the Horseman and me.

(it's always been between the Horseman and you)

"Listen, Ben," Brom said. "I don't want you playing in the woods. The farm or the village, but not the woods."

"She shouldn't be in the woods in any case," Katrina said. "It's hardly a fit place for a young lady. I don't think you should be going out with Sander today. You have lessons that you never completed yesterday."

I gazed up at Brom in mute appeal. Nothing sounded worse at the moment than a day trapped in the parlor, plunking my fingers over the piano or learning how to make tiny, precise stitches.

"Oh, I think Ben's all right to go out with Sander, my love," he said, understanding my silent cry for help. "I just don't want them playing in the woods. Only for now, all right?"

I nodded. I didn't plan on playing in the woods.

"Promise?" Brom said, sticking out his hand for me to shake.

"I promise not to play in the woods," I said, letting his huge hand engulf mine.

"Take care of my Ben, all right?" he said.

He sounded unusually serious, which gave me a little spurt of guilt. I wasn't *lying*, not really. I'd promised not to play in the woods, and I had no intention of playing out there. Investigating, though—that was another matter altogether. Brom hadn't made me promise not to investigate, and my investigations might take me into the woods, but that wouldn't be my fault if so.

"Can I walk with you into the village?" I asked.

"I'm going on horseback," he said. "You can ride with me."

I wouldn't be able to talk to Brom on the horse. But I didn't have too many chances to ride with him anymore, because I was getting bigger and soon I wouldn't be able to fit behind him on the saddle.

Katrina followed us out to the front of the house, and the groomsman was already waiting for Brom, holding Donar by his reins, so I had no chance to bring up Cristoffel.

Brom swung into the saddle and then put his hand down for me, heaving me up with one arm. I wrapped my arms around him and leaned my head against his back. There was no place on earth where I felt safer than when I was with Brom.

He kicked his heels and Donar took off at a gallop, because Brom generally considered any pace slower than that a waste of time. I held tight and listened to Donar's hooves pounding into the dirt road that ran from the farm to the village.

Th-thump th-thump th-thump

Don't think about the Horseman.

The woods lined the right side of the road, and the opposite side was all Van Brunt land for miles, the fields full of ripening crops ready to harvest. After our farm there were a few smaller farms, but they all faced the woods. The woods closed off the Hollow from one direction, so that anyone approaching the village had to either go around them or through them.

The forest had always been my playground, the place where I built my dreams. Today it seemed gray and ominous, a secret hive of creatures that should not be.

That strange being, the one that was bent over the sheep in the field—that had to have come from the woods.

I remembered the way it seemed to whisper my name, and I remembered, too, the time I'd stepped off the path and all those eerie voices had called to me.

Is this creature, whatever it is, something from the place beyond the trail in the woods? The place everyone from the Hollow fears?

Nobody from the Hollow ever went beyond that place where the track ended. That was the realm of beings that we didn't want to disturb. If my idea was true, if the silhouette with the glowing eyes came from the deep woods, then why had it emerged now? Had someone disturbed it? Had someone disturbed the Horseman?

(Don't think about the Horseman)

We passed the cemetery on the outskirts of the village, a small fat hill dotted with stone markers. My own father and mother were buried there. I wished Brom would ride a little slower so I could ask him about Bendix. Beside the cemetery stood the church, sturdily constructed out of brick and mortar to withstand the howling winters that blew into this country. And just a little beyond the church and cemetery was the brook, and the bridge, and the place where Ichabod Crane had tried and failed to outrun the Headless Horseman.

When we reached the village, Brom slowed to a canter. Sleepy Hollow proper was nothing more than a single lane lined on either side with buildings of various shapes and makes, though most of them were one- or two-story wooden constructs. Offices and storefronts populated the first floors, and generally the owners and their families lived above. Sometimes, in lieu of a second floor, there was an addition on the back part of the building for the family quarters.

Very little about Sleepy Hollow had changed since its founding. It was like the Hollow was caught inside a soap bubble, or maybe a spell—always the same, never growing or changing. There weren't even that many visitors, generally—people sometimes passed through, but they rarely stayed. Any newcomer was like grit in the Hollow's eye, and the people of the village would rub at it until the grit was removed.

That had happened to the crane schoolmaster, I gathered. He came to the Hollow and couldn't find his place, and so he was removed.

By the Horseman.

(No, not by the Horseman, Brom said that the schoolmaster just left suddenly.)

Brom doesn't believe in the Horseman. Brom didn't hear him galloping last night.

Donar easily wended his way around the carts and people filling up the street. Brom halted in front of the notary's office. For a moment I wondered why he'd done this, and then I remembered that I'd told Brom and Katrina I was going out to find Sander. My friend was likely upstairs, helping his mother with his younger sister or reading, one of his favorite pastimes.

Damn, I thought. I only used one of Brom's favorite words in secret, because Katrina would wash my mouth with soap if she caught me cursing like that. *Now I'll have to ask Sander to come out and then find some way to shake him off. Although if I'm lucky he won't want to come out at all. If he's reading he might not want to.*

I couldn't understand why anyone would choose to be stuck inside with a book when there were trees to climb, but Sander always said that he went further inside a book then I ever did on my own feet.

"Thanks, Opa," I said, sliding off Donar's broad back and landing clumsily.

"I'll see you at supper," he said, and kicked Donar into a trot.

I half-considered following him to see where he went, but then decided there wasn't a good way for me to do this without Brom noticing. Still, I might be able to get away without Sander finding out I'd ever been here.

I darted away from the notary, in the opposite direction Brom had gone. Nobody seemed to take any notice of me. I put my hands in my pockets and my head down, avoiding the gaze of any adults on the boarded walkway. I had a vague idea of returning to the place where Cristoffel's body had been found. Perhaps there were some clues in the woods. Nobody from the search party had looked very hard when they'd found the boy's body the previous day.

What clues do you think that a monster would leave behind? If it was the same thing that killed the sheep . . .

Brom had thought that a person killed Cristoffel, though. So I would proceed in an orderly and logical manner. First, I would check and see if there was any sign that a person had hurt Cristoffel. If there wasn't, then I would search for signs that something inhuman had killed Cristoffel.

What if you encounter that creature?

"I'm Ben Van Brunt," I said to myself. "I'm not afraid of anything."

I nearly reached the edge of the village when I heard someone calling my name.

"Ben Van Brunt!"

A boy's voice. I recognized it without turning around. Justus Smit.

I rolled my eyes and turned, expecting him to be surrounded by some of his little toadies. Sure enough, two other boys our age stood on either side of him. I didn't know the other boys' names. Since I didn't attend the school in the village, I couldn't always remember everyone by sight.

"What?" I asked, making my voice as bored as possible.

He stalked toward me, his intent clear. Justus Smit was dumb as a post but he was strong from helping his father at the blacksmith's forge. Still, he was shorter than me, and slower, and he'd never managed to beat me in a fight yet.

"Your grandfather is spreading rumors about my father,"

he said. "Saying that my father is a fool, that my dad has got it in for those stupid savages."

"So?" I said.

I was sure that Brom wasn't spreading rumors but rather the opposite—trying to halt the spread of any idiocy that Diederick Smit might be trying to push around.

"So he has no right to do that! Just because your family is the richest in town doesn't give you the right to say and do whatever you want."

I didn't often think about the fact that we were rich, though I knew it was true. Brom tended to put most of the money he made back into the farm, and none of us dressed particularly fine.

I shrugged. I didn't have time for Justus Smit's petty disagreements at the moment. He was spoiling for a fight and I wasn't in the mood.

"What do you want me to do about it?" I asked.

He didn't say anything, just stood there with his hands curled up into fists. He was angry and didn't know what to do with it, or what to say. I braced myself, ready for the blow that was coming, and watched the other two closely. Justus had probably told them to hold me down while he punched.

"Well?" I asked again.

Justus let out an incoherent yell and charged toward me like a bull. I darted out of the way and stuck out my foot so that he tripped and flew off the sidewalk into the dirt.

I jumped off the walk and onto his back, pinning his arms to his sides with my knees. I grabbed the back of his hair and pulled hard, bending his neck backward toward me. He cried out, half in pain and half humiliation. I knew there was nothing worse for someone like Justus than being beaten by me.

"I think you should take your little friends and find something else to do with your time," I said.

"Bitch! Bitch!" Justus shouted. "Stupid Van Brunt bitch!"

I pushed his face down into the dirt. He shouldn't be using a word like that at all, and certainly not to me. I was a little shocked that he even dared. There was a horse apple just under his chin and he got a good mouthful of it as I squashed his head down.

"What did you call me?" I asked, pushing his face into the ground even harder.

Justus made some garbled noises.

"Bente Van Brunt!" A woman's voice, full of shock.

I looked up and saw Sarah van der Bijl, one of Katrina's friends. Her blue eyes were wide and horrified. The other two boys had darted off the moment that I tripped Justus. Apparently they hadn't accounted for the fact that I might fight back.

"You get off that boy this instant!" she said.

"No," I said. I didn't have to listen to Sarah van der Bijl. She would take this tale to Katrina, and Katrina would no doubt punish me, but I would submit to no authority but that of my own house. "He tried to attack me and now he has to pay."

Justus bucked underneath me, like a horse trying to throw me off, but I kept my weight on him and leaned down toward his ear, whispering so Sarah van der Bijl, that interfering busybody, couldn't hear.

"I hope this incident will help you reconsider taking your annoyance out on me in future," I said. I thought that sounded very grown-up, and also slightly menacing.

I lifted Justus' head out of the muck so I could hear his answer. "Goddamn bitch! I'll get you for this!"

Sighing, I pushed his head back into the ground. "Apparently we're going to have to continue until you learn your lesson properly. And until your language improves."

"Bente!" Sarah said again.

I heard the rustle of her skirts as she approached, but I wasn't concerned. She wasn't anywhere near strong enough to pry me off Justus. I just wished she'd go away. I didn't want to listen to her bleating at me. And the more she yelled, the more attention we would draw.

We were near the edge of the village, to be sure, and most of the people moving about were not nearby, but sooner or later one of them would notice. One of them might even go and fetch Brom.

Not that Brom will do anything about it, I thought with a smirk. Brom believed strongly that if you couldn't defend yourself in a fight, that was your own problem. He'd never chastise me for preventing Justus from beating me.

Sarah moved to stand in front of me. "Let that boy go, Bente Van Brunt."

"No matter how many times you say that name, I'm not going to listen to you," I said. "He tried to jump me with two of his friends. Three boys on one me—does that seem fair to you?"

I gave her my most limpid look. The effect was somewhat spoiled by Justus wriggling around, trying to escape my grip. I dug my fingers harder into his hair and he howled.

"That's not what it looks like to me," she said. "It looks like you're bullying this poor boy. I've told your grandmother time and again that she needs to take you in hand, but your grandfather lets you run wild like a savage. Well, why wouldn't he? He acted just the same when he was a boy and so did your father, but you're a girl and this isn't proper behavior for a lady."

I was only half-listening to her, having heard these remonstrations many times before from Katrina, but when she got to the "proper behavior for a lady" bit, I looked up.

"I'm not a lady. I will never be a lady. Now go away, Sarah van der Bijl. I have business to sort out with Master Smit."

Sarah's face purpled and I wrinkled my nose. She was going to start yelling.

So irritating, I thought. Grown-ups shouldn't involve themselves with quarrels between children.

"I saw it," a man said from behind me.

I twisted around. Schuler de Jaager, one of the oldest residents of the Hollow, stood a few feet away, his weight on the heavy wooden stick that he took everywhere. His gray hair was overlong and had a tendency to stick up in every direction, which lent him an air of dottiness even though his blue eyes were steady and clear. He looked like he was trying not to smile at us. Something about his appearance made me uneasy, though I couldn't quite put my finger on what it was.

"Saw what, Mynheer de Jaager?" Sarah snapped.

Schuler de Jaager walked closer and gestured at Justus Smit, who seemed momentarily resigned to his fate. He'd stopped bucking around, in any case. I didn't relax, though. I knew that Justus was probably waiting for me to do that very thing, to lower my guard so he could turn the tables on me, and I wasn't going to let him.

"That boy and his friends charged young Ben, here," Schuler said. "He was only defending himself, although I do think Master Smit's probably eaten enough horseshit for the day, don't you think?"

Schuler gave me a look that reminded me much of Brom's conspiratorial gaze. I thought about it for a moment, then nodded and jumped off Justus. I'd proved my point with Diederick Smit's son. I backed away a foot or two so that Justus wouldn't grab my ankle and knock me over. I had no particular desire for turnabout.

Justus lay still for a moment, seemingly stunned that he was allowed to go free. Sarah reached a handkerchief toward him, her manner so maternal that it made me sick. It wasn't fair that she was using up all her sympathy on a brat like Justus.

"There, now, let me wipe your face . . ." she started, but Justus knocked her hand away and jumped to his feet. His face was basically covered in horse poop from the nose down.

"Get away from me, you old hag!" he shouted and ran past her, away from the village and toward the woods, bumping his shoulder against hers as he did. She fell on her bottom in the dirt.

Schuler reached a hand toward her, much in the same way she had done for Justus. "No good deed goes unpunished, eh, Sarah?"

She glared up at Schuler, who lifted her up with more strength than his fragile-looking frame implied.

"Thank you," she muttered.

She gave me one last good glare—it was clear who she was blaming for the whole incident, no matter what Schuler said—and stalked back to the sidewalk, where she'd dropped a basket full of her shopping.

I felt a little awkward. I'd never spoken to Schuler de Jaager without Brom or Katrina around—it wasn't a natural thing for children to sit and converse with older people they didn't know. But he'd just defended me and I felt that ought to be acknowledged.

"Thanks," I said to Schuler. "For sticking up for me with Mevrouw van der Bijl."

"Oh, I've been looking out for three generations of Van Brunts. Most of the people of the Hollow aren't that fond of spirited folk like you," Schuler said. "You remind me of your father, and Brom, of course. Brom's still got twice the spirit of your average citizen, no matter how old he gets."

I felt the warm flush of pride that I always got from being related to Brom. There was just no one in the world like him. Then something Schuler said caught up to me.

"You knew my father?" I asked. It was rare that I heard from anyone who knew my parents other than Brom and Katrina. Sometimes it seemed there was a general agreement that no one besides my family would mention Bendix and Fenna except in the briefest of passing.

"Of course," Schuler said. "I've known everyone that's ever lived in Sleepy Hollow."

"What was he like?" I asked.

"Bendix?" Schuler's eyes crinkled, and some emotion flared deep in their depths, something I couldn't read. "Like Brom, only in miniature—a scamp, always raising trouble everywhere he went. Even his marriage didn't calm him— well, I suppose that's the same as the way marriage to Katrina didn't calm Brom any. Brom loved that boy more than anyone in the world."

Schuler gave me a sideways glance, and then he said,

"I expect you're wondering about Bendix now, especially since the Kludde has begun attacking again."

"The Kludde?" I asked.

"Yes. A Kludde killed that boy in the woods yesterday, same as it killed your father ten years ago."

5

I stared at Schuler. "The same as Bendix?"

He sighed—a very heavy, melodramatic sort of sigh. "I suppose Katrina insisted you hear that story that Bendix died of the fever, same as your mother."

"Yes," I said. There was something about Schuler de Jaager that didn't quite ring true—like he was performing a kind of theater for me.

I wondered why this might be so. It almost didn't matter, because Schuler de Jaager knew things, knew things that Brom and Katrina had kept from me. My heart was thrumming in my chest. Schuler de Jaager knew about my father. He could tell me what had happened, what had *really* happened.

And then I won't have to ask Brom about it, and hear that sadness in his voice like yesterday.

That had bothered me more than I wanted to admit. Brom was supposed to be impervious to feelings that other, more ordinary humans might have.

"Well, come along," Schuler said, gesturing with his stick.

"Come along where?" I asked.

"To my house, of course. Do you want to hear about Bendix or not?" Schuler said, gesturing at a tiny house tucked next to and just a little behind the last large building on Sleepy Hollow's main street. The house had a view of the church and the cemetery, and the infamous brook and bridge.

I gave Schuler a doubtful look. I didn't know him that well, and the deeply suspicious part of my nature didn't think it was wise to go off with him. What if he poisoned me? What if he hit me with that heavy stick he carried? What if he didn't really know anything about Bendix at all?

"I think you can overpower me, if it comes to that," Schuler said, and gave me a sly look, as if he knew exactly what I was thinking.

I flushed. "I'm not afraid."

"Of course you're not. You're Brom Bones' grandchild, aren't you?"

I knew he was manipulating me, because nothing worked on me like being connected to Brom. Still, surely this old man didn't intend me any harm.

But I wasn't about to relax my guard, in any case.

Schuler led the way to the small wooden cottage. I glanced up and down the main road. Nobody else was near. Nobody would know where I was going.

You can take care of your own self, Ben.

Still, I wished Sander was with me. I should have knocked on his door after all.

Although he probably would have run when Justus and his lot went after me. Sander doesn't like getting in fights.

I followed Schuler into the cottage, listening to the slightly ominous sound of his heavy walking stick banging against the wooden floor. It reminded me too much of the heavy thump of my heart, or the sound of hoofbeats.

Everything doesn't always come back to the Horseman. It wasn't the Horseman who killed Cristoffel, or the sheep in the field. Or my father.

The cottage was only one room. One corner had a heavy iron woodstove, and a fire was burning inside. Sweat dripped over the back of my neck and I swiped at it with my dirty jacket sleeve. The inside of the cottage was much warmer than it was outside, and there was a strange smell lingering underneath—a tang almost like rotting meat mixed with the sulfur of a freshly struck match.

Another corner of the cottage had a small wooden table with two chairs. Nearby was a shelf that clearly served as a pantry—there was a canister of tea, a basket of apples and a few other sundries. In the opposite corner was a bed and a large wardrobe. A door led out the back of the cabin—probably to an outhouse. There was a rocking chair beside the window that faced the road.

Schuler followed my gaze and he smiled. The smile, like

his sigh, didn't seem quite real. He was like a being who didn't know how people behaved and was trying to copy them. "Yes, I was watching from my chair. I would have been out to help you sooner but I don't move particularly fast these days. And that busybody Sarah van der Bijl can sniff out trouble faster than a dog sniffing out a rabbit."

Hearing him call Sarah a "busybody" was a pleasure, as no word described the woman better. But I still couldn't relax. There was something not right here, and I had to wonder if my desire for answers was overwhelming my common sense.

I hovered near the door as Schuler put a kettle on top of the woodstove. I heard the water sloshing around inside—likely he'd filled it up earlier in the day and was reheating what was left over.

He moved slowly around the cabin, taking down mugs and tea and teapot, carefully putting slices of bread and butter on a plate.

"Sit, sit," he said as he put the bread on the table. "I know young people are always hungry."

I looked at my filthy hands. Not even I would eat with them, and my standards of cleanliness were far below what they ought to be, according to Katrina. I wasn't sure if I should be accepting food from this man. Perhaps I could get away with not eating because my hands were unacceptable.

"There's a water pump out back," Schuler said.

I decided then it was best to be polite, drink some tea and

see if I could get my desired answers. I went out the back door and found the pump in between the cottage and the building next door. The water was cold but I scrubbed my hands under it until they looked more or less socially allowable and then wiped them dry on a clean bit of my shirt.

By the time I was done and back inside, Schuler had his tea all set up, with a mug for each of us and small plates for the bread.

I sat in the chair opposite, feeling unaccountably nervous again. It wasn't like me to feel nervous or unsure. But I'd never sat like an equal with any adult who wasn't part of my household—and even then, most of the adults in my household didn't treat me as an equal. I was, depending on the person, either their master or their ward. Neither resulted in balanced dealings.

"So," Schuler said, as I buttered some bread and stuffed it in my mouth. I was hungrier than I'd realized. "You'll want to know all about the Kludde."

I swallowed the bread. "I've never heard of a Kludde."

He shook his head. "That's Katrina's doing. She doesn't like the old tales. Well, I can't suppose I blame her—not when something out of the old tales killed her son."

My stomach clenched to hear Schuler talking so casually about my father's death. I wasn't quite ready to talk about Bendix, I realized. I needed a few moments—some more bread, some more tea, some more time to collect myself.

"She doesn't like the stories about the Horseman, either," I said. "Every time someone mentions the Horseman, she gets annoyed."

Why had I brought up the Horseman when I could barely acknowledge his existence to myself?

To my surprise, Schuler chuckled. "Ah, well, she's never quite forgiven Brom for not playing fair with the schoolmaster."

"The schoolmaster? The crane?"

"Ichabod Crane," Schuler said. "That was his name. And Brom thought the schoolmaster was getting just a little too cozy with Katrina, though any fool could see that she was only using Crane to make Brom jealous. Anyway, it worked—and Brom told Crane the story about the Horseman to scare him off."

"Yes, I know about that," I said. Everyone in the Hollow knew about that.

"Ah, but did you know that Brom rode out that very night dressed as the Headless Horseman, and that he gave Ichabod Crane such a fright that the schoolmaster ran from the Hollow and never returned?"

"Brom did?" I stared at Schuler, wondering if this was some kind of joke.

"Of course Brom did. Not everyone knows about that, naturally, and those that do have kept it a secret because Brom asked them to do so, and when Brom Bones asks you to do something, you do it. But Katrina sniffed the truth out of him. Women always find out the truth."

"So that's why Brom always laughs whenever anyone mentions the Horseman," I said slowly. "But it didn't anger the real Horseman?"

A startled look went across Schuler's face. It was half confusion, half something else—was it fear? It disappeared before I could divine his true feelings. "The real Horseman? There is no real Horseman. It was just a story, one that had almost been forgotten."

"No," I said. "The Horseman is real. I heard him last night."

"That might have been the Kludde trying to fool you," Schuler said. He had the same heavy accent as my great-grandfather Van Tassel, whom I barely remembered. He'd come from the low country long before the country we lived in was even thought of.

"The Kludde do that, you know. They're supposed to be wolves with wings, demons that pull children into water and drown them, but they can change their shape, become something else. They sometimes leap onto unsuspecting passersby and become heavy, weighting the person down until they die. It must be like drowning on land."

I didn't like Schuler's speculative tone. He didn't sound as horrified as one ought to be at the idea of drowning, on land or water.

"The Kludde can look like a wolf, or it can change into a

raven, a snake, a bat, a frog. It can be a tree that grows so high its leaves touch the sky. I'm sure that if it wanted to be a Horseman, it could. Some say the Kludde pretends to be human, even."

Was that all I'd heard the previous night—this Kludde creature that Schuler spoke of? No. When Brom left me alone in the field I felt something different from the feeling I'd had when I saw the creature bent over the dead sheep. That thing might have been Schuler's Kludde. But it wasn't my Horseman.

My Horseman, I thought, and my heart skipped a beat. It was a little fear and a little bit of something else, some feeling I was just barely beginning to recognize. The shadow of memory flitted across my brain again, and I had a vision of a dark shape on a horse, leaning down to me. Then Schuler spoke again, and the vision disappeared.

"The Kludde came here from the old country with us," Schuler said, his mind already moving on from the Horseman while my brain seemed to be caught in a loop, hearing the hoofbeats that echoed the pounding of my heart.

"But it lays quiet most of the time in the deep woods," he continued. "Sometimes, though, it wakes. It woke ten years ago, when your father died. And it has woken again, and it took that boy."

"But why does it wake?" I asked. "And what happened the last time it woke?"

"What happened besides it killing Bendix, you mean?"

"I wish you wouldn't speak of it so baldly," I said. "He was my father, even if I can't remember him."

"If I'm gentle about it will that make him any less dead?" Schuler said. "Are you interested in the truth or in your feelings?"

I glared at him and then, for lack of anything else to do, took a sip of tea. It was scalding and tears sprang to my eyes as I tried to swallow it instead of spitting it back into the mug.

"Fine," I said, because I wanted to know. "The truth."

"The truth is that I don't know for certain why it wakes," Schuler said. "Oh, don't give me that 'you've wasted my time, old man' look."

This was the exact look I'd been giving him, so I glanced down at my plate and busied myself buttering another piece of bread.

"It's nice to see a young person with a proper appetite," he said, watching me.

The way he watched me made my skin itch, made me long to run out the door.

He cleared his throat. "As I was saying—the Kludde. I don't know for certain why it wakes, but it seems it wakes intermittently, and chooses a victim."

"This has happened before? Before Bendix, I mean?"

Schuler nodded. "Many, many times."

"But why does nobody speak of it?" I asked. "Or why didn't everyone move away after the first time it woke? There was no reason to stay here. It's a wide country."

"Nobody speaks of it because the people here are superstitious, and they've accepted that living near a haunted wood is their lot. They believe that to speak of the Kludde will draw it to them, to bring bad luck upon them."

"How come you're talking about it with me, then?"

"I'm old now. I have no fear of nightmares any longer."

He sounded very tired when he said this, and he seemed much older than he had a moment before, but I was again struck by the feeling that he wasn't as tired as he pretended, nor as old. Nothing about Schuler de Jaager rang completely true, but there were hints of truth in his story. The truth was somewhere, if only I could dig down and find it. It didn't seem right for me to speak into the silence, so I waited. Then he shook his head and continued.

"As for why they didn't leave—well, you can't really understand. You're too young, and you've always lived here. But many of us gave up our lives at home for a chance in a new place, a chance to build something of our own. We crossed an ocean for that chance. We endured a war for that chance. And we staked our claims in this place because we found it good."

"But the Kludde . . ."

"Followed us here, and would follow us anywhere," he said firmly. "It was our haunt, and our responsibility."

"So you just accept it?" I asked.

"It only asks for one sacrifice," Schuler murmured. "It always only takes one. One every so often is a small thing."

I slammed my mug on the table with such force that the table wobbled. "It's not a small thing if it's your loved one who's taken. Have you no sympathy for the way Cristoffel's mother must feel right now, or the way Brom and Katrina felt when they lost Bendix?"

"Of course I do. I had a wife and child, once."

I hesitated, but the way he'd said this made it obvious that I should ask. "What happened to them?"

"Our daughter was taken by the Kludde," Schuler said. "And my wife died of grief. We had her very late in life. Very late. My daughter was about the same age as Bendix."

"I'm sorry," I said lamely. I didn't know what else to say.

"Don't be sorry for me," he said, his tone brisk. "I'm only telling you this so that you understand this is the way of things in the Hollow. The Kludde has taken its sacrifice, and while I'm sorry for the mother of that poor boy—she suffers enough with that husband of hers—I want you to know that it's over now. There won't be any more deaths, so there's no reason to sneak off to the forest looking for answers."

"How did you know I was going to . . . ?"

"Do I not know Brom? Did I not know Bendix? Aren't you just the image of them—lively, curious, interfering? I could tell by the way you were slinking out of the village with your hands in your pockets, hoping to be invisible."

I flushed, annoyed that he saw through me so easily. I was also annoyed because I realized the point of this meeting was not to give me the answers I looked for, but to warn me off seeking for more. Then my thoughts snagged on something else Schuler had said.

"You said the Kludde only takes one," I said. "One death, and that's it."

"Yes."

"But the Kludde—it killed one of the sheep at our farm. Last night," I said.

"How do you know it was the Kludde?" he said. "It could have been some prankster, or even a real wolf."

"It wasn't a wolf. I saw it."

He froze, then reached out to grab my hand so suddenly that I didn't have a chance to squirm away. He gripped my fingers hard enough to bruise.

"Hey!" I said, trying to yank my hand back.

"You saw it? The creature?"

His voice was low and intense now, and it frightened me. I wanted to leave, wanted to get away from Schuler de Jaager and his strange stories and moods.

"Let go of me," I said, but I couldn't pry myself free no matter how I tried.

"Answer me!" he said. I swore I saw a flare in his eyes, like a flame lit up there for a moment and then banked again. "Did you see it or not?"

"Yes!" I shouted. "Now let go of me!"

"How did you escape? How is that possible?"

He didn't seem particularly pleased that I managed to get away from the creature he called the Kludde. I didn't know what Schuler de Jaager wanted, but I didn't think my continued good health was a high priority for him. I picked up the mug of still-hot tea and threw it at his face. He cried out and released my hand.

I didn't wait for him to respond. I ran, ran from the table and from his cottage, as he cursed and called for me to come back.

Why had I followed him in the first place? I'd had a funny feeling, and I should have trusted it. I didn't know what Schuler de Jaager was up to, but I didn't think he really knew why all of this was happening. All that rot about a Kludde taking a sacrifice—that sounded like a lot of nonsense to me. And people in the Hollow loved to tell stories about ghouls and goblins and beasties that lived in the woods, and I'd never heard any of them mention a Kludde before.

I ran hard, knowing that Schuler wouldn't be able to catch me. I vowed there and then never to listen to him again. I'd find my own answers.

Anyway, he doesn't believe in the Horseman. He thinks it was only some trick of Brom's. But I heard the Horseman last night, and I know he's real.

My feet automatically led me to the woods, to the place where I could hide from everything and everybody. The woods had always been my sacred refuge, a place where I could be myself—Ben Van Brunt, not Miss Bente. I was nobody's miss, and never would be, no matter how Katrina tried.

I turned over everything that Schuler had told me—which, on balance, wasn't very much. It amounted to nothing more than a ghost story, really, and he hadn't given it any kind of flair at that. He'd had some plan of his own, drawing me into the cottage, but I couldn't for the life of me decide what it was. Was he only trying to amuse himself by claiming to know what happened to Cristoffel and Bendix? Had he meant some harm to me?

The whole encounter had been strange and disjointed, like we were players performing in two different plays.

Yes, I thought. *It was exactly like that, like Schuler expected me to have information that I didn't have, like I was speaking lines he didn't expect.*

There was nothing for it. I was going to have to talk to Brom about everything, and that meant I'd have to wait until Katrina was busy with some household occupation. Otherwise she'd try to nose in, the way she always did, and I'd never get any answers that way. She never wanted me to know anything. Look at how she acted when anyone brought up the Horseman.

My footsteps slowed. Something about the way Schuler had spoken about Katrina and Brom and Crane—something about that had seemed true. Had Brom really pretended to be the Horseman just to scare off another man trying to court Katrina?

It explained a few things—the way Katrina always pursed her lips whenever the topic came up, and the way Brom always laughed so knowingly.

But it doesn't mean the Horseman isn't real, for all of that. It only means that Brom pretended that one time. I know the Horseman is real. It's not my imagination.

But perhaps I would keep that to myself when I talked to Brom. I didn't want him to dismiss me. Brom didn't, as a general rule, but still . . . I wanted to know the truth about what happened to Bendix, and I didn't think bringing up the Horseman was the best way to find out.

I went to my favorite place by the stream, where Sander and I liked to play, and climbed up into my favorite tree—a large maple with lots of thick branches, perfect for nestling. I rested my back against the bark and breathed in the smell of the leaves, changing now from summer green to autumn red. The scent stirred something in me, and my heart went *th-thump th-thump.*

It was the same smell as him, of the Horseman. The smell of autumn leaves and dying things, the last gasp of summer before winter's grip closed in.

I was filled with an unspeakable longing, something I did not fully understand. I wanted to see him.

I wanted to ride with him.

My heart pounded like the rhythm of his horse's hoofbeats—*th-thump th-thump th-thump.*

I shook my head, hard. "Stop being foolish, Ben," I told myself. "You don't want to see him. He takes heads. He brings death with him."

And I didn't want to die. I didn't want to be a sad and empty husk like Cristoffel van den Berg. I didn't want Brom to crumple into grief, to age before his time. I had so many things I wanted to do. I wanted to live.

"Stay away," I whispered out in the forest. "Stay where you are."

The wind rustled the leaves, and I smelled the deep, dank scent of the earth, and thought I heard someone laughing, very far away.

6

I fell asleep in the tree. This wasn't the first time such a thing had happened, and given my tossing and turning the night before, it wasn't even a surprise that I drifted off so easily. But when I woke, the position of the sun told me it was very late in the day, which meant that I'd missed my midday meal at home and Katrina would be in a high temper.

She's always angry at you, anyway, I thought as I climbed down the trunk and landed lightly on the ground. *You can't do anything right.*

Usually I was philosophical about this, but I felt a little surge of anger. Why was Katrina so hard on me, always? I was her only grandchild, the only child of her beloved son. You'd think she'd be a little bit nicer, really. You'd think she wouldn't always be trying to find fault.

I kept to the woods until I was close to the Van Brunt land, because I didn't want to be spotted walking on the road. I'd had enough of interfering adults for one day. I was irritated with myself for getting so spooked by Schuler de Jaager earlier, too. My instincts were usually good, and they'd told me not to follow the old man, but I'd let myself be dared (a Van Brunt trait if there ever was one) and had followed him anyway. And what had I gotten out of it? Nothing whatsoever.

Despite the late hour I was strolling along, my hands in my pockets and my brain whirling. The wind kicked up behind me, sending a swirl of dead leaves around my ankles. A voice seemed to follow after, a low voice that didn't have any source.

Ben. Be careful.

I stopped, glancing behind me. There was nothing and no one there, only the watchful trees standing sentinel.

"Who's there?" I called.

No one answered.

"Right," I said, turning back in the direction of home, my temper surging. "I'm not falling for any more tricks."

I'd had quite enough of being frightened and making a fool of myself the previous night. If there was someone else out here with me, they were going to have to do a lot more than that to scare me.

The wind kicked up again, more insistent. The dead leaves whipped around my knees. For a moment it felt like the wind and the leaves were trying to lasso me, trying to hold me in place, to keep me from moving forward.

Ben, the wind said, and I shivered.

I paused, and the wind settled down again. This time I looked toward the deep part of the forest instead of along the path I'd taken, the one that ran roughly parallel to the road. My vision seemed to stretch and lengthen, tunneling into the shadows that were so far away I couldn't possibly see them. It had to be my imagination.

It had to be, because I thought I saw a figure astride a black horse, and the figure was made of shifting darkness and the light of the stars. His voice reached for me—as if his hands were extending out but couldn't quite touch.

Ben. Be careful. It's near.

I felt a chill all over, one that had nothing to do with the Horseman. The creature, the shadow—the Kludde, if Schuler de Jaager was to be believed—it was close to me. I felt its malevolence on the air, thought it wasn't meant for me.

Ben, the Horseman said.

"Yes," I said, so soft, for his ears alone, and I wondered at myself.

I wondered if I was falling under some sort of spell, if the Horseman was pretending to watch over me, pretending to care so that he could make me his own prey rather than letting me fall victim to the other monster in the woods.

Now isn't the time to think about the Horseman's intentions, Ben.

(and that's not how he is anyway he watches over you he's always watched over you)

The creature was near, but I didn't know where. I lifted my boots carefully out of the leaves, placing them down again in the dirt, avoiding anything that might rustle or crack. My breath was stuck somewhere beneath my ribs, unable to go in or out.

Then I heard it. A little ways up ahead there was noise, something that sounded like crunching.

I could avoid it. That was what the Horseman wanted. That was what the smart part of my brain screamed at me to do. I simply had to cross through the thin layer of trees that separated me from the road. I'd be able to run straight and hard for home and the nightmare in the woods would never know I'd been there.

But the curious part of me, the part of me that was so much Brom, wanted to know what the monster was doing. I needed to see.

I crept forward, and the wind circled around me again, dancing a warning.

"I know," I whispered, and waved it away.

The wind subsided but didn't disappear completely. It seemed like it was nipping at the back of my neck, irritating me like a mosquito on a summer night. I ignored it, because I couldn't afford to have half of my attention elsewhere. I was getting close—very, very close.

Maybe I could find out what the monster really was, because I certainly didn't believe it was this Kludde that Schuler de

Jaager had mentioned. Perhaps I'd discover that it was a person after all—some horrifically cruel person—just as Brom had said when they discovered Cristoffel's body.

I don't think it's a person, though, I thought. *I don't think people, even evil ones, leave this kind of feeling in the air.*

I crept closer and closer to the crunching noises. There was a hint of movement up ahead and I shifted so that I would stay in the protective cover of the trees. Whatever was happening was just ahead of me.

I glanced up. The branches above were wide enough for me to climb on. I clambered up, wincing every time I heard my clothes rustle against the bark, but the crunching noises continued unabated. In fact, they were joined now by . . . *slurping*?

It sounds exactly like the pigs at the trough when their morning feed is spread, I thought as I wiggled out onto a branch, much in the same way as I'd done the day before when I spied on Brom and the other men in the woods. Then I realized that I ought to have listened to the wind, and to the Horseman, that I might not want to see what the creature was doing, because if it was eating, then the thing it was eating was . . .

A person. A boy. A boy with a cruel, stupid face even in death. A boy who would never try to blindside me again.

Justus Smit.

And what leaned over Justus Smit? What gnawed at the

cords that bound Justus' neck to his body and sucked away all the blood that spewed forth?

I didn't know what it was. It didn't look the way Schuler de Jaager had described the Kludde, though. It didn't have a real form, but was made of shadows that seemed to writhe and contort, shifting into something larger, something smaller, but always something that had sharp, sharp teeth.

Justus' hands were already gone. My own hands gripped the tree branch so hard that I felt the curves of the bark digging into my skin, cutting through, making it bleed.

The creature stopped what it was doing, lifted its head, sniffed the air.

It looked up into the tree, directly at me. Its eyes seemed to glow, glow with an unholy light.

The blood, I thought, *oh, lord, it smells my blood*.

Then it smiled at me, and the smile was something horrible, somehow so much worse than anything else it had done, for its teeth were stained with the blood of the boy on the ground and there were pink bits of flesh caught in between.

"No," I said. "No, no. No."

I slammed backward to the trunk of the tree, not daring to look at the creature again. I glanced down long enough to make sure it hadn't darted to the bottom of the trunk and then I threw myself to the ground, landing hard. All the air blew out of my body but I scrambled up to my feet again and ran.

There was no wind to keep me company this time, no breath of the Horseman in my air. There was only my own burning need to stay alive, and underneath it my shame at being such a fool that I'd gone hunting for this creature.

If I can get to the road, I'll be fine, I thought, pushing through the wild tangles of brush, thorns pricking my hands, spiderwebs tangling in my face.

There was a drum of hoofbeats along the road.

Almost there, almost there.

I thought I felt long fingernails scrape across the back of my neck.

The hoofbeats were closer, closer, closer.

I pushed out of the brush and stumbled into the road, falling to my knees. The rider reined in his horse, who leaned back and pawed at the sky before clattering to a halt inches from me.

"Ben?"

I looked up in a daze. "Opa?"

Brom jumped down from Donar's back, reaching his hand down to help me to my feet. "What on earth are you doing? I could have killed you, you little fool, or someone else might have. What are you doing falling in the road like that? And I thought you promised me you would stay out of the woods."

"Opa," I said, pushing him toward the saddle. "Let's go. Please. Let's go now."

I could tell him about Justus Smit later, about everything

I'd seen. I'd tell him the truth, too—I wouldn't even try to pretend that I hadn't broken my promise. I only wanted him away, away from the horrible thing in the wood.

"What's the matter, Ben? You're acting strange. This isn't like you."

I took a deep breath. The creature hadn't appeared. Either it had decided that I wasn't worth following, or it had reconsidered once Brom arrived. So there was no immediate danger. The only way to convince Brom to take me seriously was to stop acting hysterical and start acting like myself.

"I'm sorry, Opa," I said. "Some, well, some very strange things have happened to me today. I'd like to talk to you about them, but can we go home first?"

He nodded, but then his face changed. He seemed to take in the dirt on my face, the cuts and scratches on my hands, for the first time. I saw his expression darken as he glanced toward the wood.

"Ben," he said. "Was someone chasing you?"

I couldn't lie, because I wanted to tell Brom everything later, and lying now would only put us on a bad footing. But I didn't want to say yes and have him go haring into the woods, ready to pummel someone in my defense.

"It's all right," I said, prevaricating. "They're gone now."

"Who was it?" he demanded.

"Please, Opa, please. I'll tell you all about it at home. I promise. But I want to wash and eat first."

He looked like he'd prefer to go charging into the woods anyway. Brom loved a brawl, and took any opportunity for one, even though Katrina told him he was far too old to still act like a rowdy boy.

Then I saw him come to his senses and remember that I was there, and that he was supposed to provide a good example for me. He sighed, and climbed up on Donar, and I climbed up behind, holding him tight.

I didn't look back at the woods, not once. I didn't want to see if anyone—or anything—watched us go.

When we arrived home, Katrina took one look at the state of me and visibly boiled over, screaming like a teakettle left too long on the fire.

I was given another bath, and another lecture, and stuffed into another dress all while Katrina ranted, half in English and half in Dutch. I kept my mouth tightly closed throughout. I wanted to talk to Brom, and I wasn't about to ruin that chance by arguing with Katrina and being sent to bed without supper.

I was sent into the parlor to work on embroidery while Katrina sat beside me and criticized every stitch. It wasn't long before I felt my temper rising.

Why won't she go away and leave me alone? I thought, seething. *It's almost as if she* wants *to make me angry, wants to see if I'll respond so she can find another excuse to punish me.*

After a while I felt my hands shaking, which didn't help the straightness of my stiches. I pressed my lips tight together and told myself not to rise, not to let her trick me into revealing something I didn't want to reveal.

Brom had disappeared as soon as we arrived home, and I imagined he was hiding in his study, far from Katrina's wrath. When she was in this sort of state she'd go after anyone for any reason. Even the servants gave her a wide berth.

When Lotte announced that supper was ready, I put my embroidery aside with more relief than I'd ever felt. Katrina ceased her ranting about my faults, my height, my slovenliness and my general lack of ladylike qualities. She usually had an idea that family business shouldn't be overheard by the servants, but everyone in the county had surely heard her that afternoon. I followed her into the dining room, wondering when I could find my chance to speak to Brom. If Katrina insisted on staying at my elbow for the rest of the evening, it would be difficult.

Brom was already at the table, though he politely stood when we entered. He pulled out Katrina's chair for her and dropped a kiss on her head.

As he sat down again, he asked, "And how was your day, my love?"

Katrina spooned a very small amount of potato onto her plate and did not answer right away. Lotte had cooked the potatoes my favorite way—sliced thin and fried in a pan with onions until the edges were crispy. I knew Lotte had done this because she'd heard Katrina going at me all afternoon.

I felt a surge of warmth toward the cook. I piled triple the amount Katrina had taken onto my own plate.

Brom was loading his own plate like he'd never eaten before, which is what he did at every meal. I hadn't eaten anything since the bread and butter at Schuler de Jaager's cottage—*what a disaster that was*—and took plenty of ham and applesauce to go with my potatoes.

"Must you eat like a feral hog?" Katrina snapped.

"I'm hungry," I said, and shoveled potatoes in my mouth before I said something I regretted.

"Let her be, my love," Brom said. "Ben's been out all day running around. Children get hungry when they're active, and it's not as if we don't have the food."

"Stop encouraging her. She's fourteen, hardly a child anymore," Katrina said, turning her ire on Brom. "It's because of you that she acts like a wild animal all day long. Did you know that your granddaughter was brawling in the middle of the village today, like some common boy?"

Ah, so that was it. Sarah van der Bijl tattled on me and Katrina's been waiting for the right time to chastise me over it.

I marveled that Sarah van der Bijl was so petty as to take the time to ride out to the farm just to tell tales.

Brom only raised an eyebrow at me.

"Justus Smit and two of his friends tried to ambush me when I was alone," I said. I didn't even look at Katrina. This information was for Brom alone.

Storm clouds rolled into his eyes. "Diederick Smit's boy? And what did you do to him, Ben?"

"He ran at me and tried to knock me over, but I tripped him so he fell in the street and then jumped on his back. I told him he should apologize for trying to attack me but he wouldn't, so I pushed his face into some horsesh— er, a horse apple."

(And he died later that thing killed him something in the woods ate him all up and I don't know what to do about it or how to say anything about it because who would believe it)

Brom threw his head back and laughed, and his laugh seemed to fill up the whole room. "That's my Ben. God, but I would have liked to do the same to the boy's father today. Ignorant fool."

Katrina slammed her hand on the table. "This is what I'm talking about, Brom! Must you undermine me at every opportunity? No wonder the child never listens to a word I say."

Brom immediately looked contrite. "I didn't mean—"

"It doesn't matter what you mean, Brom. It matters what you do. Someone has to marry this urchin someday, and nobody will if she doesn't learn to comport herself with some semblance of dignity."

"That's a long way off," Brom said, frowning. He didn't seem to like the idea of my getting married any better than I did. "She's only fourteen."

"She'll be a woman before you know it. Some of the girls I knew were married by sixteen."

Married at sixteen, I thought, and the food in my mouth suddenly tasted like ash. Married in two years? No. Brom would never let that happen.

"Why do I have to get married in the first place?" I asked. "Some people never marry."

"Of course you'll get married," Katrina said. "Don't be a fool. But at this rate whoever marries you will only want your land and fortune."

"No fortune hunter is going to marry my grandchild," Brom said in a loud voice.

"And what if she's a spinster, then? What if she sits in this house alone forever, turning to dust because she can't be bothered to learn how to sew or run a household or even clean her nails?"

I looked at my hands. They were covered in scabs from the thorns I'd battled through, but the nails were relatively clean for a change. I couldn't attribute that to any action of my own, though. Katrina had scrubbed them while I was in the bath.

Brom gave his own hands a critical look. "I can't say that cleaning my nails is my best quality, and yet you married me."

"You're a man, Brom! It's different. She's a girl, not a boy, and you need to stop treating her like one. You're not doing her any favors by pretending she's Bendix."

A spasm of pain crossed Brom's face, and I thought of what Schuler had said earlier—*Brom loved that boy more than anyone in the world.* I loved Brom more than anyone in the world, so I understood exactly how he felt.

"So what if he thinks I'm Bendix?" I said, my love for Brom making my temper finally bubble over. "I'm not a lady. I'm a boy. I'm going to grow up strong, like Opa, and like my father."

"That's it," Katrina said. "I'm throwing those trousers of yours in the fire. I should have done it sooner. And there will be no more running in the woods. You'll spend every day right here, in the house, studying and practicing music and learning all the womanly things you ought to have learned by now."

"No," I said, but one look at Katrina's face told me she was deadly serious. She'd had enough of me and now she was going to rein me in, a wild horse forced into a paddock far too small. I looked at Brom.

He didn't seem to have really heard what Katrina said. He was stuck in some memory of his own, his eyes far away.

He's thinking of Bendix, I thought, and even though I'd just said it didn't matter if he treated me like Bendix, I suddenly realized it did matter. I didn't want Brom to look at me and only see the shadow of his dead son. I wanted him to see me, exactly as I was.

"Don't go looking to your grandfather," Katrina said. "He spoils you, and I've had enough of it. From now on you'll listen to me alone or you'll suffer the consequences."

Everything inside me was a jumble—my love for Brom and my need to have him acknowledge me, my fear of the creature in the wood and the knowledge of what I'd seen, the strange feelings I had about the Horseman, my deep desire to have Katrina acknowledge that I was a boy, not the girl she wanted. It all spilled over, a great churning mass of feeling.

"You're a witch," I said to Katrina, my voice low and filled with fury. "I hate you. I hate you more than anyone in the world."

Brom started, and he stared at me in shock. Katrina's eyes widened, and I saw something in their depths that I never expected to see—hurt. Well, what did I care? She hurt me every day, tried to grind me into dust. She didn't care about me.

"I won't let you turn me into lady. I'm going to cut my hair and run away and live as a boy and you can't stop me, and that's what makes you really mad. You can't stop me from doing exactly as I like. No matter how hard you try to control me, I'll keep doing just what I want. Even if you make me sit in that parlor for the next six years I'll still do exactly as I like in the end."

"And where do you think you'll go?" Katrina said, the hurt receding as her temper reasserted itself. "Who would have you?"

The Horseman, I thought, but I didn't say it aloud. That stayed in the secret place in my heart.

"Nobody needs to have me. I'll make my own place," I said.

Brom looked like he wanted to intervene, but wasn't sure how. He reached toward Katrina, but she suddenly stood, her eyes flashing.

"Go on, then. Go if you want to go. I won't stop you."

Katrina never should have dared me. There's not a Van Brunt was ever born who could resist a dare.

"Fine," I spat. "Watch me."

I stood and ran from the table, knocking over my chair. Brom called after me, but I didn't listen. I hated Katrina. I hated her with all of my being. She wanted to craft me and mold me and put me in a place that she understood. She never wanted to see me—the me that I really was.

I ran upstairs, pulling off the stupid dress as I went, not caring if the servants saw me running about in my shift. My hair—bound in two long, thick braids—tangled in my clothes and I cursed it, cursed the stupid fashion for girls and women to have hair down to their bottoms.

But it isn't the fashion now, is it? Katrina got a paper from someone she knew—a relative in the City—and the pictures showed completely new hair styles and clothes, things that have never come to the Hollow.

There was something in that, some reason why it mattered that nothing ever updated or moved forward in the Hollow, some reason why the Hollow was out of sync with the rest of the world. But I was too angry and frustrated and sad and terrified to think why.

I told Katrina I would go and I have to, a Van Brunt never backs down from a dare, but oh that creature is somewhere out there and it knows me, and it doesn't wait for nightfall to claim its victims, either.

And then there was the Horseman. The Horseman seemed to help me, or at least wanted to keep me from the other monster in the woods. But I didn't like to think about why he was on my side.

I tugged on my trousers and jacket—they'd already been washed and neatly laid on the chair in my room—then I looked around, trying to decide what I would need if I went out into the world.

Something to keep warm, for certain. I took a thick wool blanket from the closet, but it was so bulky that it wouldn't be practical to carry. I didn't know how long I would have to walk until I found someplace safe to be.

One of the servants had carried my hated embroidery up to my room as well, along with all of its accompanying tools. Perhaps they were under the mistaken impression that I'd like to sew before bedtime, although any servant in this household ought to know better. There was a heavy pair of scissors in the sewing basket, and I laid the blanket on the floor and carefully cut it in half. Now it was the perfect size to be something like a long shawl or cloak, and the wool would keep me warm and keep the rain off.

Then I went to the mirror, pulled one of my braids away

from my head, and clipped it off just below my ear. The scissors were very sharp and the tip nicked my skin. A tiny drop of blood welled up, but I ignored it and clipped the braid off on the other side. The remaining hair on my head sprang into loose dark curls all over my head, free from the restraint of the braids. My hair was shorter than Brom's. Brom wore his in a queue that ended just above his shirt collar.

No one will think I'm a girl now, I thought. I threw the braids on the floor and stomped on them. No one was ever going to make me have long hair again, or wear a dress, or play the stupid piano. I was going to live my life my way. I was going to do whatever I wanted.

I felt the air on my nape and ran my hand over it, then stilled. There were three thin scabs there, running almost straight across the back of my neck, almost like I'd been touched by sharp claws.

That was your imagination. It didn't really touch you.

(But the night is dark and there are monsters in it and where will you go to keep the monsters away?)

I shook my head, trying to shake away these traitorous thoughts. I would find a way. I would build a house in the woods

(no not in the woods, nightmares live there)

and maybe I would become friends with the native people who like Brom, and they could help me find food.

How can they live near there with the monster in the wood?

I wondered. Perhaps it didn't terrorize them. Perhaps it was only that the monster belonged to the Hollow, had come with us from the old country, just as Schuler de Jaager said.

I don't think I should lay too much value on anything Schuler de Jaager said. The whole incident in the cottage had taken on the quality of a dream, a strange dream where nothing seemed to happen properly.

I had a blanket, and I'd gotten rid of my hated hair, and now all I needed was some food to see me through the next few days. Lotte was sure to provide in that regard, so I tied the blanket around my neck and prepared to sneak down to the kitchens.

I pressed my ear against my bedroom door, listening for the sound of anyone rustling outside or coming up the stairs. There didn't seem to be anything, so I slowly pulled the door open and peeked into the hallway.

There was no one. I tiptoed across the landing and paused at the top of the stairs. Brom and Katrina were arguing. I couldn't make out their words, but the rumble of their voices came from the dining room. That meant they would be out of my way and occupied and I could sneak into the kitchens without their noticing.

My heart gave a little pang then, because I didn't really want to leave Brom. Katrina gave me no pause whatsoever, but Brom . . . Brom had always been the sun and the moon to me. Brom had taught me how to fish and how to ride.

Brom had carried me up on his shoulders so I could reach the apples on the highest branch. Brom had always been there—smiling, holding his arms out so he could swing me up into the sky.

I didn't want to leave Brom, but Katrina was making me, so I had to go. He would understand. He was a Van Brunt himself.

I was halfway down the stairs when I heard an almighty clatter at the front of the house. It sounded like horses—maybe two or three horses—and men shouting. Then there were several hard knocks on the front door.

Brom emerged from the dining room a moment later, Katrina following behind him. Neither of them noticed me frozen on the stairs.

Brom opened the front door. I couldn't see who stood there, only that there was one man in front and one or two behind—from my angle on the stairs I could only make out their legs and feet.

A moment later, however, there was no doubt of the identity of at least one of the men.

"Where's your granddaughter?" Diederick Smit roared.

I saw Brom's shoulders swell, and Katrina went to stand beside him—a united front.

"What do you want with Bente?" Katrina asked.

"My boy is missing, and she's had something to do with it. I'm sure of it."

Stars swirled in front of my eyes, and then I saw again that terrible shape, the bloodied teeth, the blank dead eyes of Justus Smit. They hadn't found the body then. And I'd never told Brom about it, because Katrina had started screaming about the state of my clothes.

"Don't go making accusations," Brom said in a tone that would have sent any sane man running for the hills. "I warned you about that already."

"Yes, you threw your weight around the way you always do. Well, I'm not afraid of you. You can't control everything and everyone in the Hollow, Abraham Van Brunt."

"I don't have to control everything and everyone, Smit. But you should know that if you slander my family there will be consequences."

"Your little bitch of a granddaughter was seen mauling my son in the middle of the street today, and Justus hasn't been seen since. I want to know what she did to him."

Katrina stepped forward then, and I heard a hard crack. She'd slapped Diederick Smit across the face.

"You watch your language. That's no way to speak in front of a lady."

Privately I thought that slapping a man wasn't very ladylike behavior, and I felt a little swell of pride. Katrina wasn't always such a prig, after all.

I moved down the stairs, staying in the shadows. There were lamps set only at the bottom and the top, so I was able to creep low without anyone noticing me. There was enough from the candle Brom held for me to see Diederick Smit's face. He looked slightly chastened, though his eyes were small and angry.

"Yes. Of course. But it doesn't change the fact that your granddaughter is the reason my son didn't come home, and I want to talk to her."

"You'd better turn yourself around and go home," Brom said. "Nobody will be speaking to Ben tonight. Your son probably ran off and hid himself in the woods because he was ashamed that Ben got the best of him."

"Why, you damned—" Smit began, but another voice cut in.

"Come now, Brom. Be reasonable. All we want to do is ask the girl a question or two."

Sem Bakker. Another person that Brom hated. So far it was a collection of people practically designed for Brom to dismiss. Brom never listened to anyone he didn't respect.

I had to move, to speak. Diederick Smit was a horrible man and his son was a small-minded bully, but he needed to know. He needed to know that Justus was never coming home.

My legs were made of jelly. They didn't want to prop me upright anymore. I held on to the banister with shaking hands and eased my way down the stairs. I wasn't scared of Diederick Smit or stupid Sem Bakker. I was scared of the creature in the woods. I was scared that if I spoke of that horror aloud it would make it true. The scabs on the back of my neck tingled.

"It wasn't me," I said, stepping in the circle of candlelight.

Brom and Katrina turned as one. I saw Katrina's eyes widen in shock at my hair, but I hurried on before she said anything.

"I didn't have anything to do with Justus going missing," I said. "He ran away from me and Sarah van der Bijl and Schuler de Jaager. You can ask them and they'll tell you that it's true."

"Schuler de Jaager?" Brom said, an unusual sharpness in his voice. "What was he doing there?"

"He happened to see," I said, and took a deep breath. "But never mind that. Later I went into the woods and fell asleep in a tree, and when I woke up there was a strange noise nearby."

I remembered the crunching, the slurping, and shuddered.

"And?" Diederick Smit demanded.

"Let her tell it in her own way," Katrina said.

There was something in her face, something in the tightness around her eyes, something in the way her lips were so flat and bloodless.

She knows, I thought. *She knows, but Brom doesn't.* I did something I hadn't done in a very long time. I reached for her hand, and she took it, and gripped it tight.

"Your son is dead," I said. "There's a monster in the woods, and I saw it killing him."

PART TWO

On one side of the church extends a wide woody dell, along which raves a large brook among broken rocks and trunks of fallen trees. Over a deep black part of the stream, not far from the church, was formerly thrown a wooden bridge; the road that led to it, and the bridge itself, were thickly shaded by overhanging trees, which cast a gloom about it, even in the daytime, but occasioned a fearful darkness at night. This was one of the favorite haunts of the headless horseman; and the place where he was most frequently encountered.

—WASHINGTON IRVING,
The Legend of Sleepy Hollow

7

"You lie!"

Diederick Smit lunged for me, but Brom was too fast for him. Brom had been looking for an excuse to punch the blacksmith in any case, and he hit the man so hard that a moment later Smit was laid out on the front porch.

Katrina had moved in front of me as soon as Smit was in motion, and she stayed there, protecting me. The top of her golden head was just under my nose, and her hair tickled. I felt so much love for her in that moment that I thought I would burst. Little Katrina—my tiny, delicate grandmother—standing in front of her giant Van Brunt grandchild with all the fierceness of a mother wolf, and I had no doubt that if Diederick Smit had run into Katrina's fists instead of Brom's, he would have regretted it just as much.

I remembered then that Katrina used to sing to me when I was small, and that she would hold my hand as we walked outside and name all the flowers. When had that changed? When had she stopped doing those things? Or was it that I had changed, and started running when she tried to hold my hand, more interested in chasing after Brom than learning flower names?

I dropped my chin to her hair, and she reached back for my hand again, and squeezed it tight.

She didn't move from her place in front of me. No one was going to hurt me while Katrina was around.

Not that I was scared of being hurt, really. I could take care of myself. I wasn't scared of Diederick Smit, any more than I was scared of his son.

Sem Bakker glared at Brom while Diederick Smit lay stunned on our porch.

"That's assault, Brom," Sem said with an air of triumph. "And I witnessed it."

"No, you witnessed Smit charging at a helpless child and I defended her."

I resented the definition of myself as a "helpless child" but I appreciated that Brom was trying to gain the upper hand in the argument. Not that Sem Bakker was going to arrest Brom for anything. The idea was beyond laughable.

"It's not the time for petty disputes, Sem. And Brom is right—he was only defending the child." This was the third man at the door, a man standing just out of the circle of light. His slow, serious tone told me it was Henrik Janssen, our neighbor. It bothered me that he'd stood in the shadows this whole time, but I couldn't say why.

Diederick struggled to his feet, shaking off any attempt by Sem Bakker to assist him. Brom's punch seemed to have enraged Diederick more, rather than sobered him. His face was a horrible contortion of fury—eyes squeezed into slits, lips pulled back into a snarl. He started toward the door but Brom blocked it with his body. Diederick shouted at me over Brom's shoulder.

"What did you do to my Justus? What did you do to him?"

"I didn't do anything," I said, then guiltily remembered pushing his face into the horseshit. It wasn't the time for those sorts of confessions, though. "I told you—I saw something in the woods. A monster."

"The Horseman?" Henrik Janssen asked.

"It's not the damned Horseman," Brom said, his tone laced with disgust. "How many times do I have to say it?"

I realized then that at least one thing Schuler de Jaager had said was true—Brom had pretended to be the Horseman once, and this was why he always treated any mention of the Horseman with so much contempt. How could he not? To admit that the Horseman was pantomime would be to put his own self under suspicion for any crime attributed to the Horseman.

"It wasn't the Horseman," I said. "It was . . . something else. Something horrible."

Brom gave me a strange look. "Are you sure you saw what you think you saw, Ben?"

"I wouldn't lie," I said, stung. I had many faults—Katrina

had listed them all for me that very day—but I would never tell a lie about something this important. I wouldn't let a parent think their child was dead if it wasn't true.

"Of course not. But you said you were asleep in the tree—perhaps you had a nightmare, and it scared you? You'd just had a fight with Justus and there was the sheep yesterday . . ." He trailed off.

"It wasn't a bad dream," I said. "It happened just as I said. When you found me, Opa, on the road—I was running from it."

I said this last in a very tiny voice. I was so ashamed to admit to Brom that I'd run from anything.

"If all this is true then why didn't you say anything earlier, girl?" Sem Bakker said. I hated the way he called me "girl," like I didn't have a name, like that was what I was. "Why didn't you raise the alarm?"

"I was going to. I was going to tell Opa."

"And?"

"And some other things happened," I said. No need to air our family business in front of these men. "I wanted to tell him quietly, when there was no one else around."

Sem Bakker's mouth twisted in disgust. "If you'd spoken right away, we might have been able to find the boy in time to save him."

"No," I said. "No, Justus was already dead when I saw him. The monster—it was . . ."

I didn't know if I wanted to explain exactly what the monster was doing to Justus Smit's father. It didn't seem like the kind of thing you'd want to know about your child.

"Well?" Sem Bakker demanded. "Tell us just what the *monster* was doing."

It was clear that he didn't really believe me, or that he might even believe that I had something to do with Justus' death. Bakker was such a puffy little rooster at the moment that I wanted badly to punch him the way Brom had punched Diederick. Perhaps that was the problem with us Van Brunts. We hit first and talked only when necessary.

"It was eating Justus' head," I said. "And his hands were already gone. Just like Cristoffel van den Berg."

Diederick stared at me. "Like Cristoffel?"

"Yes."

He shook his head from side to side, like a dog trying to dislodge a flea. "You lie."

I stepped out of Katrina's shadow then, my hands curled into fists. "I'm tired of being called a liar. Get on your horse and I'll take you to your son, and you can see what's left of him."

I should have had more sympathy for him. He was a parent. His child had been taken from him. But I was exhausted and scared and I didn't like any of the Smits anyway.

Brom gave me a long look, then said, "I'll bring Donar around, and we'll go and see."

"Fine," Sem Bakker said, and herded the other men off the porch.

Henrik Janssen stood there for a moment, giving me a thoughtful and too-interested stare, before following the other two. I wondered what he was doing there in the first place. It made sense for Diederick Smit to call for Sem Bakker's help, but Janssen didn't live in town.

Brom shut the door behind them and said, "I'm going to get my horse. You wait in the front, Ben."

He took his coat from the hook, picked up his boots, and went through to the back of the house. The stables were closer to the kitchen entrance.

Katrina grabbed my arm, her face white. She spoke in a low voice for my ears only. "You can't go out there. Not if it's back again. I can't—I can't—"

To my horror her blue eyes filled up with tears. I never really knew what to do with tears, my own or anyone else's. But I knew what she was afraid of. I knew a lot of things about Katrina all of a sudden, things that I'd never wanted to see or acknowledge because they conflicted with things I wanted. It was so much easier to pretend that it was always her who didn't understand me and not the other way around. I'd never tried meeting her halfway, either.

"It won't be like my father," I said, pressing my forehead to hers. "I'll be with Opa, and the other men. Even if Sem Bakker is useless."

She choked out a laugh, swiping at her tears with an impatient hand. "You're so much like Brom."

"I've only ever wanted to be like Brom," I said softly. "I'm sorry that it makes you sad."

She reached up and stroked her hands over the remains of my hair. "Your beautiful hair."

"Come now, Oma. Even you have to admit that I wasn't very good at keeping it nice, and you aren't going to brush my hair for the rest of my life."

Her fingers caught one of my curls, and I felt her pull it gently and watch it spring back. "I wanted to. I wanted you to be my little friend and companion, just like Bendix was for Brom. I never had a daughter, and I longed for one. I loved your mother, and she was like a daughter to me. But she came to me as a grown woman, and it wasn't quite the same. I was so happy the day you were born."

The backs of my eyes were burning. "I'm sorry I disappointed you. I'm sorry I couldn't be what you wanted me to be."

"I've never been disappointed in you," she said with sudden fierceness. "Never. But it's hard to give up on dreams. The more you pulled away, the more you ran toward Brom, the harder I tried to pull you back. That was my mistake. You weren't a horse to be broken. I should have remembered that. I'm sorry that I made you think I didn't love you just as you were."

I heard Brom's voice then, calling me to come out.

"I have to go," I said. I was reluctant to leave her, and I couldn't recall ever feeling that way before.

"Be careful, Ben," she said, and kissed my cheek.

It was only after I closed the door behind me that I realized she'd called me Ben for the first time.

It was a strange ride through the night, with nobody speaking and more than half the party seething with hatred for other members of the same party. The only person who seemed to take it all with equanimity was Henrik Janssen. I wanted to ask him what he was doing with Sem Bakker and Diederick Smit in the first place. There was something fishy about his presence. In my mind, he didn't belong. And the way he looked at me, when he thought no one else was looking, gave me the same itchy feeling I'd had around Schuler de Jaager. But it was not for nosy children to ask questions of adults, at least not when other adults who might scold them were around.

I sat behind Brom on the saddle, my arms around him. I could feel the tension in his back, the way the muscles flexed and his shoulders rolled. He was trying not to say anything, not to shout at Diederick Smit and start another argument. Brom never repressed his opinion unless he had to, so I knew he was holding back because of me.

He hadn't said anything about my hair. I wondered if he

hadn't noticed or if he thought it suited me or if he just didn't care about such things. Probably the last, I decided. Brom was never one to worry about what anybody looked like, even himself. He did the bare minimum to keep himself presentable, and that was only because of Katrina.

Sem Bakker held a lantern aloft as we rode. The moon was half-full and the sky cloudy, so without it the road would have been impossible to distinguish. Even though I knew this, I wished he would put the lantern away. I felt it was drawing attention to us, attention I'd rather not have.

Whatever is out there, the lamp hardly matters one way or the other. It can see you in the dark, I thought, and shivered.

"All right, Ben?" Brom murmured. "Are you cold?"

"No, Opa," I said.

There were so many other things I wanted to say to him, so many things I wished we'd had a chance to talk about before we ended up on the road going to find a body. I wished I had just asked him about Bendix instead of waiting for the perfect moment.

I wondered if Brom was thinking about his son as we rode to find someone else's son, and if he had any sympathy at all for the man he despised, a man who would soon grieve his son the way Brom had grieved his own loss for a decade.

Brom pulled Donar's reins. "It was here, wasn't it, Ben?"

The other three drew their horses to a halt and looked at me expectantly.

I felt my cheeks flame under their scrutiny. I honestly wasn't certain. There was a thick layer of bush and brush that ran along the road for about half a mile. I could have come through it anywhere.

"Let me look," I said, and slid off Donar's back.

I walked closer to the tangle of branches and leaves. My legs were trembling. I hoped the others didn't notice. I tried very hard not to think about long fingers brushing my nape, long fingers that might reach out of the darkness for me. I felt very alone with my feet on the road while the rest of them were on horses.

Sem Bakker's horse sidled near as he raised the lantern high. Sure enough, there was a clearly visible break, a place where several broken branches and twigs had fallen into the road. I was amazed that Brom recognized it in the dark.

"Yes, I was here," I said, pointing.

They all climbed down to look.

"It's hardly a space for a man to go through," Diederick Smit said. "I don't want to whack through all these bushes. There are thorns, see?"

I'd hardly had a moment to be astonished that Diederick Smit was worrying about thorns while his son's body was in the woods when Brom spoke, his voice dripping with disdain.

"My grandchild crossed through here without worrying about thorns. If it bothers you, you can wait here and hold the horses, Smit."

Diederick's chest swelled, and I was sure he was preparing for another argument with Brom, but Henrik Janssen cut in.

"Someone should stay with the horses in any case. There isn't a good place to tie them up. I'll do it, unless you want to stay here, Diederick."

Obviously Diederick couldn't stay, because it was his son we were looking for, and he'd been trapped very neatly by Henrik Janssen's mild offer.

"Of course I'll go. You stay here, Janssen," Diederick said.

They all climbed down and handed their reins to Henrik Janssen. Brom moved close to me.

"Let me go first, all right, Ben?"

"But you don't know the way," I said.

"I can see the signs of your passage well enough," he said, giving me that Brom Bones smile, the one that always made my heart fill up with love. "And you'll be right behind me, in case I make a mistake."

He wouldn't make a mistake. Brom was a very good tracker, but that wasn't the real reason he was going first, and I knew it. He wanted me behind him in case there was danger, and I was ashamed to admit, if only to myself, that I felt safer behind him. I should be brave enough to walk by his side.

Brom probably is in less danger than you are, anyway. The creature in the woods has only attacked children.

(and one sheep)

Why, though? I wondered. *Why does it want children?*

Not just any children, either. Thus far it had only taken children of a certain age—my age.

Brom took the lantern from Sem Bakker, and the justice fell in behind me. Diederick brought up the rear. I glanced back before the pool of light left Henrik Janssen and the horses in darkness and saw him watching us with a strange expression on his face.

I turned back, feeling uneasy. I'd never thought much about Henrik Janssen. Why was he suddenly everywhere? He was a farmer, and not even an important one like Brom. There was no reason for him to be out here in the middle of the night.

Sem Bakker walked too close to me. Several times he trod on the heels of my boots and didn't even apologize. I heard the harsh pants of his breath, so loud that it was difficult to hear anything else. It was obvious to everyone that he was terrified and doing a very bad job of hiding it. Any uneasiness I felt soon faded into irritation.

"Stop making so damned much noise, Bakker," Brom said. "I can't hear myself think."

Brom was moving slowly and carefully, following my trail. The pace actually made the passage through the thorn bushes worse, for there was more chance that they would stick and hold our clothes. But Brom didn't complain, so neither did I. I hoped stupid Sem Bakker would have to spend the next day picking thorns out of his coat.

Diederick Smit said nothing. I wondered what he was

thinking. I wondered if he was dreading what we would find in the woods.

What if it was Brom we were going to find? How would you feel about it then?

I shook my head hard, trying to dislodge that terrible thought. It seemed like a curse to even think it. Nothing could ever happen to Brom, anyway. He was proof against all harm.

(Please let him be proof against harm)

I was seized by a sudden impulse to grab Brom's arm, drag him backward, make him hide behind me.

(Don't let anything happen to Brom)

Brom would never let me protect him. I didn't even know if I could.

What would Katrina say if you returned home without him?

That would never happen. Brom would always return home, would always be standing in the foyer with his arms wide open for Katrina and me.

Brom broke through the last of the thorn bushes. His bulk had protected me from the worst of it.

Sem Bakker blundered out, cursing and pulling thorns from his clothes.

"Shut up, Sem," Diederick said, before Brom could.

Sem gave me a filthy look. "Why'd you run this way, you stupid girl? You couldn't have picked a path instead of barreling through the bushes?"

"Don't call me a stupid girl," I said.

He appeared shocked that I'd spoken to him in such a tone. "You ought to learn some manners."

"I know my manners. I'll use them on you when you deserve them."

Behind me I heard Brom snort and then cough, doing a bad job of covering up his laugh. He raised the lantern and said, "Which way, Ben?"

It was hard to make out the shape of individual trees in the dark, but I knew for sure that I'd been heading toward home when I encountered the creature in the woods. When I threw myself out of the tree I'd run in the opposite direction from home and then through the thorn bushes.

"This way," I said, gesturing to the right.

The forest rustled all around us—the sounds of little creatures scampering and dead leaves tumbling from branches. I walked beside Brom, the other two following a few feet behind. Sem Bakker was muttering to Diederick Smit. I was sure he was casting aspersions on my character, but Sem Bakker's opinion meant nothing to me.

"You know your grandmother would tell you to be more polite, even if you don't like him," Brom whispered.

"I know," I said.

"But I think he's a little worm, myself, so don't worry about it."

I grinned, but a moment later I caught a whiff of something

rotten and stopped. I reached for Brom's hand and he closed his giant one over mine.

"It's like the sheep," I said. "It smells like the sheep."

I didn't want to go any farther. I was afraid of what we might see.

"Opa," I said. "You never told me. What happened to Cristoffel?"

He shook his head. "I never found out, Ben. When I brought the body to the van den Bergs they took him inside and nobody has seen them come out since. They haven't even answered for their neighbors."

I thought about Cristoffel rotting inside the Van den Berg home. I wondered if it had happened as fast as the sheep. Then something else occurred to me. If the bodies started rotting quickly after death, then that meant Cristoffel hadn't died long before Justus found him and went for his father.

Never mind found him—Justus was probably there *when it happened. The two of them were likely playing in the woods, just like me and Sander were doing that day.*

A chill ran through me. The creature in the woods—the Kludde, if Schuler de Jaager was to be believed—could have taken Sander that day instead of Cristoffel.

Or it could have taken me.

Schuler de Jaager said that the Kludde only took one victim at a time. But this time it's taken two—three, if you count the sheep.

(You don't believe anything Schuler de Jaager said, do you? Because this thing took your father, and he wasn't a child when he died)

Why hadn't that occurred to me at the time? Bendix was not only an adult, but an adult with a child of his own.

Schuler de Jaager had fed me a bunch of strange stories along with his bread and butter, and now I suspected that most of them were false. But why? Why had he deliberately tried to lead me astray? Was there any truth in his tales?

"What's the matter?" Sem Bakker asked, then made a choking sound. "What's that smell?"

I'd gotten so caught up in my speculations about Schuler de Jaager and the Kludde that I'd half-forgotten where I was and what we'd come to do.

I glanced at Diederick Smit, who'd come up beside me. His face was so white it practically glowed. A muscle in his jaw twitched. I didn't want to be the one to say that the smell was coming from his son.

We moved forward slowly, Brom taking the lead again. I think he didn't want Smit to be the first one to see Justus' remains, or maybe he just didn't want us to trip over them in the dark.

The smell was almost unbearable, like we were trapped inside a bubble with it. The wind didn't freshen the air at all, only wafted the rotten tang deeper into my nostrils. I covered my mouth and nose with my hand but it somehow made the smell worse. It was seeping into our clothes, into our skin, a poisonous miasma.

Brom raised his hand so we would halt, then he said, "I don't know if you want to see this, Diederick."

Smit pushed past me and Brom, running into the little clearing ahead. I didn't want to see, but I felt like I had to.

I crept forward, peering around Brom's arm. There was a boy's body there, or the shape of one, anyway. The head and hands were gone, and just like the sheep, the remaining flesh seemed to be melting away. The white bones of Justus' ribs already showed, and between them the wriggle of worms inside the pink muscle.

His clothing seemed to have melted, though by what craft, I couldn't determine. Had the worms eaten his clothes, too? The only thing that was identifiable was his shoes. His heavy leather shoes had very worn-down heels, because when he walked he slammed the back of his foot hard into the ground with every step. His father was always having his shoes resoled and the shoes were always worn again less than six months later.

It seemed like something was very wrong, even more wrong than the simple fact of the murders. The creature's effect on Cristoffel's body had taken more time, the sheep much less, and Justus even less than that.

Why is that? Is its power becoming more potent?

I shivered, realizing how close it had come to harming me earlier, how just the very pointed tips of its claws had scraped across my neck. What would have happened to me if it managed to actually touch me?

Diederick Smit stood over the mess that used to be his son and stared.

I looked up and saw the same branch that I'd perched on earlier. I wished I could climb up there, escape the inevitable outpouring of grief to come.

But there was no howl of pain, no crying for his boy. Instead, Diederick Smit grabbed me by the arm and yanked me away from Brom, into the clearing.

"What is this? Some kind of trick? Where's Justus? What have you done with him?" He punctuated each sentence by shaking me so hard my teeth rattled.

"Let go of her, Smit," Brom said. I sensed him stepping toward us but all I could see was Smit's face, twisted up in rage.

"Not until this little bitch tells me what she's done with my son!"

I heard Brom's intake of breath, knew that in a moment he'd rip Diederick Smit off me and beat Smit until he couldn't move. Brom was at the limit of his patience, and I didn't want him to hurt Smit on my account. Especially with that fool Sem Bakker gaping at the three of us. He'd probably try to arrest Brom, and then there would really be trouble.

I stomped Smit's foot with all of my strength, and when he shouted and released me, I raked my nails over his cheek, drawing blood.

"You stay away from me," I said, giving Diederick Smit my best Van Brunt glare. I'd had enough of him calling me a bitch, and a girl. I'd had enough of him trying to bully me.

Brom laughed, and later I decided it was the laugh that really set Smit off. Smit knocked me aside and charged at Brom, his head down like a bull's. Smit was strong, and about twenty years younger than Brom, but my grandfather had forgotten more than Smit would ever know about brawling. He saw Smit coming, grabbed the other man's shoulders and used Smit's own momentum to heave the other man to one side before the blacksmith ever touched him. Smit rolled in the dirt and landed pressed up against the mass that used to be Justus.

He screamed then, rolling away, and bits of flesh clung to Diederick Smit's clothes, stretching out like long bands—almost as if what was left of Justus reached for his father, trying to hold on to him.

Horrified, I covered my mouth and looked away, anywhere but at Diederick Smit now struggling out of his coat, screaming.

My gaze landed on the tree branch that overhung the clearing. It had been empty a moment before.

Now there was someone there.

Someone made of shadow, with eyes that glowed.

I stared, and the monster stared back at me.

8

I went rigid, my tongue locked inside my teeth. I couldn't scream, or breathe, or cry out a warning to anyone else. They wouldn't have noticed me in any case, because Brom was trying to grab Diederick—I think he wanted to calm the other man down—and Sem Bakker had started babbling about something. The creature could have reached down from the tree and taken me away without them seeing a thing.

A shadow seemed to drift down from the branch, a shadow shaped something like an arm, a hand. It swept almost lazily through the clearing, slid over the backs of my legs, up my spine, closed its fingers around my neck. Except it wasn't really touching me. It was the exertion of the thing's will, a charm to pull me to its grasp.

There was nothing I could do. I was caught there, in its eyes, and I remembered the way it had stared at me from across the field, the way it tried to catch me before.

I thought I heard music, something very faint and old-fashioned, and the music made my footsteps move toward the tree as I was pushed—almost gently—in the direction of my doom.

Ben.

The voice drifted from somewhere deep in the woods.

Ben.

Then, in a different tone: ***Ben is not for you.***

The shadow-hand at my neck seemed to release its pressure for a moment, as if the creature were listening, and thinking.

Ben is not for you, he said again, and the implication was very clear—***He's for me.***

A shudder went through me, and I didn't know if it was because I was scared the Horseman would come for me, or if it was because deep down a part of me wanted him to come. There was something about the Horseman, some connection there that I didn't understand and wasn't sure I was ready to understand.

The creature's hand squeezed tighter then, more insistent than before, staking its claim on its prey.

Far away, I heard the whinny of the horses we'd left behind with Henrik Janssen.

As if in answer, the hoofbeats sounded deep in the woods, and my blood beat in time with their pounding.

I forced my frozen lips open, made them shape the words as I stared at the monster Schuler de Jaager called the Kludde.

"He's . . . coming . . . for . . . you."

The pressure on my neck increased, as if in anger. Then it abruptly disappeared, and a moment later the shadow was gone, slipped into the darkness.

The hoofbeats faded back into the woods, and my heart slowed. I swayed on the spot, stars shooting in front of my eyes, and took great gasping breaths.

The three men were face-to-face, arguing about how to bring Justus back to the village. While the monster had tried to take me away, the question of whether or not it was actually Justus appeared to have been settled.

Nobody, not even Brom, took any notice of me. I put my back against a tree and sank down until my head was between my knees. I swiped at the back of my neck, trying to get rid of the feeling of the shadow-hand on my skin, those fingers cold as death.

I took several deep breaths. I was safe from the creature—for now, anyway. Whatever the Kludde really was—and I was not convinced by anything Schuler de Jaager had told me about it being a nightmare from the old country—it seemed to be scared of the Horseman.

And the Horseman wanted me for himself.

It's not a pleasant sensation, to feel that you are hunted. People are accustomed to being the hunters, to feel they have control over the beasts of the wild, that there is nothing superior to a human.

But the woods near Sleepy Hollow were not the same as other woods. There were places deep and dark that no one dared go. No one dared go there because it was known that those places were the haunts of creatures not of this earth. To go there was to invite their notice, and these were not things that you wanted to notice you.

I'd always thought of myself as tough and strong and larger than life, just like my grandfather. But at that moment I felt like a very small person, and very young. I was only fourteen, after all. But these were problems and worries much bigger than any child was meant to contemplate.

I fell asleep there, my head resting on my knees. The next thing I remember is Brom lifting me up in his arms so my head rested against his chest and carrying me back to the horses. I remained half-asleep throughout this, listening to the deep rumble of his voice without paying attention to the words he spoke to the other men. He waited for the others to mount and ride away, and then he carefully placed me on my wobbly legs so he could mount Donar.

"Can you stand here a minute, Ben?"

I squinted up at him sleepily. "Only a minute."

He swung into the saddle and then pulled me up behind him. He set Donar at a slow walk home.

"What did they do about Justus?" I asked.

"Smit is going to return for him tomorrow. Though I don't know what will be left of him by then. When I went out to look at the dead sheep before breakfast this morning all that was left of the skeleton was a few bones. It was as if it had melted into the earth."

I had never asked Brom what he'd done about the sheep. I sat up a little straighter, more awake now.

"Why do you think that happened, Opa?"

He didn't answer my question, but asked one of his own. "Just what did you see out in the woods today, Ben?"

My arms tightened around him. "I don't know if we should talk about it here."

He patted my hands, folded under his ribs, so I would relax. "It's all right. You're safe. You don't need to crush me."

I knew he was only joking to try to make me feel better, because I could never crush him. But it didn't make me feel better. It made me want to cling harder to him, because I wasn't safe. The monster had tried to take me from right underneath Brom's nose. There wasn't anywhere I was safe from it.

Except maybe on the back of the Horseman's saddle.

I shuddered, because while I might be safe from the creature there, it still wasn't a safe place.

"It's all right, Ben. You can tell me."

I'd always intended to tell Brom, but I felt a sudden reluctance. Brom wouldn't understand. Brom wouldn't understand because he didn't believe in the haunts that lived in the woods. He'd always said they were nonsense. But Katrina . . . Katrina had seen the creature, too. I was sure of it. I could tell Katrina. She would understand. For the first time in my life I was certain she would understand.

"I don't want to talk about it right now, Opa."

"All right," Brom said.

He shifted restlessly in the saddle, and I felt his tension. He wanted to fix the problem, even though he wasn't entirely sure what the problem was. He wanted to run at it and beat it into submission, because that's what Brom always did. But this wasn't the kind of problem you could punch. I didn't even know if it was the kind of problem that would submit. What could anyone possibly do to make the Kludde stop?

I'd started using Schuler de Jaager's name—the Kludde—for the creature for lack of anything better to call it, and thinking of Schuler de Jaager reminded me of something else he'd said.

"Opa," I said. "Did you really pretend to be the Headless Horseman to scare away Ichabod Crane?"

He started, then said, "Who told you that?"

"Schuler de Jaager. Is it true?"

Brom muttered something that sounded like "damned interfering old bastard" before saying, in his normal voice, "There is no Horseman."

"That's not what I asked you, Opa."

Brom laughed, his laugh ringing out on the silent road. "You sound just like your grandmother, ready to scold me."

Even a few hours before I would have bristled at the idea

that there was anything like Katrina inside me, but I didn't now. Some understanding had sprung up between us while we waited at the door for Brom earlier. I couldn't fool myself that it would be easy from now on, but at least we would try not to be so hard on each other.

"Well?" I prompted, when Brom didn't seem inclined to go on.

He heaved a great sigh, one that seemed to come up from the bottom of his toes.

"I don't think your grandmother would have married him. Crane, I mean. Not really. She was only trying to make me jealous, and it worked.

"I'd been courting Katrina long before that schoolmaster came to the village, you know. Her father approved of the match. My father was a farmer, like him, and I'd be a good steward for the land. Baltus Van Tassel knew that, and encouraged me in his daughter's direction, but Katrina wouldn't say she'd marry me. I think she thought things came too easily to me, and that I should have to work to earn her love. I did love her, you know. I always had. I still do, more than anything in the world.

"The first time I saw her it was like a lightning bolt went through me, and I decided then and there that I would marry her someday. You know how old we were when I decided that?"

"No," I said. I'd never heard Brom speak like this before, with so much tenderness.

"I was six years old, and she was four," he said, and he laughed. "Our family was invited to a party at the home of the great Van Tassel. My mother made me put on my best clothes, and I remember fussing and arguing and finally being forced into a horribly itchy suit. I acted a lot like you when your grandmother tries to stuff you into a dress.

"We rode to the Van Tassel place, and I complained the whole way about my collar and my coat, but when I saw the house I stopped. I'd never seen such a grand house before. And there, waiting on the porch to greet their guests, were Baltus and his wife.

"My parents said hello and then pushed me forward, introducing me. And then Baltus called for someone, and a little girl peeked her head around the open door frame. All I saw of her was the top of her head and her eyes—those blue, blue eyes. Then she disappeared again. She was shy, if you can believe it."

I couldn't really believe it. I couldn't imagine Katrina ever being shy.

"Her father called her again, but she wouldn't come. I wanted more than anything to see those eyes again, so I shook off my mother's hand and ran into the house without waiting to be invited."

I could imagine what happened then—the chagrin of Brom's parents, the laughing dismissal of the Van Tassels, Brom's mother calling his name while Brom ignored her.

"She was just inside the door, trying to hide behind the coats hung on the wall. She was about the tiniest thing you ever saw—you know how small she is, even now—and she looked like a fairy just sprung from beneath a mushroom. And I was so big, even when I was a young boy I was big for my age, just like you. I felt like a big clumsy bear blundering into her house. Her eyes were so, so big and blue, and when she saw me there she just froze. I didn't want her to be scared of me. I never wanted her to be scared of anything. From that moment I wanted to keep her safe from everything in the world. So I held out my hand just like I'd seen my father do and told her my name. She didn't say anything for a long time, and I could see that she was working out whether or not to trust me."

I could almost see them there—six-year-old Brom, wearing a suit that was too tight, his wild dark hair cleaned and flattened to his head in an attempt to make him look civilized; and the tiny porcelain doll that was Katrina—all blue eyes and golden hair, wearing some dress covered in ruffles and lace and her tiny feet encased in tiny slippers.

"Finally she said, in such a little voice, 'My name is Katrina Van Tassel. I'm very pleased to meet you.' And she said it in that way that meant she'd been practicing, you know—like her mother had made her repeat it over breakfast so she would say it right.

"She held out her hand to me, and I was going to shake

it just like I'd planned, but then I kissed it instead. I'd seen grown men do this sometimes when they met ladies. I felt sort of a fool, but I couldn't help it. Her eyes got even bigger, and for a minute I thought I'd done something really wrong and that she wouldn't speak to me again. But then she smiled at me, the sweetest smile I ever saw, and I knew then I'd move heaven and earth for her.

"We were inseparable after that for a long time. We played together every chance we got. She used to be a little wild, your grandmother—she'd run in the woods with the boys and climb trees and come home muddy just like you. And my heart was always happiest when I was with her. I can't really explain it. It was just a sense that things were right when we were together, that all was just as it was meant to be. But everything changed when we got older. Her mother wouldn't let her run wild anymore, and I could only see her if we sat in the parlor and talked about things I couldn't care less about—art or poetry, things like that."

I couldn't imagine Katrina as a wild child, running free like Brom. But he'd said it, so it must be true. I felt sorry for little Katrina, made to give up the sky and the trees and the grass under her feet so she could sit quietly in the parlor and do her needlework.

She's trying to tame you the way she was tamed, because it's the only thing she knows, because she thinks it's right.

"And it was never just me and her anymore. There were

other boys—though we thought we were men—and there
were a lot of them. Your grandmother was a pretty little girl,
but she was a very beautiful young woman. All those boys
wanted that beauty for their own, wanted her big blue eyes
and, of course, her father's money. I never cared about the
money, and if I loved her eyes, I loved her spirit more. And
only *I* knew that spirit. *I* was the only one who saw the real
Katrina, underneath. She'd never have been satisfied with one
of those pudding-faced fools.

"I cleared the field of suitors, one by one. I made it obvious
that I was the only one for her. Her father agreed. And she
wanted me—she really did. But she didn't like that I'd gotten
rid of all my rivals so easily. She thought I should have to
fight for her. She didn't realize I'd been fighting for her my
whole life, that I'd been courting her from the first day, that
there was never anyone for me but her. Only Katrina, always.
I never even looked at another woman. I couldn't even see
them. I only saw her.

"And then Ichabod Crane came to town."

Brom's voice changed. He'd been speaking almost dreamily
of himself and Katrina, but when he said Crane's name I heard
the iron underneath.

"He was a fool if there ever was a fool, for all that he was
the schoolmaster and supposed to be smart. Looked like a
jerking puppet on a string when he walked—too much arm
and too much leg, and it was like his body was so long he

didn't know where anything was. Ate like a horse, too, and was skinnier than a broomstick. And he was poor as a church mouse. Schoolmasters don't make any money to speak of, and he had less than most, but he liked money. Oh, yes, he did. He liked it very much, liked the idea of being a rich man if he could only see his way to becoming one. Then he saw Katrina.

"She was beautiful, but more importantly, she was rich. Crane locked on to her like a hunting dog after a fox. And he was so determined that he didn't even see me standing in his way. Thought he could woo her and win her and become master of the Van Tassel land. As if he'd know what to do with a farm that size. He'd have run it into the ground. And he would have made Katrina miserable, I have no doubt of that.

"Now, I don't think she really meant to have Crane, but I couldn't see that at the time. She didn't want everything in her life to be inevitable, I think. And there wasn't much she could do. Girls were supposed to be quiet and biddable, to do as their fathers said. Though Baltus spoiled her utterly—if he approved a match and she didn't want it he would have taken his consent back in an instant. But he liked me, and he wanted me as his son-in-law, and he knew Katrina liked me, too. Baltus didn't think much of Crane, but he kept his opinions to himself. He was good that way. He was a good man."

Brom sighed, and I knew he was missing his father-in-law. They had, by all accounts, gotten along famously despite their differences in temperament—the boisterous Brom and the reserved Baltus. I didn't really remember Katrina's father—he'd died when I was quite young—but I remembered Brom's sadness after.

"So Katrina encouraged Crane, and every time I saw him offer her his arm or have a turn dancing with her, I got madder and madder. Somewhere deep down I knew what she was doing, I think, but I couldn't stop feeling angry. He didn't deserve her. He didn't deserve to walk next to her, never mind marry her."

Brom was growing angry about it while he talked. My ear was pressed against his back and I heard his heart speed up, heard the gentle rumble of his voice turn into the growling of a bear.

Crane must have been a fool, I thought. *How could a man like that think he compared to Brom, and how could he not be terrified at the sight of a furious Brom, anyway?*

"I started to think that the only way I'd ever be rid of Crane was if he left the village. Threatening him the usual way wouldn't work."

I gave a little start at that phrase. Brom did so much threatening that there was a "usual way"? I imagined that it involved the promise of Brom's fist in the other person's face, but it seemed, from the way Brom talked, that Crane was impervious to those kinds of threats.

"Now, you know the people around here are the most

superstitious lot you've ever seen. They believe anything and everything they hear. Crane was even more credulous. If it had to do with curses and spooks and magic, he believed in it. And I started thinking that the best way to get rid of him was to scare him out of town. There had always been a story in the village about a horseman that lived in the woods, a nightmare made of shadow that brought death. I just, well, embellished it a bit. Started talking about the Headless Horseman who rode every night looking for a new head to take. And it caught fire—every person in the village told the story to someone else, who told it to someone else, who told it to someone else. In no time at all the story of the Headless Horseman was part of the fabric of Sleepy Hollow. Everyone believed it, and most importantly, Crane believed it.

"One night Katrina's father had a big party to celebrate the harvest. Now that I think on it, the Van Tassels must have been having their harvest celebration the day I first met Katrina. They used to do it every year. Katrina and I would, too, until . . ."

I didn't need him to say why they'd stopped the tradition. Everyone knew part of Brom's heart died on the same day that Bendix died.

Brom cleared his throat. "People got to telling stories that night, and I admit I encouraged it. And with every story that was told Crane's eyes got wider and wider and his hands shook more and more. One of the last stories told before everything broke up was the story of the Headless Horseman. It was the perfect time to put my plan into action.

"I waited near the road just past Wiley's swamp. I'd made a kind of rig for myself with a coat and wire, and cut out small holes to see through—I knew Crane would never notice these. It looked, when I sat on my horse, like I was a figure without a head. That day I'd carved up a pumpkin so it looked like it had a face, and in the dark I held it in my lap, so it looked like I was holding a head. Half the work had been done before Crane ever saw me there in the road—he'd been so spooked by the stories we told that he was ready to believe in anything.

"Well, I didn't speak when he called out to me, and then when he tried to go past I started trotting alongside, just out of sight. When he walked his horse, I walked mine, and when he galloped, I galloped. I could see that he was more terrified by the minute, and I had such a time holding in my laughter, I'll tell you."

I could see it all—see the terrified schoolmaster on his horse and Brom barely containing his mirth, and I thought suddenly that it was a cruel trick Brom had pulled. I know he said that Crane was after Katrina, and I'd heard the saying that all was fair in love and war, but still—this was more than just a prank. Crane might have been seriously hurt. Perhaps that was why Katrina's eyes flashed whenever the subject of the Horseman came up.

"After a while the damned fool panicked and kicked his

old horse into a run—or what passed for a run, anyway. He'd borrowed some old farm horse of his landlord's. He was making for the bridge near the church, because I'd said in the story that if he crossed the bridge the Horseman would disappear in a puff of smoke, unable to cross. Of course I'd told it that way, because I knew he had to cross that bridge to get back to the place where he was staying."

I'd seen that very bridge earlier, when I'd looked out the window of Schuler de Jaager's cottage. It was just past the church and it ran over a little brook that eventually found its way into the woods—the very brook where Sander and I liked to play.

"I let him gain the bridge, knowing that the fool would turn back once he reached the other side, wanting to see the Headless Horseman disappear in a flash of fire and brimstone. As soon as he did I threw the pumpkin at his head, and it struck true. Crane tumbled off his horse—taking the saddle with him—and passed out. I took Crane's hat and threw it on the bank of the brook, and trampled over the saddle. Then I led the old horse home and took the bridle off him, knowing that everyone would wonder how the horse got there without a saddle and bridle."

We were nearly home now. I saw the glow of light in the windows. Katrina must be waiting up for us. Brom seemed to be walking Donar much slower than usual. I think he wanted to finish telling me his story without interruption.

"I went back for Crane, thinking to frighten him some more, but he wasn't where I'd left him. He disappeared that night, never to be seen again."

"Opa," I said. "You don't think he . . ."

I couldn't finish my thought. It was too terrible.

"No," he said. "I don't think he died. That was what other folk thought later, that he'd fallen into the brook and drowned. But they never found his body. I think he woke up while I was gone and just ran. He ran so far and so long that no one ever heard from him again."

Brom laughed then, and it was not his usual laughter. It was something more derisive, and it seemed to be directed at himself.

"I could have saved myself the trouble, anyway. Katrina told me later that Crane asked her to marry him that very night, and she told him no. She'd always meant to marry me."

I didn't know what to think. Brom had been triumphant, and to my mind that was how it always ought to be. But it was a sad story for Crane, however awful he might have been.

"I'm not proud of myself," Brom said, as if he knew exactly what I was thinking. "I know it was beyond the pale, even for me. And I was old enough by then to know better. I just couldn't bear the thought of Katrina with anyone else, and I think it made me a little mad."

Brom led Donar up the drive that circled in front of the house.

"But, Opa—if you did this and nobody helped you, how did Schuler de Jaager know about it?"

Brom snorted. "He saw me when I rode back looking for Crane. His cottage is within sight of the bridge, you know. He'd heard the horses and the fuss and come out to see what happened."

"So he knows what happened to Crane?"

"He says that by the time he came out, Crane was gone," Brom said slowly. "Although I've always suspected that he knew more about what happened to Crane than he let on."

Brom rode past the house, directly to the stables. He dismounted and then reached up to help me off Donar's back.

"But why would he never say anything about Crane's fate, then? And why would he keep your secret?"

Brom said, "I don't know why he kept it at the time. Schuler de Jaager has always had reasons of his own for everything his does. But I know why he kept it later. His daughter, Fenna, was your mother. She married Bendix."

I stared at Brom. "So he's—"

"Yes," Brom said, and there was a deep-rooted fury in his voice. "He's also your grandfather. And the reason you've never talked to him alone before today is because he's the reason Bendix died."

9

"I know you have questions. I can see them on your face," Brom said, putting the saddle away and making up a bucket of oats for Donar. He rubbed the horse's muzzle affectionately. "But it's late, and we both need sleep. And I think your grandmother should be a part of this conversation, too."

I didn't want to go to bed. There was no part of me that was ready to rest. My brain was whirring with everything that had happened that day, and everything that Brom had just told me. And he couldn't just tell me that Schuler de Jaager was related to me and then pat me on the head and send me to bed.

But that, it appeared, was exactly what Brom intended to do. He shuffled me inside, ignored my questions, and only allowed me to say good night to Katrina before sending me upstairs.

Katrina, for her part, kissed me good night and gave my hair a sad look. (I imagined she wouldn't stop doing this for some time—Katrina had always loved my hair even if I did not.)

She didn't even ask why Brom was hurrying me upstairs—they did that silent communication trick that they had, where they spoke complete sentences with their eyes, and Katrina understood exactly what Brom wanted.

I thought about that connection between the two of them as I dressed in my nightgown and climbed into bed. I'd always thought the two of them were almost uncannily joined, and the uncanny was something that you didn't easily dismiss if you lived in Sleepy Hollow.

The connection was something Brom had felt from the start, from the time they were very small, and Katrina must have felt it, too, or else she wouldn't have pushed so hard against it at the end. I found myself feeling sorry for Crane again, though by Brom's account the schoolmaster had never been truly in love with Katrina—only her wealth. Still, it had to hurt when someone strung you along for her own purpose. Katrina's purpose had only been to make Brom jealous, and according to Brom her plan worked.

But the strangest part of the story wasn't that Brom had pretended to be the Horseman—I'd always thought he knew more about that story than he let on—or even that it had grown to a legend in the Hollow. It was that Schuler de Jaager had seen Brom as the Horseman and never told anyone, and that Schuler de Jaager was somehow responsible for my father's death, and that Schuler de Jaager was my other grandfather.

I'd never really thought about my mother's parents. I don't

know why. Maybe it was because Brom and Katrina filled my view so completely that I'd never felt the lack of anyone else. Maybe it was because they never really talked about Fenna, except to say that she was fair and sweet natured and that Bendix had loved her, and Katrina sometimes reminded me that I was nothing like Fenna at all.

To find out that I had another living relative and that it was Schuler de Jaager, of all people—I couldn't believe Brom expected me to go to sleep after hearing that. Schuler was so old—much older than Brom. Schuler was seventy if he was a day, and he looked even older—withered and gnarled like an ancient tree.

He did say earlier that he had his child late in life. But it must have been very late for him.

I couldn't imagine calling Schuler de Jaager "Opa," or laughing with him the way I did Brom. I couldn't imagine him being a father, never mind a grandfather. There was something crafty about him, something deep and almost eerie. He'd never have the kind of arms you'd run into and feel safe. He wasn't Brom.

Well, Ben, there's lots of people in the world who aren't Brom. It's not a character flaw.

I'd had a feeling the whole time I was with Schuler de Jaager that I was missing something, that we were speaking at cross-purposes. He knew he was related to me and I didn't, so that might have accounted for the strangeness of the conversation.

(And why didn't he say anything about it to me? That seems like the sort of thing you might mention, the sort of thing that you wouldn't keep from a child.)

But that wasn't *completely* the reason our conversation was so odd. There was something else—something Schuler de Jaager knew that nobody else did.

I needed to find out what he knew. It might have to do with Crane, or the Kludde, or it might be some other secret that he'd scooped up and kept close to his heart for the day when it would be useful to him.

How are you going to convince him to tell you what he knows when he never even told Brom?

Well, there was that. If Brom couldn't get him to talk, then what powers would I have to persuade that secretive man?

Brom is not the blood of his blood. You are.

I shuddered. I didn't like the idea of Schuler de Jaager's blood running in my veins. I didn't like the idea of being connected to him at all.

Connections. Between Brom and Katrina, between Brom and Schuler, between Bendix and Fenna, between me and all of them. There was something in that web, something tangled deep down, and that something was the source of all the trouble happening. Those boys were dead because of it.

Brom had said Bendix was dead because of Schuler de Jaager.

I rolled over and buried my face in the pillow. I wasn't

getting anywhere—my brain was spinning in circles. I determinedly closed my eyes and thought, *Sleep, sleep, sleep.*

But I didn't sleep. *How could I sleep when I was under the stars, under the big dark night? How could I sleep when the horse was running underneath me, running so fast that it seemed impossible? How could I sleep when I could hear his heart—his wild, wild heart?*

No, not his heart. My heart. Because my heart was his heart and his was mine. We were the same, the same under the skin.

I sat straight up in bed, my eyes wide open. The morning sun blinded me. I had slept, but I didn't feel as though I'd rested. I'd dreamt the whole night of him, of riding on his horse, of listening to his laughter.

I crossed my hands over my own heart, felt the rhythm of the galloping horse there.

Stop thinking of the Horseman as freedom.

But the Horseman had saved me in the woods. He'd called the Kludde off me.

(because he's always watched you always since you were a little child and you made him out of nothing)

I stopped, tried to grab that thought, but it was smoke that dissipated before I could breathe it in. Sleepy Hollow was a magical place, a place where enchantment could drift on the air, but sometimes that enchantment could blow dust in your eyes, make it hard for you to see what was right in front of you.

(Remember you need to remember him there's something important to remember)

I shivered, and got out of bed, dressing in the same clothes I'd worn the day before. I felt a strange sense that I was doing that day over again. I was dressing in my boys' clothes. I had many questions with no answers. I needed to talk to Brom. Another boy was dead.

Please don't let every day be like this from now on. Please let the Kludde have gotten what it wanted from us.

At some point I'd decided I didn't believe what Schuler de Jaager had said about a curse taking victims. It was ridiculous, and besides—it would be impossible to keep something like that a secret in Sleepy Hollow. Everyone was always so willing to believe in the strange and unnatural, and they liked telling stories about those strange things best of all. If a creature regularly emerged from the woods and snatched up a child then there would be a story about it. Henrik Janssen had said that the people of the Hollow accept those sorts of things as part of the fabric of their lives here, and it was true. There was no story; therefore it wasn't true.

(Or maybe it was true and you just never heard about it. That happens here, too. There are blind corners, and secrets that never bubble up. Look at the very fact of Schuler de Jaager, that he's related to you and you never knew.)

I shook that off. Yes, things were hidden in Sleepy Hollow, things I might never learn. But this wasn't one of those things.

This was too big. So why had Schuler de Jaager made it up? Why did he tell me something I could easily check? All I needed to do was ask any of the village gossips and they would gladly tell me the story if they knew of it.

Not that I would bother with such a task, I decided. Schuler was clearly lying, and there was no need to waste a whole day inside, buried in dusty parlors, having tea foisted on me and being forced to listen to stories that I hadn't come to hear.

But I could do some poking around, and listening to adults talk when they didn't think anyone was about.

I had a sudden idea that I ought to go to Cristoffel van den Berg's house. I could say that I came to say sorry about Cristoffel, and his mother would have to invite me inside for a few moments, and then I could find out if Cristoffel's body had melted like the sheep and Justus Smit.

It would be horrible if that had happened, because Brom said he'd taken Cristoffel right to the Van den Berg house. That meant that his parents would have watched him rotting right before their eyes.

Nobody was at the breakfast table, though all the dishes had been left out for me. I took all that I wanted and ate until I felt really full for the first time in ages. It was so wonderful to eat without Katrina watching and tutting over the amount of food I put on my plate.

Katrina. I had some things I wanted to ask Katrina, as well. I pushed away from the table and went looking for her.

She was in the parlor, sewing. She sat in her favorite chair beside the window, where she could see the front drive and know if anyone rode up to our door.

And where she could also keep watch for wayward grandchildren who came home later than they ought, I thought.

The sun was shining and her golden hair caught its rays, making her look like she'd been crowned with sunlight. She looked up when I entered. Her eyes flicked up to my hair again and I saw her suppress a sigh.

"You slept late," she said. "It's nearly ten."

"I was eating," I said, though I had still slept much later than I usually did. I was normally up with the sun, because that was when Brom rose. He said a farmer needed to keep the sun's hours, and since I wanted to be a farmer just like him, I did the same.

But you don't really want to be a farmer just like him anymore, do you? You want to ride through the woods under the starlight.

"Well, I'm glad you're finally up. I need to see if these will fit you."

She held up what she was sewing and I realized that she was making new breeches for me.

She saw my expression and said, "It's only that I'm tired of you ruining every dress you own."

But I knew that wasn't why she was making them, and I loved her so much just then I thought my heart would explode.

"Come over here," she said.

I obeyed, and she held the breeches up to my front.

"However," she continued. "I've been thinking that we should change the cut for you. Even though you don't care in the least what anyone in the village says about you—you're like your grandfather that way, he's just as impervious."

The way she said this made it clear that it wasn't a compliment.

"But I don't want people thinking you're indecent. You're still young but you're going to have a woman's body someday whether you like it or not. I'd like to make these a little longer for you than other breeches, and perhaps not so tight as the mens'."

Normally I had no interest in clothes-making, but I was intrigued by the idea of breeches just for me.

"A little extra room would make it easier to climb," I said. "I wouldn't be so likely to tear them. But not so much that the fabric gets in my way, like a dress."

Katrina ordered me out of my bottoms then and had me put on the breeches. There wasn't much to them yet—only a waist with bolts of cloth hanging off—and she spent the next several minutes pinning and adjusting while I stood with my arms overhead. This process would usually have me fidgeting uncontrollably, but I made myself stand very still. Katrina had decided to make something I really wanted and I wasn't going to throw that generosity into jeopardy by irritating her now.

After a while she had what she wanted and I was allowed to put my (now obviously too small) breeches back on. I watched her for a few minutes as she made careful, neat stitches despite the thick cloth. I'd never been able to make stitches like that. I wondered if my mother had.

"Oma," I said. "What happened to my father?"

She put her sewing down and looked at me, and something in that look told me she'd been waiting for me to ask that very question from the moment I stepped into the parlor.

"You know that a fever swept through the Hollow many years ago?"

I nodded. "And you always said that my mother and father both fell sick because of it and died."

Katrina stared out the window, but I don't think she saw anything beyond the glass. Her eyes had gone someplace— no, some*time*—far away.

"Your mother did fall ill because of the fever, and she died because of it, too. But your father died because he went into the woods looking for a way to save her, and you."

"Me?"

Katrina nodded. "You were just as sick as your mother. It was a terrible thing to see. So small, you were, just a few years old, and your little body limp from the fever. You wouldn't even cry. Poor Bendix, he was out of his mind with worry."

"Opa said that Schuler de Jaager is the reason why my father died," I said, watching her carefully. Katrina could explode very suddenly, like a cannonball tearing through a line of soldiers.

Her eyes hardened. "That old bastard. I wish he'd die and go to the devil where he belongs."

I stared at her in shock. Katrina never spoke like that. Brom, yes. But not Katrina.

She saw my expression and gave a short laugh. "Believe me, Ben. If anyone deserves to take a direct route to hell, it's him."

"Brom said Schuler was my mother's father?" I put the question mark at the end because I was still hoping it wouldn't be true.

"And you're wondering why we never told you that. Well, you met him. Would you want him as your grandfather?"

"No," I said, so quickly that Katrina laughed again.

"Even before what happened with Bendix and Fenna we didn't want you near him. I loved your mother very much but I never understood how she came from the same blood as that man."

"He made my skin crawl."

"He does that to everyone. I think even his wife felt that way, though she only lasted long enough to birth Fenna and then she died."

So that was a lie, I thought. *He told me that his wife died of grief when Fenna was taken by the Kludde. I can't trust a single thing he told me yesterday. What did he want me there for, if he was only going to tell me stories?*

"Even Fenna was a little frightened of him. She didn't speak often of her home life, but I had a strong impression that Schuler de Jaager was not an ideal parent."

Katrina fell silent again, brooding.

"But what happened to my father? I don't understand how Schuler de Jaager could have been responsible if my father died like Cristoffel did. If he was killed by the"—I almost said *Kludde*, and then decided not to use Schuler's word for it—"creature in the woods."

"You have to understand your father. He was like Brom, and like you. Bendix could never bear to be still and wait. He wanted to do something. He needed to do something. He couldn't just sit in the sickroom and watch his wife and child waste away. Schuler knew that. He took advantage of Bendix's nature."

Katrina sighed. I recognized the grief creeping into the corners of her eyes, a thing that she kept hidden most days—as if she wouldn't allow herself to feel it.

"Brom hated having Schuler visit, would always avoid it if he could, but with the man's daughter ill we felt we had to allow it. Schuler insisted upon it, in fact, and Brom was so tangled up in worry himself that he assumed the old man felt the same way.

"But Schuler de Jaager did not come here to pray over his daughter or his granddaughter. He didn't come to hold our hands and speak words of comfort together. He came here to whisper a tale into Bendix's ear, and I can only believe that, given the outcome, Schuler meant harm to our son."

Katrina paused for a long while, and I tried very hard not to yell, "But what did Schuler de Jaager *say*?" because I knew that she would get to it in her own time and that if I showed any sign of impatience now she might give up on telling me the story altogether.

"He hardly seemed to notice Fenna at all, or you, for that matter. He was in the sickroom for a few moments before coming out again, and though none of us went in with him, I can't imagine that Schuler wept any tears of grief. Then he asked to speak to Bendix alone, and again we permitted it, because we thought it was appropriate for Bendix's father by marriage to have a few quiet words with him. They went into Brom's study, and they stayed there for an hour—long enough that Brom and I began to wonder what they could be saying to one another.

"When they came out Bendix had a light in his eye that hadn't been there since before you and Fenna fell ill, and the sight of that spark unnerved me. But it was Schuler's expression that truly placed terror in my heart—he looked satisfied. I didn't think a man should look like that when his daughter was so ill with fever she hardly knew where she was. He shouldn't look as though he'd gotten his way, and was pleased with it.

"Brom noticed, too, and as soon as Schuler de Jaager left

the house we asked Bendix about it. But Bendix wouldn't say anything, wouldn't even hint at what the two of them discussed. Well, there wasn't a thing we could do about it. Bendix was a grown man, and his business was his own if he wanted to keep it. But I worried.

"The next day was the worst of the fever. You'd stopped crying altogether, and would lie there so still that sometimes I held my hand under your nose to make certain you were breathing. Fenna thrashed and screamed and shook so hard that sometimes she rolled off the bed, and I couldn't keep the cloths cool enough—as soon as they touched her skin they would heat through and be useless. Bendix and Brom and myself were the only ones who went into the sickroom—we felt that we couldn't risk the servants who weren't already sick themselves. We each took a few hours in the room with the two of you. I remember that day that Bendix was with you for all of the morning, and I came in around noon and stayed until evening, and then Brom arrived to relieve me.

"I went out to check on the sick servants. Two of them had died that day—the cook that we had before Lotte came to us, and a scullery maid. There were many preparations that needed to be made and so I was fully occupied until well after dark. I hadn't seen Bendix since that morning, but I didn't think anything of it—Brom and Bendix were sharing the farm duties, and I presumed he was out on the grounds somewhere.

"I went up to my bedroom to wash and rest. I was at the washbasin near the window when I saw a figure leave the house out the kitchen door. The night was clear and the moon was full, and it was obvious that it was Bendix. What's more, he was trying to be furtive. I saw that immediately. He was always terrible at sneaking, even when he was a boy.

"I don't know what made me do it. I pulled on my darkest-colored shawl and made sure my hair was covered and went out after him. He hadn't gotten very far—his silhouette was clearly headed for the road that ran along the woods. He looked back several times, but he never seemed to notice me. For a while I kept just far enough away to follow without being seen, but then I realized that I was being silly. Bendix was my son. I was his mother, and I had every right to ask him where he was going in secret, after dark. I called out to him.

"Bendix was so tense that he leapt into the air on hearing the sound of my voice. Then he realized it was me, and when I approached he began shouting at me for following him. Bendix was always even-tempered so it was a shock to hear him speak to me that way. But I was also angry, and he'd never been able to stand up to me when I was in that state, so I managed to worm it out of him.

"I wish that some of our last words were not angry ones. I wish I'd told him how much I loved him."

She wept as she spoke, and I felt torn. I didn't want her to go through this, to relive the last moments of her son's life.

But I thought, too, that I needed to know—that I *deserved* to know. Bendix was her son but he was my father, and all my life I'd been told a lie about him.

I put my arms around her and hugged her tight, and she clung to me as she cried. I had never, *never* seen Katrina show such weakness like that, and it scared me. It was as if Bendix had died the previous day, not ten years ago.

For her it probably always feels that way, I thought with sudden insight. *When do you ever get over the loss of a child?*

Schuler de Jaager doesn't seem to be especially bothered by the loss of his, and this thought was followed by a spurt of anger.

After a while Katrina composed herself, and waved me into the chair across from her. She continued the story as though there had been no interruption.

"Bendix told me that Schuler de Jaager claimed there was a creature who lived in the wood, in the place beyond where the trail ends, the place where no one in Sleepy Hollow ever goes. Schuler told Bendix that if he went to this creature and"—her voice hitched here, but she steadied herself and went on— "sacrificed himself to it, that the creature could heal Fenna and you, and everyone in town, as a matter of fact. The creature could end the fever, Schuler said, if only someone brave and true would give himself up for everyone else. Bendix would have done anything for Fenna, anything for you. He loved you so much, and he wanted to be doing. He wanted to feel he could solve the problem. Bendix didn't tell us about it because he knew we would object and he'd already made up his mind. If I hadn't seen him sneaking out of the house then I never would have seen him again. He would have disappeared into the woods without a trace."

"But why?" I burst out. "How could he believe anything that Schuler de Jaager said? There's no guarantee that Schuler was doing anything except sending my father to die for some reason of his own."

"And that's exactly what I told him," Katrina said, with a touch of her usual tartness. "There's magic in the woods, and danger, too, but there was no possible way to know if this creature would actually heal you or Fenna. It was madness, but I could not persuade him to return home.

"He couldn't persuade me, either, though he raged at me for some time. I finally told him if he wanted me home he'd have to bring me there and stay there himself. Of course he wouldn't do that, because he'd screwed up his courage and if he went home then Bendix wasn't certain he'd come out again. He didn't say this, but I knew. So we went on together.

"The woods seemed darker that night than they'd ever been, and every step we took filled me with deeper dread. I wasn't certain what I could do to stop it but I had no intention of letting Bendix sacrifice himself to some monster in the woods. We're not pagans. That was old country nonsense that Schuler had planted in his head. Bendix didn't say a word to me until we reached the place where the path ends. Then he turned to me and said, 'Mama, it's time for you to go home now.' I shook my head at him and he got angry again and said, 'I don't want any harm to come to you,' and I replied that I didn't want any harm to come to him, either. He threw his hands into the air and he went off the path into the deep part of the forest.

"I couldn't let him go, so I followed. But Ben, there was something *wrong* there. I felt it immediately. It was as if something was pulling at me, but trying to tug in all directions, and there was a sound, a sound like . . ."

She trailed off, and I said, "Like something buzzing in your ears, like it was pressing in on you, and there were many voices at once."

Katrina gave me a sharp look. "You've gone to the end of the trail, where you're not supposed to."

I gave her a sheepish look, one that I'd seen Brom use many times. "I didn't go any farther. I only stepped off for a moment, so I could see what it was like."

She muttered something in Dutch, then sighed, and went on.

"I clung to Bendix, because all the noise made me disoriented and I felt things tugging at me, tugging at my skirts, pulling at my hair. I don't know what Bendix felt. He didn't speak to me, but I could just make out his labored breath over the strange sounds in my ears. I don't know how long we walked on, but I heard something like singing. I say 'something like' because it wasn't quite speaking, but it didn't have a melody, either. It drew me in a way I didn't understand. I felt my grip on Bendix's arm loosen, and somehow I drifted away from him in the dark.

"As soon as I lost hold of him I came to myself again and called his name, but he didn't answer. The only sound that came back were many voices calling me, saying, 'Katrina, Katrina, Katrina.' I knew they were trying to lure me, trying to put me under their spell, but I wasn't having any of it. I needed to find Bendix. I needed to save my son. But I couldn't see anything in the dark, and now the calling voices were laughing at me, and I spun and stumbled and cried out for Bendix but there was nothing except the dark and the woods and the creatures that lived there pressing all around me, keeping me from my child.

"Then I heard him scream.

"His scream was so long and so terrible that it was like a trail for me to follow, and I chased after it. Somehow I was able to shake off the horrible little creatures that tugged at me with their grasping fingers and I ran, ran, ran toward the sound of Bendix.

"I stumbled into a clearing. There was a perfect opening in the canopy of trees, a circle, almost as if it had been cut there on purpose, and the moonlight shone down through the opening and I saw it."

"A shadow," I murmured. "A long shadow that shifts and

shimmers and doesn't seem to hold its shape, but somehow it has sharp teeth and eyes that glow."

"Yes," she said. "And it had already taken Bendix's head and his hands, and it was hunched over him, drinking Bendix's blood—my blood, Brom's blood, the blood that was created from our love for each other. I screamed. I screamed and screamed so long that I didn't know when I would stop. And the creature stopped, and looked up at me, and Ben—I had the strangest feeling then. I felt that I'd seen it before, and that it *knew* me."

She shuddered, and I reached across and took her hand. Her fingers were like ice.

"What happened then?" I asked.

She shook her head. "I don't know. I fainted, I think, and when I woke it was morning, and the creature was gone, and all that was left of Bendix was a body without its head and hands.

"I had to do something, had to get my boy back home. I didn't want to leave him there in that terrible place. And I knew that Brom would be half out of his mind by then, with both me and Bendix missing. But I wasn't certain how I would do it. I couldn't possibly carry Bendix.

"The noises I'd heard in the night had faded but not disappeared entirely. I felt, though, that they weren't as malicious as the voices in the dark. They seemed like they were, oh, I don't know—encouraging me? But none of the voices' owners appeared to help me."

"Oma," I said, then hesitated. I didn't know if she knew about what happened to Justus and the sheep. "In the morning, when you saw my father's body . . . was it whole? Whole except for the head and hands, I mean."

"You're thinking of Justus," Katrina said. So Brom had told her, then.

"Yes. Was my father—" I couldn't say it. I couldn't ask her if her son's flesh had melted away like soft candle wax, if there was nothing left of the boy she loved except bones and wriggling worms.

"Bendix wasn't like what you found last night. I don't know why that happened to those boys, to Cristoffel and Justus."

"Do you think that it's because the creature in the woods has changed somehow? Gotten stronger?"

Katrina frowned. "I don't know if this means it's stronger. But something certainly has changed."

We were both quiet for a while, thinking about what the changes could mean. Then Katrina went on.

"I'd started to despair that I'd never get Bendix home, that I'd have to leave him there in the woods. I didn't know how I'd find that clearing again, or if I'd even be allowed to. The spirits in the woods might not let me. Then I heard the sound of a horse, clop-clop-clopping soft over the dirt and grass, and a little whinny."

My heart raced. Had Katrina met the Horseman—the *real* Horseman? Had he helped her bring my father home?

"Then a black horse appeared before me, almost like a miracle. It was Daredevil, your grandfather's horse—the one he had before Donar."

I felt a spurt of disappointment, but didn't say anything.

"He was the smartest horse I've ever seen. If your grandfather hadn't had Daredevil he never would have managed that Headless Horseman stunt. No other horse could have run like that in the dark, with his rider half blind from that silly costume."

I gave her a surprised look, and she smiled.

"Yes, I know Brom told you. I've always hoped the story of the Headless Horseman would fade away but the people of this village won't let it go. They've made Brom's prank something real—at least in their minds."

"But nobody knows it was a prank," I said. "Except us. And Schuler de Jaager."

Her eyes narrowed. "That man. He's like a demon who's haunted us ever since that night. He *knows* what happened to Ichabod Crane, but he won't tell anyone."

He just likes having power over Brom, I thought. *He likes knowing something nobody else knows.*

"I know that God will think me wicked, but I've wished every day that the old man would just die. When the fever swept through the village, and so many young people went—your mother, and so many others—all I could think was, 'Why won't that man die?' He must have made some compact with Lucifer. That's the only possible reason he could still be alive when so many good people are gone."

Her voice was laced with venom. This wasn't a Katrina fit of temper—it was hatred, deep and wide. I think in that moment a little of it infected me, too, a drop of poison in my blood. Schuler de Jaager had done his best to make Brom and Katrina miserable, and he'd certainly been the reason that Bendix went into the woods that night and met the terrible creature of shadow.

"So Daredevil found me in the woods, and I somehow managed to sling Bendix over his withers, and then I got onto his back and Daredevil took us home to Brom."

A tear rolled onto her cheek, and she swiped it away with an impatient hand.

"It was all for nothing, too, just as I'd thought, for when I returned home I discovered that Fenna had died while Bendix sacrificed himself in the woods because of that terrible man's whim."

But I lived, I thought. I would never say this, though, especially as I didn't think that my life had been gained at the cost of my father's. I just happened to survive, the way some people do.

If only Bendix hadn't gone out that night, I thought. *If only he had waited one more day. Fenna would have died and he would have known that no sacrifice of his could make a difference. I would have had a father, at least.*

I shook those thoughts away. Bendix might have died anyway, might have caught the same fever that ravaged me and my mother. And while I missed the idea of him, it wasn't as if I'd wanted for affection. I'd always had Brom—and Katrina, even if I didn't really always understand the way she cared for me.

Katrina shifted in her chair, bending over her sewing again. "You should go out and find Sander. There aren't many days of sunshine left this autumn."

I hesitated, but I could tell that she wasn't going to say any more. I left her there in the parlor, bent low so nobody would see her weeping.

10

At first I thought to go about on my own as I'd done the day before, but then I realized Katrina had a good idea (she was suddenly full of them) and went to find Sander. My head was whirling with everything I'd learned and I wanted somebody to talk to. I couldn't tell him everything, of course—I'd take the secret of Brom and the Headless Horseman prank to my grave—but I could tell him some things, about Justus Smit and the sheep and about the creature I'd seen in the woods.

The road to the village was busy. Many people who had farms near ours were taking their harvest to market, or bringing it to one of the many wholesalers who would buy the crop and resell it in New York City. Several carts trundled past me, pulled by slow-moving horses, and many people shouted my name and asked after Brom and Katrina. I was glad for the constant stream of company, for it kept me from thinking too hard about the woods I walked past—and the things that were hidden there.

I was halfway to the village when one of the carts slowed beside me.

"Can I give you a ride, Miss Bente?"

It was Henrik Janssen. Why was Henrik Janssen suddenly everywhere? Before the last few days I saw him perhaps a few times a year, despite the fact that his farm was next to ours. He was around thirty years old—close to the age that my father would have been had Bendix lived—and had very light blue eyes in a weather-beaten face. His shirtsleeves were rolled up and I could see the muscles in his forearms.

He gave me a strangely intent look that made my stomach squirm. I did not want to climb onto the seat next to this man.

"No, thank you," I said, and gave him my best Katrina smile, the one that was polite and full of teeth but never reached her eyes. "It's such a beautiful day and I'm enjoying the walk."

"You're certain?" he asked. "What with Cristoffel and Justus, I'd think it would be safer if you were with me."

I don't, I thought, and I only just managed to avoid saying it aloud.

"I think it's perfectly safe for me to walk to the village in the daylight," I said. "Thank you, Mynheer Janssen."

My tone was very final. He couldn't make me ride with him, short of climbing down and throwing me in the cart, and if I saw him move I was going to run.

He gave me a long look and I stared right back at him.

A Van Brunt never shows fear, but I wondered what he was thinking. His eyes gave away nothing.

His eyes are like Schuler de Jaager's eyes, I thought. *Exactly the same. Full of things he doesn't want me to know.*

Finally he nodded and clicked his tongue at the horse, and the cart moved on. I watched it go, lingering on the side of the road for a few moments so that the cart would get ahead of me.

He wants something from me, I thought as I walked along. I had no evidence of this, only the strange feeling that had come over me as he stared me down. *But what could he want?*

Henrik Janssen gave me the same sort of skin-crawling feeling that Schuler de Jaager did, and I did a kind of full-body shake hoping to get rid of it. It didn't really work. I still felt as though light-footed insects crawled up and down my spine for several minutes after.

I passed the edge of the village and saw the scrubby little cottage where Schuler de Jaager lived. The old man was at his window and our eyes met as I passed. I raised my eyebrow at him and gave him a good hard glare before going on. He smirked at me in response, and I had a lot of trouble restraining myself from doing something childish and stupid, like breaking his window with a rock. No boy in the Hollow could throw a rock as hard or as accurately as me. If I wanted to I could probably put a rock dead center between Schuler de Jaager's eyes.

He's your grandfather, some little part of me whispered. *You can't do that.*

He's no grandfather of mine, the stronger, more sensible part of me insisted. *I have a grandfather already, and his name is Abraham Van Brunt.*

I'd half considered confronting Schuler, demanding he tell me what he knew about the monster in the woods, but then decided it wouldn't be any good just yet. If Schuler de Jaager had kept the secret of Brom's ride as the Horseman for thirty years, he wouldn't give up any other secret just because I asked him. Confronting him meant having a plan, and I didn't have a plan just yet.

Sander sat on the boarded walk in front of the notary's office, his feet and legs sticking out into the street. He idly tossed a stick into the air and watched as it fell to the ground.

"What are you doing?" I asked as I came up.

He rubbed his nose with his sleeve. "Nothing special. Mama said I was getting underfoot and told me to go help Papa, because I'm supposed to be learning from him how to be a notary, too."

Sander was at the age when most boys began learning a trade or profession, and being the son of the notary, it was most natural for him to take on his father's business.

"But now Papa is talking to some men and I haven't anything to do," Sander said. "They've been in there for some time, arguing."

"Who's he talking to?" I asked, peering into the front window.

There was quite a collection of individuals in the notary's office, including Brom and Diederick Smit. They seemed to be having a heated discussion, if the expressions on their faces were any indication.

"Sander!" I said, shaking his shoulder. "Is there any place where we can listen to what's happening inside your father's office without being seen?"

His mouth twisted and his eyebrows knit together. "Not now that everyone is already inside. If we had gone in before they arrived we could have hidden in the big cabinet. Sometimes I go in there when Mama's in a bad mood."

Sander stood up. "Anyway, what do you want to go in there for? It's just boring business talk. Let's go play Sleepy Hollow Boys in the woods."

I had to remind myself that Sander didn't know about anything that had happened to me since we saw Cristoffel's body. It seemed like I'd lived two lifetimes since that morning, but it had only been two days.

"The woods aren't safe anymore," I said. "Not even during the day, or in the part we like to play."

I sat close to him on the walk and talked low so none of the nosy passersby could hear, and I told him all about finding the sheep, and seeing Justus and the creature in the woods the day before.

"You *saw* it?" Sander's eyes were about the biggest they'd ever been.

"Not only did I see it, it tried to take me, too," I said, and then I told him about last night's journey and how the creature had appeared at the clearing.

"But how did you get away from it?"

"The Horseman saved me," I said, and felt my face redden. I felt strangely shy about the Horseman.

"The *Headless* Horseman?" Sander said, practically shouting, and I shushed him.

"He's not headless," I said. "And I didn't see him, anyway. I only heard him, and the creature in the woods heard him, too."

"How do you know he's not headless if you didn't see him?"

"I just know, all right?" I said, and punched him in the shoulder.

"But . . . why did he save you and not the others?" Sander asked.

"What, do you wish he'd let me have my head and hands taken?" I said, stung.

"Of course not. But it's strange, isn't it? That he would save you specially."

It's because he only watches out for me, I thought, and shivered, and wondered how I knew that.

"So what should we do then if we can't go into the woods?"

I was always the one who came up with games for us to play and things for us to do. I didn't want to play just then, though. What I wanted was to know what was going on inside the building behind us.

An empty cart went by in front of us, and I felt the same skin-prickling feeling I'd had earlier. I looked up and saw Henrik Janssen watching me as he drove his cart past.

Just then the door to the notary's banged open. Diederick Smit stalked out. When he saw Sander and me sitting on the walk he scowled at us, or rather at me.

"There's the little witch," he said.

He'd grabbed me by my arm and yanked me to my feet before I knew what was happening.

"I know you're the reason Justus is dead. What did you do in the woods? A spell? A dance? Did you call up that demon to take vengeance on my son because you couldn't?"

His eyes were wild. Spit was flying from his mouth. I recognized that grief had driven him mad. I also knew, with a deep uneasiness, that any accusations of witchcraft might be taken seriously by the people of the village. Sleepy Hollow believed in spirits and demons, because they lived side by side with those beings. The people of the town believed in magic. And why wouldn't they? Magic was woven into the fabric of the Hollow. It drifted in the air. It rode through the night on a fast horse.

I had to stop Smit's mouth before it started. Brom and Katrina's standing would protect me to a certain degree, but if Smit started going around telling people I was the reason

Justus was dead, I'd be in terrible trouble. Most folks didn't care, but a fair number of people already thought I was strange for dressing in boys' clothes. If those people decided that the way I dressed indicated something more sinister then . . .

For the first time I realized some part of what Katrina feared for me, and why she tried so hard to make me fit in. In little villages like ours, those who don't fit in were cast out.

I didn't think about what to do next. I needed Smit to stop talking, to stop talking *immediately*.

I punched Smit in the face. My punches were nothing like Brom's, who could lay a man out before you blinked, but I knew how to hit hard and fast. Smit's nose crunched under my knuckles and he let go of my arm, staggering backward. He held his hands over his face.

"You damned little *bitch*!" he snarled.

"Don't touch me again," I said.

I was surprised that my voice was so calm. It almost felt like I wasn't part of my body, like I was watching from outside myself. I was vaguely aware of Brom appearing in the notary's doorway to my left. It would be better for Smit, much better, if I was the one to drive him off. If Brom knew Smit had grabbed me again then Brom would probably kill him right there in the street.

"I told you before, I didn't have anything to do with your boy dying," I said. "I'm sorry that you're so sad about it, but it won't do you any good to make wild accusations."

Sander had stood up when Smit grabbed me, and I heard him breathing hard near my right shoulder. Sander did not like confrontations, and he especially did not like confrontations with adults.

"Ben, you shouldn't—" he whispered.

"Go home, Mr. Smit," I said. "I think you should do your grieving quietly in your house."

"You're just like your father, and just like *him*," Smit said, pointing at Brom. "Always thinking you have the right to tell people what to do and what to say and how to think. Well, let me tell you this, Ben Van Brunt—I know what you've done and you're going to pay for it. You're going to *pay*."

Smit leaned his face close to me as he talked. I could smell the tobacco on his breath, see the wild rolling of his eyes. Smit's wife had died in childbirth with Justus, and his son was all the man had. I felt sorry for him, but not enough to take his abuse.

"I haven't done a thing," I said. "And don't you dare accuse me of something I haven't done again, or you'll be the one who pays."

I didn't know what had gotten into me. I was a skinny fourteen-year-old and Smit was a grown man. There was no way I could make him suffer. Brom certainly could, but not me. And I wasn't threatening him with Brom. I realized a moment too late that what I said could be interpreted as a threat of witchcraft, if a person was already inclined to believe such things.

All the blood drained out of Smit's face. "Witch."

"Call my grandchild a witch again and you won't like what happens next," said Brom.

"It's all right, Opa," I said. "Mynheer Smit was leaving."

I sounded like Katrina when she was in full lady-of-the-house mode. Smit looked from Brom to me and backed away, stumbling into the street.

"You'll pay," he said. "Everyone will know what you are, and you'll pay."

Several people who'd been about their morning business had stopped to stare at us. Brom stepped out onto the sidewalk and glared around until all of them suddenly remembered why they were out and about and hurried away. All of them, that is, except Henrik Janssen, who stood a few feet along the walk, leaning against a building. When I caught his eye he straightened and came closer, unaffected by Brom's fierce look.

"That's some girl you have there," Janssen said to Brom. "Almost as brave as a boy."

Brom's face relaxed, and he came close and put his arm around my shoulder. "Braver than most boys, I'd say. She's just like her grandmother."

I started. It was true that Katrina wasn't afraid of anyone. I'd seen her stare down men twice her size when she wanted to make a point. It pleased me more than it ever had, I think, to have someone compare me to Katrina. But I didn't want to talk to Henrik Janssen. The hairs on the back of my neck stood up as he looked at me.

"Some man will be lucky to have you as a wife one day," he said.

"I'm never getting married," I said, but his words had made me very uneasy. Was that why he kept looking at me that way? Did he have designs on the Van Brunt farm? Just because our lands bordered one another didn't mean that they should be joined. Anyway, if Brom wanted Janssen's land then my grandfather would just buy the other man out. That's what Brom always did.

And he's so old. At least thirty. Why doesn't he have a wife his own age already?

Brom seemed to be thinking along the same lines, because he squeezed my shoulder and said, "She's far too young for me to think about giving her up."

"Not so young for all that," Janssen said. "Plenty of girls around here marry at fourteen."

"But more of them marry at sixteen, or eighteen," Brom said, and then added, pointedly, "and they usually marry boys their own age."

Janssen only smiled at that, and it was the sort of smile that made my stomach turn. Still, whatever Janssen wanted, at least I knew Brom would never trade me for land or some such thing. I knew that this happened to some girls.

Poor Veerla die Wees—her parents were almost as poor as the Van den Bergs, but she'd been so beautiful that she caught the eye of a merchant who happened to be passing through the Hollow while she was hanging laundry outside their cottage. Veerla had only been fourteen, but she had five younger siblings and there wasn't enough food to go around. The merchant (who was fifty if he was a day) offered to marry Veerla in exchange for what was rumored to be an extremely generous bride price.

She tried to run away before the wedding, but her father found her before she'd gotten very far. The whole village turned up to see the slender, weeping form of Veerla be given in unwilling marriage to the merchant, who'd eyed her throughout the ceremony as though she were a prize cow. That had been about a year before, and I remembered feeling sick throughout the service. Katrina had her lips pressed together the entire time, like she was swallowing a furious diatribe.

"I've got to get Ben home now," Brom said, shouldering Janssen aside. "Katrina will skin us both if we're late for the midday meal."

"Yes, you should take her home," Janssen said after us. "Before anyone else comes along making accusations."

"Opa, I was going to play with Sander," I said, peering over my shoulder at my friend, who waved forlornly after me.

"Not now, Ben," he said under his breath, steering me toward the barn where he kept Donar when he was in town.

"I don't think I want you in the village for the next couple of days."

"Because of what Mynheer Smit said?"

"Yes," Brom said, quickly saddling Donar and mounting. He pulled me up behind him. "I don't think most people would take him seriously, but there was nothing left of Justus except his bones when we returned to get the boy's body. Smit is flailing about, looking for someone to blame, and he's decided it's you. Nothing any of us said could convince him otherwise."

I felt a chill that had nothing to do with the weather. "But he can't do anything to me. A whole lot of people heard him threaten me right in the street."

"And they heard you threaten him, too."

"And you, too," I retorted.

"I've punched most of the men in this village at one time or another, whether in sport or in anger," Brom said, shrugging. "They expect it of me. But not of you."

"That's not fair," I burst out. "Why do boys get to do anything they want? Mynheer Smit wouldn't even be able to say I was a witch if I was a boy."

I couldn't see Brom's face, but I felt him take a long, deep breath and let it out again.

"Maybe I didn't do you such a favor, raising you the way I did. Maybe I should have let Katrina have her way. But I—"

Brom didn't finish his thought, but I didn't need to hear it.

He missed Bendix so much, and wanted his son back, so he made me his son instead. I wasn't angry about it. I *liked* being this way. It was the way I felt I really was inside, not just because of what Brom wanted. I was the one who'd turned away from Katrina when I was young, had started following Brom like a puppy. I only wished that no one knew that I was a girl at all, that they didn't think I was a girl pretending to be a boy.

Donar came to a halt, and I realized then what had made Brom stop talking. Schuler de Jaager stood on his porch, watching us as we passed.

I felt hatred burst through me, more intense than I'd ever known. Schuler was the reason Bendix was dead, and even before that he'd spent years trying to make Brom miserable. Anyone who tried to hurt Brom was unforgiveable, in my mind. I stared at Schuler, who only smirked back at me.

"I'm going to kill him," Brom said under his breath. "I should have done it years ago, and damn the consequences. He seeds nothing but misery in his wake."

For a moment I thought Brom would leap from Donar's back and strangle Schuler de Jaager right there in the street. I couldn't think of anyone who deserved it more, but I didn't want my grandfather jailed—by stupid Sem Bakker, even— for killing my other grandfather.

Donar waited patiently while Brom and I did our best to smite Schuler de Jaager with our eyes. The old man was completely unaffected—if anything, the waves of hatred rolling off us seemed to amuse him. After a while Brom clicked his tongue at Donar and we continued on our way, though I felt Schuler watching us until we were out of sight.

I leaned my cheek against Brom's back. I wasn't entirely sure it was a good thing for me to stay out of the village. Diederick Smit was probably running from door to door, telling tales. Someone ought to be there to make sure people heard a version of the story that wasn't his, and I said this to Brom.

"Don't worry about that," he said. "I'm going to take your grandmother into the village later to do her shopping. Katrina will put any wrong thinkers aright."

I considered Katrina's imperious glare, her magnificent temper and the generally mild personalities of the vast majority of people in the Hollow. *Yes, Katrina could sway them.*

"And while we're out," Brom said, "you're to stay *on the farm*, do you understand? No weaseling out of your promise like yesterday. I don't want you in the woods, or near the woods, or even thinking about the woods."

"Yes, Opa," I said. He didn't have to worry. I had no intention of going anywhere near the woods again after the night before.

But how will you see the Horseman, then? a little voice whispered. I pretended I hadn't heard.

Brom and I ate our meal with Katrina and told her about Diederick Smit. Her eyes sparked when she heard about Smit's accusations.

"Useless man," Katrina said. "He always has been. He's the same age as Bendix was, you know. Smit tried to court Fenna but she wouldn't have him. He resented Bendix for that, thought it was because Bendix was rich and he wasn't, but Fenna told me it was because Smit was cruel and stupid."

"Justus was the same way," I said.

"You can't teach your children if you have nothing valuable to teach," Katrina said. "They learn what they see."

I frowned. "So it was all right that Justus was like that, because he couldn't help it?"

"Of course not," Katrina said. "But it would take a smarter child than Justus was to learn how to change."

I picked at my stew, mulling this over. Was everyone condemned to act the same way as their parents, to repeat the same patterns and cycles over and over again? Everyone told me I was just like Brom, and I'd always been proud of that. But I also knew that Brom had many troublesome qualities—not that I would ever say this aloud to anyone.

Brom tended to run people over if they didn't give him his way. Sometimes he did it with charm and sometimes with force, but he always got what he wanted and damn anyone else. Did I want to be like that? Did I want to put my wants above everyone else's, squash them or push them out of the way just because they resisted?

I loved Brom so much, but I didn't want to be *exactly* like him.

Katrina and Brom went off to the village in the trap, for Katrina refused to ride behind Brom on Donar.

"I'm a lady, and ladies don't ride astride, and there really isn't enough room for me to ride sidesaddle," she always said.

Once I overheard Brom offering to let her ride in his lap, and this was accompanied by a look that I didn't understand but made Katrina swat him and say, "Shush."

After Brom and Katrina left I went out by the sheep paddock. The sheep acted as they normally did, no strange silent huddle. I suppose they must have forgotten what happened to their fellow the other day.

Sheep get to do that. They forget. It must make them happy, not to trail bad memories around behind them like people do.

I walked slowly along the fence until I came to one of the wheat fields. The crop had already been harvested here, and nothing remained except the rough half-stalks left behind. The sun was warm and I wandered into the field, letting my mind turn over everything that had happened.

I still didn't have any answers about why Cristoffel and Justus had died. Everything Brom and Katrina told me seemed to muddy the waters. Above all, I could not determine why Schuler had kept Brom's secret about the Horseman, or why he'd sent Bendix into the woods to die, or why he'd told me that the creature in the forest was a Kludde. Had he thought to inspire my curiosity, to send me to my death like my father?

I paused. Schuler *had* sent Bendix to his death. He'd deliberately manipulated my father, knowing what was out there and what would happen. But why? What vendetta did he have against Bendix? Or did he just hate all the Van Brunts?

No matter how I tried to find an answer, I couldn't. I wished Brom hadn't taken me away from Sander so quickly. Sander wasn't brave and he wasn't fast and he wasn't a very good tree-climber, but he was one of the smartest boys our age. If I told him about all this *(not about Brom the Headless Horseman, and not about the real Horseman either, no no no, that's for me alone)* he might be able to help me work through the problem. Later I'd ask Brom if he could bring Sander to the farm tomorrow. No one could object to our playing if we stayed on Van Brunt land and away from the forest.

I wondered if any more boys had gone missing, and would be found in the forest. I'd spent more time walking the road to the village that day than I had actually in the village. People might be talking—talking about Cristoffel and Justus, about what to do, about any other boy that might have gone missing. It seemed impossible to me that the creature in the woods would have stopped taking victims.

But if any boy taken melts away like Justus did, people might not even know that boy is dead if they don't find him in time.

I found a place in the field where the stalks had been flattened and lay down on my back. The stalks were scratchy but the ground was soft and the sun was bright. My head was spinning and I just wanted to rest a little while. No one could see me from the house out here, so no one would come and tell me I had to get up and do this or that. I closed my eyes and inhaled the smell of the earth, and the grassy scent of the wheat stalks, and the indefinable gold of the sun. Sander had told me once that the sun didn't have a smell.

"It does," I'd insisted. "It's that warm soft smell that you get on a really sunny day, and it's in the air and it sort of fills you up."

"That's just because the sun is making the grass and everything hot. That's what you're smelling—the grass and the trees," Sander said.

"No. It's the smell of the sun."

He wouldn't let me convince him that day, but I knew I was right. I breathed in the sun, let it fill up my nose and my lungs and my heart, and I felt easy for the first time since I'd seen Cristoffel's remains in the woods.

Ben.

Someone's hand was on my face, someone trailing their fingers over my cheek.

Ben, wake up.

I felt like I was struggling out of a deep pit, like my hands scrabbled for purchase, looking for an edge that wasn't there.

Ben!

My eyes flew open. He was calling me.

But it wasn't the Horseman leaning over me in the twilight. It was Henrik Janssen.

11

He sat on the ground next to me, his legs stretched out beside mine. He was close, far too close, and the look on his face wasn't right. He shouldn't be looking at me that way.

I scrambled away, realizing that the hand I'd felt on my face was Henrik Janssen's. I wanted to scrub at the place where he'd touched me.

"What's the matter, little Bente?" he asked, and there was something horrible in his voice, something hungry.

"What are you doing here?" I asked. I wanted to stand up, to run, but my legs wouldn't do what I wanted them to do.

"I came to speak to your grandfather, and I saw you lie down in the field. I didn't think you should stay out here, not with everything that's happened. You might get hurt."

The only thing around here that wants to hurt me is you, I thought, but I knew that wasn't quite right. He wanted something else from me, something I didn't really comprehend.

I was a farmer's child. I knew about procreation. And I also knew that grown men shouldn't look at young girls the way

Henrik Janssen looked at me, like he could see right through my boys' clothes to the skin beneath.

"I can take care of myself," I said.

"Yes," he said. "I saw you taking care of yourself today with Mynheer Smit."

Everything he said seemed laced with some other meaning, and every glance he gave me made me feel like bugs were crawling all over me.

"If you came to see Brom you ought to go up to the house," I said, finally managing to get my legs underneath me to stand.

He stood, too, and gazed upward at the sky. "This is my favorite time, when the sun slips away and the stars come out. Won't you walk with me under the stars, little Bente?"

I was hardly little. I was almost as tall as he was, but when he said "little," it was as if he meant something else, meant that I was something he wanted to take and hide away—like a doll, like a jewel, like a secret he wanted me to keep.

Brom and Katrina would be back from the village by now. All I had to do was run for the house. Henrik Janssen would never be able to catch me.

He shifted, just a little, and suddenly he stood between me and the house, almost as if he'd read my mind.

"I know what you want," I said. "If you touch me I'll kill you. And if I don't, then Brom will."

His eyes glittered in the half-light. "But the damage will be done, and you'll need a husband then, little Bente."

I lifted my chin, though inside I trembled. "I'd rather die than marry you, or anyone. I'm not a girl. I'm a boy."

He couldn't possibly run as fast as me. I could get away from him if I took him by surprise.

I wondered at his confidence in this gamble. He had to know that if I escaped him I would tell Brom and Katrina.

He's going to make sure you don't escape until he gets what he wants.

"You're disgusting," I said, my voice dripping with disdain. "And pathetic. You're out here in the middle of a field, trying to force a child young enough to be your daughter to marry you because—what? You don't think your farm is big enough?"

There was just enough light for me to see his half-smile as he stepped closer. "You can't possibly think this is about the *farm.*"

There was something so wrong with him when he said this, something that wasn't just about his impulse. It was as if he was being driven by a force beyond himself.

I had only a moment before he grabbed me, and I knew with great certainty that if he did I'd never escape.

I turned and ran, away from the house.

Away from the house, and toward the woods.

Behind me Henrik Janssen cursed. I heard the rustle of the wheat stalks as he pursued me, his ragged breathing.

I heard a voice calling from close to the house. "Ben! Ben!"

Brom. He was looking for me. I could tell by the way he called my name that he was worried.

I glanced behind me. Henrik Janssen was much closer than I thought he would be. Terror coursed through my blood. I couldn't let him catch me.

But you're not to go into the woods either Ben you promised Brom that you wouldn't and there's something in there much worse than Henrik Janssen something with long fingers that wants to take your head and your hands something made of darkness that wants to swallow you up.

"Help!" I screamed as I ran. "Help me!"

I didn't call out because I thought help would come in time. I didn't think Brom would magically swoop down and find me. But I wanted him to know that I was out here, that I was in distress, and I also thought it might drive Henrik Janssen off if Brom came looking for me.

He must be mad, I thought as I ran. Whatever Henrik Janssen wanted, he was off his gourd to suddenly act this way. Did he think he wouldn't be caught out? Did he think that Brom wouldn't beat him bloody for even trying to touch me?

What if he is mad? What if something from the woods— some magic, some miasma—has seeped into him, is making him act this way?

There was no time to think, to wonder, to solve the problem. I heard Janssen put on a burst of speed behind me, and I ran harder than I ever had.

I crashed into the woods, a flailing intruder, and immediately the trees closed around me and shut out the starlight.

I clambered up the nearest tree, feeling out the limbs in the darkness, and tried to slow my breathing.

A moment later Janssen blundered through the bush, making so much noise that he was probably heard by every creature for miles. I couldn't see him, because I'd climbed as high as I could safely go in the dark, but I heard the rasp of his breath and the scrape of his boot soles over the dead leaves littering the forest floor.

"Come out, come out, little Bente," he crooned.

He didn't sound like himself. Not that I'd spoken to him so many times, but Henrik Janssen was normally quiet and soft-spoken. Had he been hiding this monster inside him all this time? I couldn't imagine keeping such malice stuffed inside a human skin. Perhaps he'd grown tired of it, longed to let the darkness inside stretch and burst its seams.

I stayed very, very still as he fumbled and scraped around in the darkness. After several minutes I heard him cursing, and then the sounds retreated—back in the direction of the fields.

I wondered if he'd run into Brom there.

The forest was quiet all around me—not the eerie silence that meant something terrifying was coming, but a soft hush that enveloped. All the little creatures were tucked up in their beds, and I imagined tiny squirrels and chipmunks and field mice being kissed by their mothers, or told stories by their fathers. I felt safe, the way I'd always felt in the woods before I saw the creature devouring Justus Smit.

A chill brushed across my skin. The trees felt safe now, but they wouldn't keep that way. I should leave, go back to the house, tell Brom and Katrina what happened in the field.

I was alight to any possibility of a trick as I eased my way out of the tree. Henrik Janssen could have pretended to leave noisily while returning in silence to wait for me to emerge. But I jumped to the ground and heard no movement other than my own.

Still, I thought it best to stay in the woods a while, and walk parallel to the fields until I was closer to the drive that led up to the house. Janssen could be lurking in the fields. I listened hard for any sound of a search, for Brom calling my name, but there was nothing except the wind.

I moved along slowly in the dark, placing my feet carefully so I didn't rustle the leaves any more than necessary, my hands out before me so I wouldn't run headlong into any trees.

A horse whickered softly in the darkness, and I stopped walking. It came from somewhere ahead.

Was it Brom? Was he out with Donar, searching for me?

I thought this but deep inside, in that secret place I kept only for me, I knew it wasn't Brom. I knew because the moment I heard the horse my heart soared, and my feet moved faster, moved toward him because there was nothing else I could do.

I stumbled into a clearing, tripping over my own legs in my haste, and he was there, standing in a shaft of moonlight.

He wasn't headless, and he didn't laugh the way that Brom had when my grandfather pretended to be a demon horseman. He sat absolutely still upon his horse—a breathtaking horse, a horse the color of the sky at midnight, taller even than Donar.

His legs were long and so were the fingers that held the reins, and he seemed to be dressed in the same darkness as his horse, except there was just a hint of something racing over his skin, something that looked like fire.

His face was turned away from me. He knew I was there, though. I waited, my breath caught in my throat, for the moment when he would look at me.

He turned his head toward me, and I was lost forever.

He was the most terrible, the most beautiful thing I'd ever seen, and yet I couldn't describe the shape of his face. He was so glittering, so unearthly, that human words were wholly inadequate. I'd been wrong about him, wrong because the stories said he came with a sword and took your head away. The Horseman wasn't death. He was life, more life than I'd ever imagined.

He held out his hand.

I understood. It was my choice.

It was always my choice. He was here before, a long time ago, reaching his hand down to me. There was almost nothing of him then—just a shadow, just a thought—and I was so small. But when I touched his hand, touched that shadow, he was real and solid and part of me and I was a part of him.

The thought flitted across my mind, a silverfish dancing in a sunlit stream. I'd forgotten. I'd forgotten that I knew the Horseman of old.

(not just knew him made him)

There wasn't time to take that out and examine it, to look at that idea from all sides. There wasn't time because he was here, and all I wanted was to ride.

I put my hand in his, and he took me up on his horse in front of him. He squeezed the horse's sides with his legs, and then we were running, running so fast it seemed impossible. There were trees in the way but he glided around them so smoothly it was as if they weren't even present.

Then we burst out into the open, and we were galloping across the fields, and we were fast and free under the stars.

I wanted it to last forever, to stay there with him on his horse and run until there was nothing left of me.

But then I saw Brom, standing in the middle of a field, calling my name, and I felt a moment of regret.

The horseman knew, somehow he knew, and felt it. The horse slowed, and cantered around back toward Brom, and a fist squeezed my heart and I didn't know what I wanted, I didn't know if I wanted to go back to being a child or if I wanted to stay with him.

"Ben, Ben!" Brom called.

I wanted to stay with the Horseman. I wanted to go back to Brom. The Horseman felt the push and pull of my heart before I did, and I heard him whisper, *Not yet. It's not time yet.*

Why did you come for me, then? I thought, and everything in me yearned to stay with him, to ride fierce and free and be exactly who I wanted to be without any expectation.

I came for you so he wouldn't take you. And so you would remember me.

A noise came out of my mouth, half-sob, half-laugh. So I would remember him? How could I ever forget him? How could I have forgotten him before? He was seared inside me.

He steered the horse toward Brom, standing in the field calling my name. We stopped a few feet from Brom but my grandfather still strode forward, bellowing, "Ben! Ben!"

He can't see us, can't see the Horseman, I thought, and slid from the horse's back. Brom's eyes widened as I appeared practically under his nose, seemingly out of thin air.

"Ben?" he said uncertainly, and reached toward me, but I turned away from him, my heart breaking.

Don't leave, I thought, but he was already gone, and nothing remained but the rush of wind to show he'd ever been there at all.

I don't remember much after that. I remember Brom bringing me inside, but for the first time in my life I wasn't comforted by his presence. There was only one thing I wanted, and I wasn't going to find it safe in my house, under the watchful eyes of Brom and Katrina.

I hated the Horseman then, just a little, for he'd made me want. He'd made realize what I had wasn't enough. He made me long for something unexplainable, indefinable.

The next morning I was up well before the sun. I'd hardly slept again, and knew that sooner or later this lack of rest would betray me, but every time I'd closed my eyes my mind raced out the window and into the night, searching for him.

I dressed and sat quietly in my room until I heard the household stirring, then went out to find Brom.

Lotte was busy preparing breakfast when I passed through the kitchen. She nodded at some apples on the table. I took one to please her even though I wasn't interested in eating it. Everything roiled inside me, making me feel sick and unsettled.

Brom was in the barn, currying Donar. We had a stableboy but Brom preferred to groom Donar himself, leaving the carriage and field horses to the boy.

Donar whickered softly as I approached and I thought of the great black horse standing in the moonlight, and the rider on his back.

No, I thought. *Not now. Don't think of him now. There are words that need to be said and you won't be able to say them if you're dreaming of the night.*

"Ben," Brom said, and I noticed blue shadows under his dark eyes. I wasn't the only one who'd had trouble sleeping.

"How are you feeling today? Your grandmother and I were worried about you last night."

"I'm better," I lied. "Opa, listen. I have to tell you what happened."

I told him about falling asleep in the field, about Henrik Janssen attacking me, how I'd escaped into the woods. A storm moved into Brom's face until he looked like an angry thundercloud about to burst. I'd worried a little about what I would say about the Horseman, how much I should or shouldn't explain, but I needn't have bothered. I never got as far as talking about the Horseman at all.

"I'll kill him," Brom said, slamming the currycomb into a nearby bucket with unnecessary force.

Donar, used to Brom's moods, ignored this. I stroked his nose and he nudged my shoulder in an expectant way, so I gave him my apple.

"I'll kill him," Brom said again, and the way he said it made me uneasy.

Brom was always threatening people, but he didn't really mean it. It was his—admittedly strange—way of venting his feelings. This time, though, he sounded serious—as if he really would murder Henrik Janssen. I stepped in front of Brom before he went barreling out of the barn in a rage.

"Wait," I said. "Wait. I didn't tell you this so you would hurt him."

"Get out of the way, Ben. I'm going to strangle him, and

no one in Sleepy Hollow would blame me if they knew what he'd done."

"Wait!" I said again. "Please."

"Why? Why should I let that piece of filth breathe one more moment upon this earth?"

"Because I don't think it was him, or at least not *all* him, at any rate."

I had a strong impression that Henrik Janssen did hold some seeds of those horrible feelings deep inside, but I don't think he would ever have let them take root. There was something else at work, something that came from the woods, something that had woken the sleeping monster that killed Justus and Cristoffel, something that fed the evil Henrik Janssen would have smothered and let die.

"What do you mean? You're talking nonsense, Ben. Who attacked you if it wasn't him?"

I took a deep breath, because I knew how Brom would react to my idea. "I think it's something to do with the woods, with the magic in the woods. It, well, it seemed like he was being spurred on, that he wasn't exactly himself."

"Don't tell me you believe that rot. Monsters in the woods, fairies in the garden, spirits at the door. I thought I raised you better than that. We're not small-minded fools."

"It's not nonsense," I said. "How can you think that when you saw what happened to Justus? How can you say it isn't real when you know what happened to Bendix?"

Brom looked away. "Your grandmother shouldn't have told you that story. It's put ideas into your head."

"Don't act like Oma is confused," I said, and I was shocked to hear the anger in my tone. I'd never been angry with Brom in my life. "You're the one who's confused, who doesn't want to believe. Strange things come true in the Hollow. Everyone knows that. Everyone except you—and even you know it, you just don't want to admit it's true. Because if you do admit it then that means Bendix died and there wasn't anything you could do about it."

I regretted this the moment I said it. Brom's face turned the color of old parchment, and looked just as brittle.

"I'm sorry. I'm sorry, Opa, I didn't mean it."

"Yes, you did. I didn't teach you to lie."

"All right. I did mean it. But I didn't mean to *say* it."

Brom snorted. The color returned to his face.

"Listen, Opa, please. Every time you've seen one of the dead boys you've been too busy arguing with Diederick Smit to really think about what happened to them, and why. Oma told me you never really believed what she told you about how Bendix died."

"It's nonsense," he muttered, but for the first time I noticed his eyes didn't reflect what his mouth was saying.

"Ten years ago my father went into the woods, to try to save me and my mother."

"Yes, on the advice of Schuler de Jaager." Brom spat. "So?"

"So when my father went there he woke something, something that attacked him. But nothing like that has happened since, at least not until recently. There have been no other deaths like that, or people going missing with no explanation in the woods. Have there?"

Brom frowned. "There's always a few going missing every year—usually kids that wandered too far while playing. They've mostly been found, though. And a few adults that were turned around and wandered in circles until someone else happened upon them."

"Anybody that went missing and was never found?" I should know this, since Sleepy Hollow wasn't such a large village, but I often drifted away when Brom and Katrina were talking, lost in my own world and my own thoughts.

As a child does, I thought. *Not bothering about anything an adult might say.*

I felt a little pang of mourning for that child that I was, for the innocence I'd never have again. I'd never be able to play in my own land again without thinking of the country beyond, all the world pressing up against my door.

"Elizabeth van Voort. She was never found," Brom said, startling me out of my thoughts. "She was a teenage girl, though, and most folk decided she'd run away with some boy from another town. I never really believed it. She wasn't the type, and even if she did run away, I think she would have written to her parents, and they never had word of her again."

"What do you think happened to her?"

Brom's mouth twisted, like he was rolling something unpleasant on his tongue. "I don't know if I should tell you this or not, but you've seen some of the ugliness of this world already, and I can't shelter you forever."

I waited expectantly.

"I think one of the men of the village, er, compromised her and then got rid of her. I never could find out who did it, though I tried."

I did my best to disguise my shock. Of course I was aware—in a dim, childish sort of way—that such things happened. It was that they seemed like things that happened far away, in places that weren't like Sleepy Hollow.

Brom seemed eager to move on from the subject of Elizabeth van Voort before I asked any uncomfortable questions. "And there was William de Klerk. That wasn't so very long ago, and he's your age. I'm surprised you don't remember."

"William de Klerk," I said. A memory bubbled to the surface, hazy and incomplete. "I didn't really know him. But he was a farmer's son. He went missing at the beginning of the summer?"

Brom nodded. "He was playing in the woods with some other boys, and William was separated from them. There was an enormous search. It seemed like everyone in town was out looking for him."

I remembered now. I also remembered my shameful

indifference, my conviction that it hardly mattered to me if some boy I barely knew disappeared. Brom had been out all day for several days in a row. Sander and I were told to confine our games to the farm in the interim. It was decided, in the end, that William had wandered too deep into the woods and was lost forever. No one would dare search for him there, beyond the safety of the trail. Everyone in the Hollow knew that if William had gone there, he would not return.

But I forgot, and nobody talked about it again. This was one of those blind corners, a dead end that nobody spoke of. It was hazed by magic that tied everyone's tongues. But they didn't forget, exactly. The knowledge was still there, else Brom wouldn't have spoken of it so easily. I don't know why, but I thought of Schuler de Jaager—thought that somehow he was the reason why this happened. Then I pushed Schuler de Jaager away, because I realized something.

"He must have done it," I said, thinking hard.

"Who must have done what?" Brom asked.

"William de Klerk. He must have woken the creature in the woods. Attracted its attention. Whatever he did caused the creature to go looking for more boys, to stray from its usual place."

"I don't know, Ben. If there is some haunt out there taking children, and it's been awake since the beginning of the summer, why didn't it go after you and Sander? The two of you practically live in the trees from dawn to dusk."

Because the Horseman's been watching over me all this time, I thought. *Even if I didn't know he was there.*

But that wasn't the only reason Sander and I had been safe. There was something more. "You said William de Klerk was playing with some other boys? What if those boys were Justus Smit and Cristoffel van den Berg?"

"What is it you're thinking? That they trespassed where they shouldn't, and so the boys were punished?"

I could see the effort it cost Brom to admit there might be something dangerous in the wood to do this theoretical punishing.

"Maybe," I said, but I still felt I wasn't grasping all of the puzzle. I hesitated before I spoke again, because I knew my next words would kick open a hornet's nest. "I bet Schuler de Jaager would know."

Brom's whole head reddened, from hairline to neckline. "I don't want you anywhere near Schuler de Jaager."

He took a big heaving breath before continuing. "Ben. Whatever he knows, don't believe for an instant that he'll tell you of it. He keeps his secrets and only reveals them if he thinks it's to his benefit. You won't learn anything from him, and you might even come to harm."

Brom was thinking, I knew, of Bendix. Bendix, who'd been closeted with Schuler de Jaager and emerged convinced that the only way to save his wife and child was to seek a cure in the deep, dark woods.

"I'm not concerned about that old devil at the moment in any case—only Henrik Janssen. At the very least he ought to be reported, even if Sem Bakker is useless. And then I think I'll ride over to the farm and have a word."

"Opa, I don't think it will do any good. It really won't." The more I thought about this, the more I was convinced it was true. Henrik Janssen had not been himself—decidedly not himself. Something had taken hold of him, something that meant me harm. Perhaps it was the shadow creature in the woods, or perhaps it was just a lingering stench of evil that infected Janssen when he went near the woods that night we searched for Justus.

Why didn't it affect Brom, though? Then I answered my own question. Brom was too good to be tainted by a seed of evil. He was full of mischief, a trickster, a brawler, sometimes a bully, but he was never evil—not deep down, not in his heart.

But Henrik Janssen—he had something inside him that the darkness flowing out of the wood had been able to grasp. And so did Diederick Smit, I realized. When Smit accused me of witchcraft that had killed his child—there had been something in his eyes that had never been present before. There had been the expected anger and grief, but there had also been hate, and cunning. The realization of that cunning chilled me now. What was Diederick Smit planning?

Sem Bakker had been in the woods the night we searched for Justus, too, though he seemed as unaffected as Brom.

I attributed this to stupidity rather than inherent goodness. It was strangely comforting to think that most of the people in the Hollow would be untainted by the creature's influence because of this same quality. Brom always said that while kindness was ingrained in the people of the Hollow, intelligence was not.

Most folk wouldn't go near the woods in any case. They feared the ghosts and ghouls and phantoms that dwelled there. And that was good. Their fear, their superstition, would keep them safe.

"Even if you think some, er, *presence* overtook Janssen last night, I still believe he could use a good thumping."

Brom sounded so sulky that I laughed. "Opa, you always think thumping is the solution. I think it's more important to find out who was in the woods with William de Klerk, and exactly where they went and what they did."

"Well, we can't exactly ask Cristoffel van den Berg or Justus Smit," Brom said, and I winced.

I realized then why Katrina so often hushed Brom when they were in mixed company. He didn't have that polite line in his head that made most people stop speaking before something off-color slipped out of their mouths.

"What other boys ran around with those three?" Brom asked.

"I don't know," I said. "I'll have to ask Sander. He might know."

Most of the boys ignored me—except for the few who

tried to bully me, and those, I realized, were all dead now. The boys thought I was strange for dressing like them and acting like them and they avoided me because of it. All of the girls ignored me for the same reason. Consequently, I didn't bother myself about learning much about most of the other children of the village. Katrina hired various teachers to educate me at home with varying degrees of success so I didn't even attend the local school with everyone else.

School. The schoolmaster.

For a moment I thought of Crane, pursued through the night in terror by Brom on his black horse. Then I shook it away. Crane had nothing to do with this, and nobody was sorrier than Brom for what happened after.

"The schoolmaster might know," I said. "Or he would be able to ask the children at the school who William de Klerk was friendly with besides Justus and Cristoffel."

"That's a good idea, Ben. I'll ride out to his quarters and ask him today."

"Then you believe me? Believe that there's a monster out in the woods?"

Doubt flickered in his eyes. "I don't know if I believe in your shadow creature. But there's clearly something strange afoot. I said it before and I'll say it again—I don't want you in the forest, for any reason. Whatever is happening, you've already gotten too close to danger for me to feel easy. You take care of my Ben, all right?"

"All right, Opa," I said. I would have agreed to anything. Things were moving, finally. The mystery would be unearthed. We would solve it, Brom and me.

Brom decided I ought to spend the day learning about running the farm, so I trailed after him like an eager puppy until midday. I suspected he only wanted an excuse to keep an eye on me, but I didn't mind. I didn't mind anything at all, because I was with my opa and my head was full of all the triumphs we were going to have together when we vanquished the creature in the woods.

I was in the best mood I'd been in for days. At least, until Brom had Donar brought around after lunch so he could ride into the village and then informed me in no uncertain terms that I was to stay home.

12

"Are you going to talk to the schoolmaster?" I asked, following him outside.

"Yes," he said, mounting Donar.

"But I want to come, too. It was my notion to speak to him in the first place." I tried, and failed, to keep the outrage I felt out of my voice. What happened to our team, to me and Brom fighting the darkness that threatened our town?

Brom glanced behind me before answering, as if seeking support from Katrina, but she had not followed us out.

"I don't think it's safe for you in the village just yet. Rumors were thick in the air yesterday, and Katrina was able to do less to quell them than she hoped. It was strange, really. Even some of the people I'd normally consider less credulous appeared to believe."

A chill ran over my skin though I stood in a patch of sun. "It's not strange. It's that *thing* in the forest. Whatever infected Janssen, infected Smit, is passing from person to person like a sickness." Perhaps the people of the Hollow weren't quite so ignorant—nor innocent—as I'd hoped.

But I still didn't understand *why*. Why was the darkness of the wood suddenly spreading? Why did the creature in the woods seem to be circling around me, coming ever closer? Was it because the Horseman had marked me? Or because I'd seen it attacking Justus? Was it some curse of Schuler de Jaager's? I ground my teeth. There was something I was missing. No matter how I tried I couldn't see the whole picture. And now Brom wanted to leave me out of it, have me sit at home and embroider while he went out hunting for clues.

"If evil is spreading like a sickness then that's all the more reason for you to stay at home," Brom said. "You're the one who believes Henrik Janssen wasn't responsible for his actions last night."

"I didn't say that. I mean, not completely responsible," I said. "I don't think I explained properly."

"You explained plenty, and if I see him I'm not going to feel guilty about any damage that might be done to his person," Brom said. "Whatever is happening seems to revolve around you, and I don't want you in the middle of it. I can't defend you from an entire village of angry folk. You'll stay here, where you're safe."

He tapped his heels lightly against Donar's sides and the horse broke into a trot. I went after them, running until I caught up and could jog alongside. This was my investigation and it wasn't fair for Brom to go off without me. Besides, he hadn't seen what I'd seen. He didn't know what I knew.

"But Opa," I said. "If I go with you I can talk to the other children while you speak with the schoolmaster."

Brom scowled. "I said no, Ben. Stop acting like a child."

That stung, but it made me realize what really bothered me about Brom's refusal. After all, he could be in just as much danger as me—he was my grandfather, and people might decide he was guilty of something just for that. Yet off he went, blithely taking his horse to the village.

"You want me to stay home because you think I'm a girl, not a boy," I said, and I couldn't keep the disgust out of my voice. "You think I'm not capable. You think I can't defend myself."

"How can I have lived with your grandmother for thirty-two years and believe such foolishness? Of course it's not because you're a girl."

But his eyes cut away and I knew for certain that was the real reason, no matter what he said. And it hurt me, hurt me in a place I didn't know I could be hurt, for Brom had always treated me like his boy, and defended me when Katrina said I ought to act more like a lady. Brom wasn't supposed to be the one to think of me as lesser, as weak, as someone who needed defending. Brom was supposed to know who I really was.

I'd followed him all the way down to the road, where the woods ran alongside until the road reached the village. Brom glanced uneasily at the shadows shifting between the trees and said, "Go back to the house now, Ben. I expect to find you there when I get home."

Brom never spoke to me that way, never ordered me to do things I didn't want to do. I opened my mouth, ready to argue, to protest the deep unfairness of *everything*. But before I could say a word he kicked Donar into a gallop and left me behind with a face full of dust.

I swiped at my eyes and stared after him, half of me wanting to run after him just to prove he couldn't stop me if I really wanted to do something. I recognized this as childish, realized it would only undermine the trust I wanted him to have in me, and kicked a large stone in frustration.

I saw Katrina standing on the front porch, gazing anxiously down the drive after me. I waved so she would know I was on my way back to her.

It happened so suddenly that in the moment I didn't really grasp what had occurred. One second I was waving at Katrina, moving back toward the house, and the next second there was darkness, a hoarse triumphant laugh, the smell and taste of burlap, and strong arms carrying me away.

My first thought was that it was Henrik Janssen, still in the grip of whatever madness had possessed him the night before. I had an inkling of what that madness intended for me, and I kicked and elbowed and did anything I could to shake myself loose.

The man only squeezed me tighter and said, "Quit that, you little bitch." The voice wasn't Henrik Janssen's. It was Diederick Smit.

I knew then exactly where he was taking me, and why. He was holding me in front of him, his arms around my waist, and I drummed my boot heels into his shins. He cursed and clouted me on the side of the head. I thought I heard Katrina's voice calling me.

She'd seen everything. She had to have done. I'd been looking right at her, waving, so she would have seen Diederick Smit drag me into the woods. She'd raise the alarm. She would get Brom. Someone would find me before it was too late.

Please let someone find me before it's too late.

Smit barreled roughly through the brush and the bramble, heedless of branches and thorns. I felt them catch and prick at me but I didn't care. The only thing I cared about at that moment was loosening his unnatural grip. I was certain I could outrun him if only I could get free. There wasn't a chance that Smit was fast enough to catch me running.

Once we were clear of the brambles he threw me to the ground, so hard that all the breath flew out of my lungs. My brain screamed at me to *Get up, now's your chance, run,* but my body wouldn't respond, and a moment later Diederick Smit clubbed me in the head with one of his meaty fists. Stars exploded behind my eyes, and before I could think, he grabbed me again and tossed me over his shoulder as if I weighed nothing.

The boxing and the tossing made my head spin, and the burlap-scented air had me gagging. I coughed hard, felt the catch in my throat, and realized it would be incomprehensibly horrible to get sick while my head was still stuffed inside a bag.

I shook my head and shoulders from side to side in a panic, frantically trying to loosen the bag. My stomach bounced against Smit's shoulder with every step.

He stopped, shifted me slightly, and growled, "Enough. Be still."

I levered my knee into his chest with all the force I could muster—which, at the moment, was not very much. Still, it was enough to make him grunt and loosen his hold. I rolled gracelessly off his shoulder, crashing to the ground.

I scrabbled at the sack and managed to push it off just in time to see Diederick Smit's fist descending toward my face. Blood spurted from my nose and I reeled in agony. Getting hit by a grown man in the full flush of anger was not like fighting with one of the village boys, with their small sharp fists and childish force. This was like being clobbered by a boulder, or kicked by a horse.

Tears sprang to my eyes and they made me angry, angry enough to want to fight back. It wasn't the time to cry, to weep like some weak, gentle thing. I needed to survive, to get back to Katrina and Brom.

My fingers groped in the dirt for something, anything to defend myself from the monster looming above me, his fist descending again toward my face. He mashed my cheekbone and I screamed, or tried to, but the pain was so breathtaking only a pathetic little squeak emerged.

I felt a flood of shame. He was grinding me into nothing, pummeling my pride in my strength, my ability, my absolute certainty that I was a Van Brunt and therefore was invincible.

His fist raised again. His eyes shone mad blue against the canopy of autumn leaves above us. Saliva frothed at his lips.

He's going to beat me to death, I thought dully. *Whatever his original intent, it's gone now. All he can think of is Justus, and how he's decided his boy is gone because of me.*

The sun dripped through the leaves. I smiled. I was glad I could at least see the sun, at the end.

I'm sorry, Oma, Opa.

My fingers closed around a stone. No, not a stone—a miracle.

I smashed it into Diederick Smit's temple before I even realized what I'd done. My body had kept fighting without me.

Smit rolled to one side and I felt all the breath I'd been holding burst out of me, and with it came a surge of frantic energy. I managed to push myself halfway up and slam the rock, still gripped hard in my fist, into Smit's face.

He made a choking noise, and his hands flailed out, trying to grab me, but I hit him again.

Somehow I was kneeling on his chest, pressing my knees down so he couldn't breathe. It felt vaguely familiar, and I realized I'd done something similar to his son only a few days before. But this wasn't some chance to humiliate a bully. It was my life at stake. My life, or his.

I pounded the rock into Diederick Smit's face over and over. Over and over until I realized he wasn't moving. I looked at the stone in my hand. It was coated in red slick fluid, and so was my skin. Diederick Smit was an unrecognizable mass of swollen, purpling flesh and blood. He was completely still.

I dropped the stone to the ground in horror and scrambled off him, breathing hard. Had I killed him?

I didn't mean to.

What would happen if he was dead?

I didn't mean to.

Would Sem Bakker arrest me? Would I be tried for murder?

(But I didn't mean to I was only defending myself he was going to kill me it's true it's true you didn't see his face he was going to kill me)

That's right, he was going to kill me, he was either going to feed me to the monster in the woods or he was going to beat me until I couldn't move any more just like I've done to him

(he isn't moving oh god what have I done)

I needed to see if he was still breathing. I reached toward him, then pulled my hand back. No, I needed to get away, that's what I needed to do. I needed to run before someone found evidence of my crime.

(but it isn't a crime, you were only defending yourself, only keeping him from harming you)

Nobody will believe that. They'll say there's something wrong with you. Unnatural. And everyone will believe its true because they already think you're unnatural, you're a girl who wants to be a boy.

They'll say you're a witch. They'll say you killed Diederick the same as you killed his son Justus.

(But Katrina saw, Katrina saw him grab me and take me away)

Everyone will whisper that it's only the Van Tassels and the Van Brunts throwing their weight around again, they think they could do whatever they want and their grandchild is just the same, she's nothing but a shameless witch.

"No, I'm not," I said, but there was no one to comfort me, no one to tell me any different, and I was afraid.

I was afraid and I wasn't supposed to be. Van Brunts weren't supposed to be afraid. I was nothing but a disappointment to Brom, nothing but a scared little child who got taken when I was supposed to be a big brave boy like Bendix, like Brom's first Ben.

Dimly I was aware that I'd staggered away from Diederick Smit's body.

(Maybe he's not dead maybe you should stop and see and

make certain and then maybe you should run and get help no the only running you should be doing is away away AWAY before they find you and call you a murderer you're a murderer what kind of person are you you're a murderer)

I couldn't run even though I wanted to, couldn't force my body to move that fast. My right eye had swollen shut and sweat ran into the left eye. I could barely see, barely grasp where I was going, and knew only that it was essential for me to escape.

Brom. I needed Brom. Brom could fix it. Brom could fix everything.

No, he can't. He can't make a dead body go away. No one can do that except the monster in the woods, the one that makes flesh melt and bones soften, the one that's hunting boys in the wood and you still don't know why. All you've done since the beginning is run around in circles, get underfoot, accomplish nothing. Nobody needs you. Even Brom didn't want you with him today.

(but if he'd taken me this wouldn't have happened so who's fault is it really)

Brom doesn't need some small, pale imitation of Bendix. He wants the real Ben and you'll never be it, you'll never be good enough.

I grabbed my head and shook it from side to side, almost as if I could dislodge the poisonous thoughts embedded in my brain. Where were these coming from? Of course Brom didn't think that. Of course Brom wanted me. He loved me the way I was, even if I wasn't Bendix.

(But does he?)

"He does," I said to the birds that fluttered onto high branches as I crashed past, to the chipmunks that scurried from me with acorn bounty swelling their cheeks.

I stumbled, almost blind, without any sense of the direction I moved in. All the trees appeared the same, the trees I knew so well, the forest I'd loved and played in since I was a small child.

Diederick Smit *(Diederick Smit's body you mean no don't think that he might not be dead)* was somewhere behind me, or perhaps to the side of me. I'd gone the wrong direction, that was certain. The farm wasn't this way. If I kept walking I'd be in the part of the forest I wasn't supposed to go.

That's why William de Klerk went missing. He strayed from the path and forgot his bread crumbs. I wondered if I ought to keep going. I didn't have any bread crumbs, either. Perhaps I should just sit down and wait for someone to find me, wait for Brom or the Horseman or even the monster in the woods, wait for someone to help me or scold me or change my fate.

Or maybe I ought to cross the border we were never supposed to cross and become part of the woods, fold myself into shadow, meld with the trees until my breath was only the rustle of wind in the leaves. And the Horseman would be part of me, too, because the woods were him and he was the woods, he was all that was beautiful and terrible in the world and I wanted to be beautiful and terrible, too.

I don't know how long I wandered like that, half out of my mind and only vaguely aware of my surroundings. Suddenly I was aware of two things—the rumble of a horse's hooves, far away, and that I could only hear the horse because everything else had gone silent.

I stilled, the reflexive freezing of a small animal scenting a predator, but it was too late. The monster was already there.

13

I couldn't see it yet, but I could feel it. It was the ice in my spine, the frantic seizing of the muscles under my ribs, the water that replaced the bones in my legs.

I only had sight in one eye and I squinted into the dappled shadows, certain the creature lurked out of sight on my blind side, enjoying the taste of my fear in the air. I was convinced that each quarter-turn of my head had the monster dancing away before I caught a glimpse of it, and that soon I'd feel the creep of its fingers along my nape. I wanted to run, to move, to go anywhere that it wasn't, but I didn't know how. Malice permeated the air, draped itself over me like a suffocating cloak.

The wind shifted, and the air was suffused with the tang of rotting meat, of blood, of the sulfurous curl of a freshly struck match. I knew that smell. But I didn't have time to place it because suddenly the monster was there, rising up before me, the leaf-filtered sun hardly making an impression on the deep pools of darkness inside it.

It seemed such a strange and incongruous thing, for this night-terror to be out in the day. Such a creature should never be revealed in sunlight, should never be touched by something as warm and good and wholesome as the sun.

Then I recalled that I had seen it twice during the day already, and that it was a foolish thing, a childish thing, to think that monsters only showed their teeth at night.

The creature seemed to draw all the shadows to it, to shape itself of the same stuff, but somehow there was a mouth where there hadn't been a mouth before, and eyes that burned red and wanted something from me that I never wanted to give.

I didn't know how to save myself, or how to even start. I couldn't fight my way out of this, couldn't punch it until it submitted like Brom, or ice it over with my frosty gaze of disapproval like Katrina. The Van Brunt name meant nothing to monsters in the wood, and the Van Tassel name even less. Everything I'd always relied on—my sense of worth, the skills I'd inherited, the lofty branches of my family tree—meant nothing. There was no value in all the things I'd always valued when faced with something that shouldn't even exist.

The figure before me blurred, seemed to elongate, and then was more solid than it ever had been before. From a creature made of shadow and nothing there was something like a man, something at least man-shaped, though still insubstantial.

It was a strange-looking man, to be sure—a very tall man, tall as Brom but with none of Brom's bulk, so he seemed like a bird perched on very long thin legs. There was a flash of an extended chin, a hooked nose like a beak, and I thought again, *Bird, he's like a bird, a long tall bird with its wings tucked in*, and then I knew.

"Crane," I said, and didn't realize the thought had escaped my mouth until the creature before me jerked back, as if startled to hear such a name in such a place.

"You're Crane," I said again, and I forgot everything in that moment, forgot that it was a monster who could hurt me, who *meant* to hurt me, who'd killed three boys already. All I felt was a surge of elation because I knew something nobody else knew, knew what the monster in the woods was even if I didn't know why or how it had come to be. There was a reason behind it all—a reason why all those boys died, why my father died, and the reason was before me.

This is why Katrina thought the monster was familiar, that it knew her. She thought that because it did *know her, because it was Crane.*

"Ichabod Crane," I said.

Saying the name for the third time triggered some kind of change. The creature—Crane—grabbed for his own head to cover his ears, or the place where the ears ought to be on a person. He was somehow less shadow and more flesh than he had been before.

"I'm not," he said, and the voice wasn't that of a human, but the snarl of a monster in the night. "I gave up that name, gave up that body, gave up that life."

"Why?" I asked, even as I thought, *I should be afraid, I should be running.*

But I couldn't help myself. I wanted to know. I needed to know. How had the man who'd disappeared so mysteriously thirty years before somehow become a demon in the woods?

"*You* ask why? You ask, child of privilege, child of the child of that damned Brom Bones?"

He reached toward me, and his long fingers were less of shadow and more of man but they could still hurt me. I knew with all of my being that they could still hurt me. I don't know what made me say it but the words tumbled out of my mouth before I could think.

"Child of the child of Katrina Van Tassel, too."

The hand stilled, an inch from my neck. His face was clearer than it had been before, a blurry image coming into sharp focus. That face was covered in grief, and regret, and the burning eyes weren't burning red anymore, but enormous brown eyes too big for the long bony face. He was a person then, not a monster, even if bits of shadow trailed around him, softening his sharp planes and edges.

"Katrina," he said, and covered his face with his hands. "My Katrina."

She was never your Katrina, I thought, and luckily my

foolish tongue didn't give me away. I imagined his rage would have been incomprehensible, unstoppable, if I said that Katrina had never been his, even if it was true. This man was stupid beyond all reason if he ever thought he had a chance with Katrina. But then, I supposed, he *had* been stupid beyond all reason. He'd asked her to marry him, so he must have believed she might accept him.

Still, Katrina and Brom *belonged* to each other in a way very few couples did. You could see it when you looked at them. Even a delusional schoolmaster should have been able to see that.

"If it wasn't for Brom," he said. "If it wasn't for Brom she could have been mine. She told me no but I could have changed her mind. I don't even know if she really meant to say no. Perhaps she was only being a coquette, as some women are. I could have persuaded her. I know I could have. But then the Horseman chased me, the blasted Horseman. I know it was Brom Bones' doing. He cursed me. He set the Horseman upon me to take my head, to clear the field for himself."

I would not, for all the world, have told Crane in that moment—or ever—that the Horseman who chased him that night was actually Brom. The presence of a real Horseman in the woods kept Brom's secret safe.

"I managed to escape him, though. I made it across the bridge, though I don't remember how. But Gunpowder threw me, threw me and the saddle both, and everything was black for a while. Then there was a man leaning over me, a strange old man."

A chill swept over my skin. There was only one strange old man in this story, only one who'd been on the spot that night. Schuler de Jaager.

I should have known that Schuler would be involved. He seemed to be in the middle of everything, a part of every tragedy related to my family. And looking at Crane, at what he'd become, there was no doubt that this was another tragedy.

I'd barely been aware of Schuler de Jaager until a few days before, and now he seemed to be everywhere, under every rock, like something that shouldn't see the light of day.

Crane had stopped speaking. I held my breath, unsure if I wanted him to continue or not. He seemed to have forgotten I was there, to be speaking to someone who wasn't me. Every word brought his nebulous form more strongly into focus, made him more of a man and less of a wraith.

"I don't know what that old man did to me. I can't recall everything that happened. He asked if I wanted the power to avenge myself on Brom Bones, and I said yes. Of course I said yes, because I thought that if I destroyed Brom that Katrina would be mine. He put me on a horse—not Gunpowder, Gunpowder was gone then—and brought me to these woods. I remember him speaking words in a language I'd never heard before, words that were surely not of this earth. Then my blood was on the ground and there was pain like I'd never imagined, and somehow my body was gone, gone, gone.

"I was nothing but a shadow, a shadow without form or meaning, and when I tried to weep, to curse him, the old man told me he'd given me power and it was up to me to use it. Then he left me. I was alone in the woods, and Brom wasn't destroyed—I was. I wasn't revenged at all. Brom married Katrina and got everything he wanted, and I had nothing. I had no body, no Katrina, no understanding of how to use my power to do anything about it.

"A long time passed. I don't know how long. Time means nothing here, where there are no schedules to keep. I floated here and there, a ghost made of grief, and words drifted to me, about Brom and Katrina's happiness, and their child, and how everything Brom touched turned to gold. I always felt fury at hearing these words, these soft things that drifted on the wind from the Hollow, but I couldn't do anything about it. I was powerless, for all that the old man had promised me power."

I thought I'd hated Schuler de Jaager before—for letting my mother die, for killing my father—but I found my hate bubbling hotter than before. Schuler had made this monster, transformed that foolish Crane into a creature of blood and nightmare, and for what? For his amusement? So he could watch and laugh?

"Then, one day after so many days had passed, the old

man returned. He was disappointed in me, disappointed that I hadn't fulfilled my purpose, the purpose for which he'd made me. I protested that I didn't know how, that he'd never taught me. He said that perhaps I only needed the proper motivation, and he went away.

"More time passed. It might have been an hour or a day or a week or a month or a year. Another man came to the woods, and this man seemed to be looking for me. The moment I saw him I knew who he was, could smell it in the air. The man was made of Brom's blood, of his flesh and bone. He was Brom's child. I could have Brom's child, take his blood and give myself a real form again. I could hurt Brom, hurt him in his heart, because the taking of a child is the worst of all harms.

"I fell upon Brom's child. The powers that had sat latent inside me sprang forth as if I'd always known what to do with them. I took his head—took his hateful eyes that were so like Brom's, took the line of jaw that reminded me of his father, took the tongue that spoke like my rival. I took the hands that would have defended his body even in death.

"But then—but then—*she* was there. How could she be there? Katrina, my Katrina, my beautiful cruel Katrina. She saw that I was a monster. She saw me eating her son. I couldn't take the rest of him, not while she was watching. I couldn't finish it. His blood would no longer feed me, and I fled. I fled to the deepest part of the forest, where not even the others go."

The others, I thought. The ones who creep in the shadows, the ones who speak in whispers. The ones I felt the day I stepped off the path. Part of me wondered who the others were, but the sensible part knew that it was likely best if I didn't know. That kind of knowledge was dangerous.

"I hid away from the light, even from the things that lurked in the darkness. I hid, in sorrow and in shame. There was no moment in my life more terrible than that when Katrina looked upon me as a demon. I'd forgotten, you see, that he was her child, too. I'd only thought of Brom, as if the child had sprung fully formed from Brom's head like Athena from Zeus.

"My form receded again. I thought to die, to disappear, but whatever that old man had done to me wouldn't allow me to die, at least not in that shape. I wasted to almost nothing but I still existed, nothing but pain and misery and hunger. Oh, how I hungered. I wanted something, something that would fill the emptiness. I came out of my barrow, searching, longing. And then those boys wandered into my reach. Foolish boys, stupid boys—the sort I was always reprimanding when I was a schoolmaster. Nobody would miss such boys. The world had no need for those sorts.

"I took one of them, thinking to use his meat to feed me. But something had changed. My touch melted his flesh. I was only able to take his head and his hands, like Brom's son.

"I felt myself filled with fury again, a rage I'd not known in so long. Somehow taking Brom's child had changed me, broken something inside me. The only sustenance I was permitted was the head and the hands, and without it I would wither, but not die.

"The two boys who'd been companions of the first had fled in terror, but some weeks later they returned, looking for their fellow. It was clear they did not expect to find him, but felt they should do something to make up for their cowardice. They did not find him. They found me."

Crane smiled at me, a terrible smile, a smile unrelated to humor or joy. I shuddered, and not only because of the smile. I shuddered because I'd hoped he had forgotten I was there, that he was only speaking to himself, and if I was lucky I could take him by surprise and bolt.

There was still a chance that I might dart away, but any wish that Crane was unaware of me was unfulfilled. He knew I was there. He wasn't so deep in his memories that he would forget that.

"When I took the second boy the same result occurred. I couldn't eat his body or let the substance of his meat feed me. Then I thought only of Brom, of punishing Brom. I went to the farm, the farm built by Katrina's father, the farm that should have been mine by all rights."

"It would never have been yours," I said, and regretted my words instantly. Crane turned his malice-filled eyes and malice-poisoned heart on me.

"You saw me there, didn't you, little child of Brom's line?

Another Ben, they say, though you are a strange one. Half in a dress, half in breeches, don't know where you belong. Not a proper lady. Not a proper man. Not a beauty like Katrina, either. I can see Brom stamped all over your face, and it doesn't favor you.

"I killed the sheep to warn Brom of what was coming, but then I saw you. I knew if I took you that Brom's heartbreak would be complete. This, then, was the least I could do. I could not have Katrina but I could ensure that Brom Bones' line had no future. I would have, too, if it wasn't for the thrice-damned Horseman. Always in my way. Always thwarting me. He tells me I am not to harm you, that you belong to him."

Belong to him. Did I belong to the Horseman? Was that my place in the world? I felt the pull inside me, the thing that longed for him, and I also felt that what Crane said wasn't quite right. I didn't belong to the Horseman, not the way Crane said. I belonged to myself, and to the Horseman, and the Horseman also belonged to me, but somehow none of it really meant possession. It meant some other path that wasn't clear to me yet.

"But it does not matter what the Horseman says or what the Horseman does. The Horseman cannot ride in the day, cannot keep form under sunlight. I didn't know that was true the day I met you in the woods. He fooled me with his threats from afar. But I won't be fooled now. And that means there is nothing he can do for you now."

So the hoofbeats I'd heard earlier were only in my imagination, nothing but wishful thinking. Nobody was going to ride to my rescue, to burst out of the trees on a horse made of the night sky. I was a foolish child, and I would die here.

But he spoke to you once, when it was day and you woke in the tree and you found this Crane leaning over Justus Smit. So maybe it isn't true. Maybe he could still come for you.

(there's a big difference between communicating on the wind and appearing under sunlight, you nit)

Crane watched me, his face avid. He appeared almost human at that moment, the only proof of his transformation those trailing bits of shadow that clung to his skin like cobwebs.

"You've realized, haven't you? That you are alone in the woods with me and you'll never escape."

My body and face ached from Diederick Smit's brutality, and I was exhausted from everything I'd seen and heard. Part of me wanted to give up, to give in, because there was no hope of winning.

But then I looked again at Crane's face, at the deep seed of surety in his eyes, and wanted to take that away from him. I wanted to hurt him, to make him suffer.

This is what Brom felt when he saw the smug expression on the schoolmaster's face, when he saw Crane's certainty that he would win the battle for Katrina's heart.

I couldn't blame Brom, not really. What was a man

supposed to do in the face of such complacency? Playing the Horseman seemed merciful.

Crane was certain he would win. I couldn't allow him to.

I raked my nails *(broken, filthy, Katrina would say unacceptable)* over his cheek, just to see if I could hurt him, and came away with his skin and blood. Was it because he was almost human now? Or was it because my father's blood was in him, had fed him, and now tied Crane's physical self to mine?

He screeched *(like a bird, he always seems like a bird to me)* and slapped his face in shock. I ran, not waiting to see what happened next. The important thing was to get out of his reach. I darted between trees and crashed through shrubbery.

My fingers burned where I'd touched him and I glanced down. The horror of it nearly halted me on the spot, but I swallowed hard and forced myself to keep going.

The tips of my middle three fingers were burning away, the nails melting, the skin and fat dripping off like water to reveal the naked bone beneath. Suddenly it hurt like fire, hurt like nothing I'd ever felt before, and I bit down hard on my bottom lip so I wouldn't scream uncontrollably.

Would it stop? Or would my hand melt away, too, and my arm, and my shoulder, and my chest, and my heart?

I thought I heard a horse again. It was nothing but a wish, a child's hope, but it was my talisman and I ran toward it. Behind me I heard the sounds of Crane's pursuit.

He has a body again. I don't know how, but he can be hurt. I hurt him. If he can be hurt then he can be killed.

Touching him again was out of the question. I was afraid to look at my left hand. The remaining skin on my middle three fingers tingled, though it had stopped burning. I heard the *click-clack* of my bones knocking together, and shuddered.

I made myself look down. The burning stopped just before the second knuckle of each of my middle three fingers, leaving the muscle and veins exposed underneath. Blood dripped over the shorn bone. If I survived, my hand would never be the same.

But first, survive. Look for a weapon.

A rock was useless. I could throw it, but I might miss. My eye was too swollen to accurately gauge distance, and I didn't trust the grip of my skeleton fingers.

Something else, something long and sturdy. There were branches everywhere, but they were all frail deadwood.

The sound of hoofbeats grew louder. I knew it was my imagination—perhaps I was dreaming, terror and pain had made me mad—but I still heard it.

Don't listen. It isn't real.

I needed a long branch heavy enough to stun. My intention was not to kill Crane. I didn't imagine that in my current state it was even possible. Stopping his chase long enough to allow me to escape was my only goal. I couldn't touch him again.

No matter how human he appeared now, his body was made of poison that would kill.

Poison. Poisoned by Schuler de Jaager, poisoned by hate and jealousy.

Crane thrashed through the woods in pursuit, all elegant floating forgotten. I ran into a small clearing and paused, trying to reorient myself. All would be lost if I kept heading deeper and deeper into the forest.

I heard it again—the sound of a galloping horse, and with a jolt I finally realized it wasn't in my head. Someone was coming.

The Horseman, and my blood thrilled at the thought.

Crane barreled in my direction, and the Horseman approached. In a moment they would meet, clash, and the Horseman would triumph. Of that I had no doubt. Crane was frightened of the Horseman. I smiled, because the Horseman was on my side.

But Crane said the Horseman can't reveal himself under sunlight. It can't be him.

I shook away any doubt. It was him. It had to be him.

I climbed a nearby tree, thinking to watch the battle from above. This wasn't as easy as it usually was, with my injured hand and injured eye and general feeling of having been run over by a wagon. But I managed to heave myself up and settle onto a large branch. No sooner had I done so when I heard his voice.

"Ben! Ben!"

Oh no. No. No. No.

"Ben! Can you hear me? Ben!"

Not him. Not now.

"Ben! If you're out here, answer me!"

"No." I moaned. "Opa, no!"

I scrambled out of the tree—practically fell out of it, if truth be told, between my haste and the poor grip of my fingers.

"Ben!"

He was so close. Too close. I didn't want him anywhere near Crane.

A moment later Brom burst through the trees and reined Donar hard a few feet from me.

"Ben!" His eyes widened when he saw the state of me.

Even though I was terrified for him, wanted him away from this place, I ran to him and threw my arms around him.

"My Ben," he murmured, holding me close. "My boy."

I held him even tighter then, because Brom had always understood the secret longing of my heart. No matter what he'd said earlier, Brom knew. Brom knew who I really was.

Then Crane stumbled out of the trees, and they saw one another for the first time in more than thirty years.

"You!" Crane shouted. His face contorted, a mixture of fury and glee that made me want to grab Brom and run.

Brom's expression was momentarily puzzled, as if trying to place the face before him into a sensible context. Then his eyes cleared, and I saw relief—and regret.

"Ichabod Crane!" Brom boomed, and it was his hail-fellow-well-met voice. "We haven't seen you for so long in Sleepy Hollow! I hope the years have been kind to you."

Brom didn't seem to realize that Crane wasn't human anymore. He didn't seem to notice the trailing edge of shadow all around Crane's body, or the unnatural way Crane moved. He was just a boy trying desperately to pretend he'd never done anything wrong, that he hadn't bullied his schoolmate, and if he pretended loud enough then his victim would have to believe it, too.

"You should come into the village with me," Brom continued. "There are many folk there who would be pleased to hear from you, and discover what you have done all this time. The most extraordinary rumors followed on the night you disappeared . . ."

He trailed off, for it appeared he'd grasped that Crane's appearance was not normal.

I kept one arm tight around Brom and said, "Opa, don't go near him. He's not a person anymore."

Brom looked down, and he seemed to really notice my swollen face for the first time. "Did he do that to you?"

"No, that was Diederick Smit. But Opa, look." I stretched out my deformed hand to him.

"What in the name of all that's holy?"

There was a hint of fear in his eyes that hadn't been there before, hadn't been there ever in my lifetime. It was as if

Brom suddenly realized that all the superstitious people of the Hollow weren't simply superstitious, but aware of something he'd carefully ignored. I don't know why the sight of my hand should do this instead of the bodies of Justus and Cristoffel— I only know that something seemed to connect in Brom's mind that hadn't connected before.

"It's because I touched him," I said, jerking my head at Crane. "He's not a person anymore. He's the one—he's the monster in the woods. He's the one who killed those boys. He's the one who killed my father."

Crane stood motionless, seemingly transfixed by the sight of Brom. He still appeared mostly human, though the shadow that clung to him seemed more substantial. There was black blood, darker than ink, coating his face where my nails had raked down. Some of the blood fell to the ground, where it sizzled.

"Stay away from him, Opa. If you touch him, he'll burn you."

I wasn't certain Brom heard me. He had a strange expression on his face—part disgust, part fascination, and underneath it all, thoughtful.

"So it's you that killed those boys."

"Yes," Crane said, and the "s" was longer than it should be, the sibilant hiss of a snake. "Very good. You always were just smart enough to recognize the completely obvious."

The old Brom, the one Crane had known when they were

young, might have risen to the bait. He might have flown at Crane in fury at the insult. But Brom had grown up, grown older, grown sensible—at least, what passed for sensible in Brom.

Crane was the one locked in the past, the same person he'd been thirty years before. For Crane it was still the night that the Headless Horseman chased him, the night that Katrina said she wouldn't marry him. Brom was still his rival.

"Ben," Brom said quietly, unwinding my arm from his ribs. "I want you to take Donar and ride home. Stay with Oma."

"No," I said, shaking my head. "I won't leave you."

"You're hurt, and you have to be cared for. Listen to me. I need to know that you're safe."

"And I need to know that *you're* safe. We'll both go. Whatever you're thinking, Opa, you can't do it. If you try to hurt him he'll hurt you instead. You can't punch your way out of this."

He gave me a crooked grin. "You sound like Katrina when you say things like that."

He might have said more, but Crane let out a long, low moan.

"Katrina," Crane said. "I lost Katrina to you. To you! A man so stupid, so selfish. A swollen-headed bully. How could *I*, a man of intelligence, of refinement, lose to one such as *you*?"

"She didn't love you," Brom said. What he didn't say, but was obviously implied, was, *She loved me instead.*

I didn't think he ought to say things like that at the moment. Crane looked like a cannon with its fuse nearly burned down. He was on the verge of an explosion, and Brom and I would be the ones receiving fire.

We should leave, ride away, leave Crane here to roil in his jealousy. Come back only if we have a plan to deal with him properly.

Even as I thought it, I knew it wouldn't happen that way. That was a sensible plan, and Van Brunts didn't do things sensibly. We were led by our hearts, always, never our heads. Heads were only for banging through walls with brute force. I didn't think Crane would succumb to that kind of force, though.

Crane rose up, and I was reminded of a snake uncoiling, fangs bared. Brom drew the knife he always kept in his belt. Donar stamped his feet and blew out a snort. I backed against a tree, felt the texture of the bark pressing through my clothes. All around the forest seemed to hush, to watch, to wait.

"She might have loved me," Crane said.

He shifted to one side, taking a few steps, and Brom matched him. Brom didn't bother trying to send me home again. All his attention was focused on Crane.

"She might have loved me, if not for you," Crane said.

"No," Brom said. "She saw your heart. You wanted money, status, the privilege of being a Van Tassel. She could never have chosen a man like that."

"And what of you?" Crane spat. "You didn't want her farm, her fortune? The great Brom Bones was above such venal concerns?"

"No," Brom said. "I didn't care. I always loved her, even before I really knew what money was, or what it meant. I love her still. And a man—if you are still a man—who claimed to care about her would never have broken her heart by killing her son."

Crane quailed, turned his head away, and when he spoke it didn't quite have the force he'd possessed a moment before.

"It was your heartbreak I wanted, not hers. Never hers."

Brom shook his head. "Did you think you'd win her this way? Make her think better of you?"

Crane grabbed his head, shook it from side to side like there was something huge and painful inside that he was trying to get out.

"No, no, no! It was you. I only wanted my revenge on you. You were the one who deserved to hurt. You were the one who deserved to suffer. Not my Katrina. Not my beautiful, perfect, capricious Katrina."

"A child is born of two people. You should have known that your choice would only make her hate you."

"Hate me? Hate me? No, Katrina, no. She saw me, saw I was a monster. There was horror, disgust in her eyes." Crane seemed to grow smaller as he spoke, like he wanted to shrink away and disappear.

"What did you expect? Bendix was her child. He came from her body. Half of his blood was hers. You hurt her beyond all reason."

Brom worked his way slowly across the clearing as he spoke. His movements were careful, deliberate, so slow they didn't appear to be movements at all. He was several feet from me now, much closer to Crane.

I bit down hard on my bottom lip so I wouldn't cry out a warning that would attract Crane's attention. The man (*Demon? Spirit? What was he?*) appeared wholly lost in thoughts of Katrina, and I knew that Brom was taking advantage of that. My mouth was swollen like an overripe grape from Diederick Smit's beating and the pressure of my teeth burst the skin, sent blood pouring over my chin.

Stay away from him, Opa, I thought desperately. *Stay away.*

Brom took a firmer grip on his knife, slid toward Crane. Crane threw his head up, smiled too wide.

"You think I didn't notice you? You're not that smart, Brom."

He reached for Brom and I screamed.

"Don't let him near you! Don't let him touch you!"

It was too late. Crane had his hand flat against Brom's barrel chest and I heard something sizzle, smelled the horrible melting. Crane's smile grew wider and wider, stretched impossibly across his face until it seemed he was only made of teeth and eyes.

Then Brom moved and the smile faltered, and there was

another smile to match it, only this one swiped across Crane's long thin neck, and black blood poured from it like rain.

Brom staggered back from Crane's touch and I heard him gasping for breath. I ran to him and propped myself under his shoulder. Sweat dripped down his cheeks and his teeth were bared. I didn't want to look, didn't want to see what Crane had done, but it was impossible to avoid. Crane had burned a hole in Brom's chest right over the heart.

"Opa!" I cried.

"It's . . . all . . . right . . . Ben," Brom said, but it wasn't all right, it would never be all right again.

Crane covered his neck with his hands, confusion on his face. He fell back onto his bottom, kicked away from Brom and me. His head seemed to wobble on its axis, like Brom's cut would cause the whole thing to fall off.

"But how? But I'm special. I'm immortal. Nobody can hurt me."

"The . . . Horseman . . . always . . . takes . . . his . . . head," Brom said. There was a terrible wet rattle in his chest, and blood bubbled at his lips.

Crane was fading before our very eyes, dwindling into nothing. This was the monster in the woods? This was the terror that I'd run from?

His head jerked at Brom's words, and he said, "You."

Brom smiled. His teeth were red. "Me. Always . . . me."

And then Ichabod Crane—who came to Sleepy Hollow

to be a schoolmaster, who dreamed of becoming the master of the Van Tassel fortune, who was chased by the Headless Horseman and became a nightmare that committed four murders—died in the woods outside the Hollow, forgotten by everyone except as the victim of a legend.

The moment Crane fell backward and lay unmoving in a pool of black blood, Brom fell to his knees.

"Opa, Opa," I said. I wanted to do something. There had to be something I could do. "Don't die. Don't. I need you. Oma needs you. You have to stay with us. You have to stay here."

His hand swiped over my hair, full of affection, full of love, the way he always did. He smiled at me one more time, and then he fell to one side, and the light went out of his eyes.

"No," I said, rolling him onto his back, shaking his shoulders. "No, you can't. You can't. Come back, please, Opa, please come back. It's not supposed to happen like this. You're not supposed to die like this."

How could Brom be dead? How could the great Brom Bones, a true legend of Sleepy Hollow, be killed? A man like Brom was too great, too powerful, too indestructible to be killed.

I bent over him, covering the hole where his heart used to be.

"Opa," I said, and my tears ran over his neck and mixed with the blood there.

I'd never hear his laugh again, echoing through the house, never hear his great big voice call my name, never feel him grab me and raise me high into the air no matter how big I got. I'd never see him kiss Katrina when he thought no one was looking, or see him babying his herd of sheep like they were his own children. I'd never see him galloping on Donar's back, or striding through the fields of wheat in the summer.

He was gone. He was gone. He was gone.

I don't know how long I was there, but after a while I heard the sound of a horse picking its way gently through the woods. The horse paused, and there was an intake of breath, and I looked up.

Donar, as wise as his predecessor, had gone for Katrina. She sat on his back, regal as a queen, her face carved in marble as she looked at me, at Crane, at Brom.

Then she climbed down without a word. She patted Donar's neck and I noticed her hand trembled.

I hunched over Brom as Katrina approached. I didn't want her to see what Crane had done. I didn't want her to see Brom like that.

She stopped on the other side of Brom's body. She'd never seemed so small, so frail as she had in that moment.

"Let me see him," she said.

I shook my head.

"Let me see him," she said again, but this time in that tone I couldn't ignore, the one she always used when I was misbehaving.

Slowly, reluctantly, I pulled away, and Katrina saw.

She knelt down beside her husband, the love of her life, and took his hand in hers, and kissed it.

Then she said, in a voice clogged with all the tears that she would weep later where no one could see, "Let's take him home now, Ben."

PART THREE

Brom Bones too, who shortly after his rival's disappearance conducted the blooming Katrina in triumph to the altar, was observed to look exceedingly knowing whenever the story of Ichabod was related, and always burst into a hearty laugh at the mention of the pumpkin; which led some to suspect that he knew more about the matter than he chose to tell.

—WASHINGTON IRVING,
The Legend of Sleepy Hollow

14

TEN YEARS LATER

I watched the man, one James Hardigan, bend over the piece of parchment and carefully sign his name. Sander watched, a familiar expression of consternation on his face. I knew how Sander felt about this, how he felt about everything I'd done in the last decade, but it wasn't for him to say in front of Hardigan, and he knew it. Sander's job as a notary was to witness the real estate transaction, not to pass judgment on it.

Not that he'd hold his tongue altogether. I knew Sander too well. He'd have plenty to say once Hardigan was gone.

Hardigan stood and handed the pen over to me. I dipped it in the inkwell and signed my own name on the line—*Ben Van Brunt*. I stared at it there, next to Hardigan's.

Hardigan. Not even a Dutch name. There were more and more people in the Hollow now who'd not lived here since its founding, more and more people with names from places other than our home country. I didn't mind. It was only that it was strange to me. The Sleepy Hollow of my childhood— that insular, superstitious valley—was disappearing.

Though in many ways, the Sleepy Hollow of my childhood had died the same night as Brom.

Sander pulled the parchment toward him, sealed the document in wax with the stamp of his office, and pronounced the transaction completed.

Hardigan held his hand out to me.

"A pleasure doing business with you, Mr. Van Brunt."

I shook his hand. "Likewise, Mr. Hardigan."

Hardigan jammed his hat back on his head, made some comments about a long ride back to the city, and swept out of the office and into the street.

I watched him go, if only so I could spend an extra few moments avoiding Sander's expectant stare.

"Ben," he said.

I had to look at him then, and saw just what I'd expected on his face—worry, and something else. Something else I didn't want to talk about again.

"Don't, Sander," I said, holding up my hand. "Please don't. We've been over and over this. Every time I come in here having sold another piece of the farm we have the same conversation."

Sander took off his spectacles and cleaned them on his shirt, a tactic he'd used to collect his thoughts ever since he started wearing spectacles.

"I only want to be certain that you know what you're doing."

There it was. The same objection that he always had.

"Would you be asking the same if I was Brom?"

And there it was—the same response I always gave. We'd had this conversation more times than I could count. I didn't understand why Sander wouldn't stop bringing it up.

"Frankly, yes," Sander said. "You have—had—vast and valuable farmland. That land was bought by Mynheer Van Tassel and expanded by Brom. If you didn't want to tend the land yourself, you could have hired an estate manager, someone who could handle it for you. There's no reason for you to sell off your children's inheritance."

I sighed. "How many times have I told you that I'm not going to have any children, Sander? Half the people who live in the Hollow now think I'm a man, and the other half have grown so used to me dressing this way that they've almost forgotten. I've made them believe. I'm not going to suddenly appear wearing a dress and rubbing my pregnant belly."

He looked down at his desk, shuffled some documents that clearly didn't need to be moved.

"You might change your mind."

And we had reached the something I really hadn't wanted to talk about ever again.

"Sander," I said. "It's past time for you to stop waiting for me. You should be married by now, with a family of your own."

The little line appeared between his eyes, the one I knew

so well from when we were children and I would propose some scheme that he knew would get us in trouble. I loved him so much in that moment, because he was the only friend I'd ever had, but I could never love him the way he wanted me to love him.

"The only family I ever wanted was with you, Ben."

I hated the way this hurt him, the way he kept putting his heart out for me to crush over and over.

"I'm sorry, Sander. I am. But the future that you want— it's not the same future I want."

Sander had always accepted me just as I was, more easily than anyone other than Brom and Katrina. But even he wanted me to conform, to change, to be a good little wife and mother. I could never be that. I could never love someone who wanted to cage me, make me something I was not.

The only thing I wanted was to run free under the stars.

But I never told him that. I never told Sander, or Katrina for that matter, about the Horseman. The Horseman was mine and mine alone.

"Ben—"

"No," I said, cutting him off. "There's no sense in going around and around like this again, Sander. We only have the same conversation every time."

"I keep hoping I can change your mind," he said, so quietly I almost didn't hear him.

"You should know that Van Brunts never change their

minds," I said, giving him a little smile, hoping to joke him out of his mood.

He sighed, and turned away, busying himself with more documents.

"Yes, I know."

I watched him for a moment, then gave a sigh of my own. "Thank you, Sander."

He didn't turn back to me. "I was only doing my job."

"Of course you were," I said. "But that wasn't why I was thanking you."

He still didn't respond, so I went to the door. As it swung shut behind me, I thought I heard him say, "You're welcome," but I didn't look back.

I didn't remember a lot of what happened after Brom died. I was in a daze, my brain wrapped in cotton wool that was punctuated only by the occasional moment of sharp clarity.

Lotte weeping, both arms wrapped around her middle, and no one could comfort her or make her stop. Katrina choosing Brom's best clothes for the funeral, her face white and sharp, all the bones pulled into relief. Sem Bakker's expression at Brom's funeral, and the sense I had that he was somehow relieved rather than sorry that Brom was gone.

Katrina knew we couldn't tell anyone about what happened in the woods—about Diederick Smit, about Ichabod Crane.

People would have believed us if we told them Crane was the monster of the woods. Of course they would have, because it was Sleepy Hollow and the people of the Hollow believed in ghosts and goblins, believed in spooks and haunts. They already believed that Crane had been taken by the Horseman. It would be nothing for them to think he'd become another legend himself.

But Katrina didn't want me dragged into any investigation into Diederick Smit's death. If we talked about how Brom really died, why he was there in the woods that night, an investigation would have been inevitable. No one must know that Smit kidnapped me, that I killed him.

For I had killed him, there in the woods. I'd beaten him to death with a rock, and it was no good telling myself that he wanted to harm me, that he was only going to do the same to me. The man was out of his mind with grief. He only wanted justice—what he thought was justice—for his son. And he'd been convinced that I was the person responsible.

I should have stopped hitting him before he was dead. I should have hit him once and run away. But I'd been scared and hurt and I only wanted him to stop punching me, stop dragging me through the woods, stop saying that I'd killed Justus with my magic.

It wasn't an excuse. I knew that. My being young and afraid wasn't enough to justify anything I'd done. And though whatever spell Smit had cast with his words seemed to fade

away, the accusations of witchcraft lingered longer than I—
or Katrina—liked. There was quite a long period where the
villagers looked at me askance, and some of them whispered
when I passed. After a while they seemed to forget, forget
about Diederick and Justus, forget about anything Smit had
said about me. Because that happened in the Hollow, too.
People decided to forget things, and those things were tucked
away and never spoken of again.

I could never forget the feeling of the rock gripped tight
in my hand, my skin spattered with his blood.

I killed him.

I killed him, and Katrina helped me cover it up. We found
his body in the woods. We buried him. I'll never forget the
horror of that long night, digging a hole for Smit's rotting
corpse. We waited until after Brom's funeral, and worried that
Smit would be discovered in the interim, but no one was
looking for Smit then. He didn't have very many friends, and
everyone was distracted by Brom's sudden death.

If ever Diederick Smit came up in conversation, Katrina
would say that he'd probably gone mad with grief, that he'd
gone into the woods looking for his son's ghost. Soon enough
this rumor was passed around at all the tea tables and sewing
circles, and became the accepted reason for the town's lack of
a blacksmith. A new one was recruited from a place farther
south, a man called Grimes who was much younger than
Diederick Smit. He had dimples and he wasn't married and

a lot of the young women of the village developed an abiding interest in his craft, contriving excuses to walk past the smithy at all hours of the day.

We brought Brom home, Katrina and me, and we washed him and dressed him and covered the hole in his chest, and we told everyone his heart had suddenly failed.

This, somehow, was the worst of the many lies we told. The idea that Brom's heart—his giant heart full of passion for life, his love for Katrina and me—could have failed was ridiculous, absurd. Brom's heart would never have failed if Ichabod Crane hadn't carved a hole there.

Whenever I thought of it, I wanted to kill Crane all over again, but there was nothing left of Crane except a few moldering bones and a black stain in the grass, like spilled ink. I knew because I'd gone back to that place in the woods. If it wasn't for Donar I'd never have found it again, but Donar somehow knew what I wanted. Brom's horses had always been like that—smarter than the humans that kept them.

Many, many people came to Brom's funeral. It seemed the whole village was there and more, that everyone for miles around had come to pay respects to the great Abraham Van Brunt. His coffin was so large that they needed eight men to carry it, but to me he didn't appear so big as he used to. His spark had made him larger than life, and his spark was gone forever.

Katrina stood straight and still at his graveside, and so

did I. Neither of us wept as Brom was lowered into the plot next to his son, whom he'd loved so much. We saved our tears for when no one could see us.

One person was not at Brom's funeral. I'd expected to see him there, gloating. I'd hoped for it, because he was the only person who could tell me why he'd turned Crane into a creature of darkness, and why he'd set Crane upon Brom.

But Schuler de Jaager was gone.

The day before Brom's funeral, Schuler's little cottage burned, burned so thoroughly that there was nothing left of it but a pile of ash. As I stood at Brom's graveside I could still smell the lingering scent of smoke, and of something else—something sour and rotten, something not of the earth.

No one ever built another house or business in the place where Schuler de Jaager's cottage had stood, even as Sleepy Hollow grew and became notably less sleepy. Within five years of Brom's death it was practically bustling, its proximity to New York City and its convenience as a stopping place to points north making it a center of trade.

But the empty plot where Schuler de Jaager used to live stayed empty. The ash blew away bit by bit, leaving only a blank-faced plot of land, but if you walked near the plot you'd still get a whiff of something rotten. Children wouldn't play there. Even the stray cats avoided it.

When I returned home I found Katrina in the parlor with her sewing. The work sat in her lap, practically untouched from when I'd left that morning. She stared out the window at the drive that led up to the front of the house, as if she was still waiting for Brom to ride up, as if she still expected to hear his great booming voice announcing that he was home.

"Oma?" I said.

I hovered in the door. Lately it seemed like she was slipping away from me, spending more time in a place where Brom never died. I didn't know what to do about it, or how to feel. Brom was dead because he'd come after me, because he'd saved me from Crane. That made Brom's death my fault, though Katrina had never said so.

If she wanted to live inside her memories of Brom, was it fair or right for me to take her from them? That was what she wanted. She wanted to be with Brom.

But it left me feeling lonely, like I was losing Brom all over again.

And I feared the day when I would return home to find Katrina breathless and still, her face turned toward the window but her eyes seeing nothing, and I would truly be alone.

But it was not that day. Katrina started, her blue eyes turned toward me, and she said, "Ben. I'm glad you're home safe."

I went to her then, and knelt beside her, and took her hand with my right one. My left hand was always covered with a leather glove and had been since I returned from the confrontation with Crane. We put it about that I had burned my skin badly and wore the glove for protection. I only took it off at night, in the privacy of my room, and the sight of my own bones never failed to make me shudder.

Katrina's hands seemed smaller than ever, frail like bird bones. At twenty-four I towered over her—not as tall as Brom had been, and of course not nearly so broad-shouldered—but I was very close to six feet, with all the proportionate limbs. Katrina seemed like a child's doll beside me, all the more so because she'd shrunk into herself once Brom was gone. She barely ate enough to keep a mouse alive, never mind a grown woman.

"Have you eaten anything?" I asked. "I could warm some soup."

Lotte had died of a sudden fever two years before. She'd been the last of our servants, and we never replaced her. Katrina and I had slowly let all the servants go, just as we'd sold off the land, just as we'd sold off most of the furniture and closed most of the rooms in the great house.

Now it was just Katrina and me, alone, rattling through the few open doors. Almost all the land was sold, save a few acres close to the house. When I looked out the window I could see other people farming the fields that had once been ours, that I'd thought I'd walk one day as Brom had, lord of all I surveyed.

That had stopped being my dream long ago. I didn't want to be tied to the earth any longer.

"Soup," Katrina repeated, and looked out the window again.

She was like this more often now, vague and dreamy. Sometimes I thought I'd give anything for the bite of her sharp tongue, even though it harried me when I was young. At least then I'd know Katrina was still inside that shrunken body.

"I'll warm the soup, and then we can eat," I said, and stood, watching her.

"All right," she said, and looked into her lap. She seemed surprised to find her sewing there, and a needle in her hand. She began industriously pulling the needle through the cloth, as if she'd been doing it all along.

My stomach twisted as I watched her, the bile rising in my throat. It was like living with a ghost, someone half in and half out of life.

I went through the foyer toward the kitchen, and had the same sensation I always had—that Brom was going to be there, his great voice booming, "I'm home!", his great arms waiting to scoop me up and swing me into the air.

But there was no Brom. There was no bustle of servants as they went around the house, no Lotte in the kitchen sneaking treats. Only me, and the sound of my feet creaking over the old wooden floor.

I heated some soup left from the night before, and sliced the bread I'd baked that morning. I was rather good at bread making, much to my surprise. Lotte had taught me before she died, and she said because I was big and strong that made it easier to knead the dough. It was the first time somebody had ever complimented my size.

I laid out the soup bowls at the table in the kitchen. The servants used to eat there, but now it was for Katrina and me. There wasn't any point in all the fuss of the dining room when we never ate grand meals anymore, and like every other room in the house it was hard to escape the feeling that Brom was there, laughing and piling his plate with more food than it seemed anyone could eat.

The kitchen was one of the few clean rooms left, in any case. Most of the furniture was covered, and what wasn't covered was coated in a thick layer of dust. I was an indifferent housekeeper, and Katrina seemed to forget most of the time.

I left the soup on the stove and went back for Katrina, who always required some coaxing to eat. She was staring out the window again, the sewing forgotten in her lap.

He's not coming, I thought. *He's not coming but I'm still here. Please be here with me.*

I was a little ashamed of this feeling, because I was a grown adult, not a child. I shouldn't need her to look at me, to see me, but I did. She was still my oma, the woman who'd raised me, the woman who fought with me and hugged me and loved me and, finally, accepted me.

And now she was slipping away from me, slipping into that place where Brom had already gone.

"Oma?" I said from the door.

She looked from the window to me. "Ben?"

I hated hearing the query in her voice, like she wasn't certain who I was, like she didn't know which Ben was standing in the doorway.

"It's time to eat," I said.

"I'm not hungry," she said, turning her face to the window.

I went to her and took the sewing out of her lap, setting it in her basket. Then I knelt next to her and took both of her hands in mine. Her skin was very soft and delicate, like the petal of a rose, and her finger bones almost insubstantial.

"Just some bread and butter," I said, carefully pulling her to her feet.

She stood for a moment, looking up at me, and something in her eyes changed. She seemed like she was actually there, seeing me, not seeing something that happened years before.

"You're so much like him," she said, and there was a ghost of a smile that I hadn't seen in a long while. "In your face. I see him in your face, and your eyes. But not as noisy. He was noisy, wasn't he?"

"You could hear his voice booming through the house," I said, guiding her toward the kitchen. She took little baby steps next to me, like she wasn't sure how to walk, or even why she should be doing it.

"Yes, booming," she said. "That's exactly right. And his laugh. You could always hear his laugh."

"He was always laughing," I said.

"You used to laugh more," she said. "When you were younger. You stopped. You became very serious."

I didn't say that there hadn't been very much to laugh about since Brom died. I didn't say that every day since that day I'd felt the weight of what he'd done, what he'd sacrificed for me. I didn't say that sometimes I woke up in the middle of the night seeing Diederick Smit leaning over me, his eyes wild with hate, and that I could feel the stone I'd used to beat him to death still gripped in my hand. Worst of all, sometimes I thought I heard Schuler de Jaager laughing his knowing laugh, and the scent of something sulfurous and rotten drifting in my window.

"He was a happy person," I said instead, because it was true.

Brom had been happy, even though he'd loved and lost a son and a daughter-in-law, even though he regretted things he'd done and wished he could change. Brom looked at the world as a place full of possibilities, every day a chance for more joy. And he'd had Katrina. No one meant as much to him as Katrina.

I settled Katrina in a chair and spooned some of the soup into her bowl—not much, because I knew she wouldn't eat much. I put out the plate with the sliced bread and a dish of butter beside it, and remembered Lotte buttering thick slices of bread for me even when she wasn't supposed to.

I sat across from Katrina with my own full bowl of soup and began eating. My body was hungry but I didn't take the same pleasure in eating as I did before Brom died. Now it was only fuel to keep me going every day. I also knew that if I ate, Katrina would copy me, at least for a little while. Her deeply ingrained manners wouldn't permit me to eat alone.

Sure enough, she began spooning soup into her mouth a moment after I started, like a little bird mimicking its mother.

I am like her parent now. I take care of her instead of the other way around.

I buttered a slice of bread for Katrina and handed it to her. She took a bite and chewed slowly. Every mouthful was a victory, another day of sustenance keeping her alive.

We didn't talk while we ate. I finished my soup and two slices of bread, and tried not to sigh when I saw Katrina had left more than half her soup in the bowl, though she had finished her bread. She sat like a docile child in her chair, her eyes distant, waiting for me to direct her to the next task.

I cleared away the plates and washed them, then wrapped the bread in a cloth so it wouldn't dry out overnight. I wished we had a dessert so that I could convince Katrina to eat a little more. I had a sudden longing for one of Lotte's fruit pies. She'd shown me how to make a pie crust, and I'd made meat pies before, but never a fruit pie.

Why make it, though? There's no one here to eat it except you, and the fruit would sour before you finished it.

Katrina let me lead her back to the parlor, where I settled her in the chair again. Her face immediately turned to the window, and I stared at her helplessly, wanting to do something, anything, to keep her present, to keep her with me.

"Shall we play whist?" I said.

It was really a four-person game, although I'd modified it in the past so the two of us could play. We hadn't played a card game in a very long time, and Katrina used to love whist. She was a fierce competitor who loved to win, and when she and Brom partnered, nobody could beat them.

"No." She sighed the word out, like it was too much effort to even speak one syllable.

"I could read to you," I said, feeling increasingly desperate. I had to do something, anything, to keep her from staring out the window. "Poetry? I could read some poetry."

"No," she said again.

The clouds were forming in her eyes again, that distance that I hated so much.

Katrina stared out the window, and I stared at her, feeling the gulf between us and not knowing how to build a bridge to reach her.

The day grew darker, and I lit the candles, but Katrina never moved, never gave any indication that she knew I was there at all.

I never went into the woods anymore. After Brom and Crane and the horror of Diederick Smit I couldn't bring myself to walk under the trees. More importantly, the woods were his place, the Horseman's place, and I never wanted to see the Horseman again.

I never wanted to see him again but still everything in me longed to see him, to understand the connection between us that I'd never fully puzzled out.

I hated him. I hated him because he hadn't come for me when could have, hadn't helped me escape from Crane. He was supposed to protect me. He was supposed to watch over me, the way he always had. And because he didn't, Brom had to ride into the woods that day. And because Brom rode into the woods that day, I lost Brom forever.

Still I dreamed, always, of that magical night when I rode with the Horseman, and how it felt to be a part of the wind and the night and the stars.

Sometimes I heard his voice, at night when I lay awake, whispering my name from very far away. But I never followed that voice, never sought its source. I'd rather be alone forever than go to the Horseman again.

I told myself that every day, and then I told myself that it wasn't a lie.

15

I had to ride into town again the next day for some supplies. Katrina settled in the parlor, eyes facing the window, as soon as breakfast ended. She didn't seem to notice when I left. I wasn't going to be gone long but I felt a little twinge of worry.

Perhaps I should ask someone to come and sit with her when I am out. She shouldn't be alone.

Then I shook away the thought. Katrina wasn't fine, I couldn't fool myself about that, but neither was her behavior potentially harmful to herself. She only sat and looked out the window. She was perfectly safe for an hour or two.

Though neither of us was eating much, Katrina and I still needed food, especially since we didn't have the bounty from the farm. I didn't even bother to keep the vegetable garden anymore, since a bumper crop of tomatoes or squash would only end up rotting on the vine before we ate it, and I didn't have any desire to take the excess into town to sell. It seemed too humiliating, the most unacceptable blow to the Van Brunt legacy. Brom never would have stooped to such small change as selling a few meager vegetables in the common market.

But you're perfectly willing to shop in that common market, I thought to myself as I selected some potatoes. People bustled all around me, some of them calling my name in greeting, but mostly they were folk I didn't know. Sleepy Hollow wasn't the place I'd known as a child, the place that seemed frozen under glass, where everyone knew everyone and most people were related to each other. It was growing just like the rest of the country, becoming something modern and unrecognizable.

I could have stopped to visit Sander, as I usually did, but I didn't want to repeat the same frustrating conversation of the previous day. Sander was my friend, my only friend, and I wanted him to stay that way.

I loaded my purchases into my saddlebags and took Zacht's reins so I could walk him until we reached the edge of the village. There were too many people about to ride even at a slow pace, though Zacht was no threat to anyone around him. My horse was nothing like his sire or grandsire. He had no fire in his eye, no wild nature. He was smart like Donar and maybe as fast as Daredevil, but I never rode him the way Brom would have. I liked his sweet nature.

I carefully weaved in and out of the crowd, raising my hand occasionally when I heard my name. As I passed the place where Schuler de Jaager's cottage used to be I caught a whiff of rotting meat, the tang of blood, and the sulfurous curl of a freshly struck match. The combination was so repugnant and yet so familiar that I paused, and I remembered a shadow rising up before me in the forest, the same strange scents filling my nose.

Crane, I thought. But Crane couldn't be near, couldn't be in Sleepy Hollow. Brom had killed him and there was nothing left. He'd melted away, thwarted by Brom Bones in life and in death.

Besides, whatever shadows that held sway over Sleepy Hollow had gone away when Brom died and Schuler de Jaager disappeared. There was a road through the woods now, through places where no one would go ten years before. People didn't fear the woods, didn't repeat stories about ghosts and magic and Horsemen without heads.

I'd heard that there were still a few dark and unexplored places, places that hunters avoided. These men always said in loud voices that this was because there were no animals in those dark copses. But when they'd drunk a few glasses of ale and the lanterns were low they'd always whisper that they'd seen a shadow, or heard a voice without a body, or felt a cold chill on their nape, and the other men around the storyteller would nod and say the same thing happened to them.

But this wasn't the woods. This wasn't some shadowed corner, some remnant of the old drowsy magic that had bewitched Sleepy Hollow. This was an empty plot of land, exposed under the clear blue sky and the brightly shining sun, and there were people all around, and Crane couldn't be near because Crane was dead.

I stared at the dirt where Schuler de Jaager's cottage used to be, noticed that it was still gray like ash, like the day the cottage burned down a decade before. The plot still looked over the covered bridge, and the church, and the cemetery where Brom and my father and my mother lay.

The scent of sulfur grew stronger, strong enough for me to cover my mouth and nose with my free hand. I felt a touch on the back of my neck, a finger sliding over my spine. I spun around to see who it was but there was no one there.

Someone laughed, a low, malicious chuckle, very close to my ear.

Then I heard a man nearby say, "Look at the smoke! Where is it coming from?"

I turned toward the speaker, and saw him gesturing toward the sky above the road that led away from the village.

His companion shielded his eyes with his hands and said, "Looks like it's out near the old Van Brunt place. I wonder if someone's field is on fire."

For a moment I stood frozen, staring at the black curl of smoke in the sky. Then I was on Zacht's back, kicking him into a gallop, shouting for anyone in front of me to get out of my way.

It's not the house, it's not Katrina, everything is all right, it's likely only a burning field just like the man said, it's been a dry autumn and a careless ember could set a whole field of wheat afire, it's not the house, it's not Katrina, everything is all right, Katrina will be all right, she'll be staring out the window just like she was when I left her an hour ago.

"Faster, faster," I whispered to Zacht, and he pounded over the road, passing plodding wagons driven by people who turned their heads to watch us as we passed.

Katrina will be fine. She has to be fine. Even if it is the house she will have gotten out. She wouldn't sit there and stare out the window while the house burned all around her.

But I still whispered to Zacht that he should go faster, faster, faster.

I rounded the turn of the road that led up to the drive. A small crowd of neighbors was gathered on the lawn, staring up at the house.

The Van Tassel house, the pride of Baltus Van Tassel, passed to his equally proud son-in-law Abraham Van Brunt, who'd always wanted it to be an heirloom for his son.

But his son had died, and now the house burned.

Black smoke billowed from the back of the building, and the flames seemed impossibly huge and high. There was a hungering roar, a consuming snarl, emitting from the fire, and I felt then that fire was a live thing, a predatory animal, not a benign friend that cooked our food and warmed our hands. This was a monster to be feared.

I galloped to the edge of the crowd, shouting at the people gathered there.

"Katrina! Katrina!"

One of the men shook his head. "She's not here."

I swung down and threw Zacht's reins at the man, whose name I could not recall. I'd sold so much land to so many people in the last several months that all their faces blurred together.

"Where are you going?" he cried as I ran past him and the others gathered there.

I didn't bother to answer. Did the fool think I was going to leave my grandmother in a burning house? Why had all of them gathered just to gawk? No one had even bothered to think that the fire might spread to the fields, and that they should be dampening the ground between the house and the crops.

There was no time for me to explain this to them. I needed to get to Katrina. I knew exactly where she would be.

The front door was slightly ajar, and smoke emitted through the crack. Had I left the door open when I left? Or had someone come into the house, started the fire and neglected to pull it shut?

I pushed the door further open and a rush of heat and smoke poured out, nearly knocking me flat. I staggered, then pulled my handkerchief from my pocket and used it to cover my mouth and nose as I entered the house. I didn't need to go far. I only needed to get to the parlor.

Smoke hung from the ceilings in a thick haze, and though the actual flames hadn't reached the front of the house yet, the heat felt like it was eating me alive. It dried out my skin and mouth in an instant, made me brittle and breakable.

If I'm breakable then Katrina is even more so, I thought as I hunched down below the thickest part of the smoke and made my way toward the parlor door.

I squinted, my eyes streaming from the smoke, my arm outstretched to push the parlor door open. But the door was already open, and I'd stumbled over the threshold before I realized it. My gaze went straight to the chair where I'd left Katrina, the place where she'd always been without fail every day for the last several months.

She wasn't in the chair.

She wasn't anywhere in the room.

Panic spiked through me. I rushed back to the foyer. Something shifted ominously toward the back of the house. I heard timbers cracking.

"Oma!" I called.

I rushed into the kitchen with a half-formed idea that she might be there, that the fire might even have started there because she'd tried to cook or to make tea, but the room was empty. All the other rooms on this floor were closed up, but I still checked Brom's office, thinking that she'd gone there to be close to him.

Every moment I remained in the house the smoke increased,

and the roar of the fire grew to a defiant howl. I felt that at any second the ceiling would collapse, that the whole structure would fall down around me, but I couldn't leave, couldn't bring myself to run like a coward when Katrina was still somewhere inside.

I ran up the stairs, calling her name, but I could hardly hear my own voice and knew she'd never hear it over the sound of the flames. The smoke was gathered at the top of the house, and I could barely see through it no matter how low I crouched. My sense memory of the house led me toward Katrina's bedroom. When I reached the door it was closed.

I grasped the knob and screamed aloud, because it was as hot as a poker that had been sitting in the fireplace. I felt my skin scorch, the pain unlike anything I'd ever known, but I'd automatically turned the knob when I touched it and so the door swung open.

A blast of flame burst out like a cannon fire and it hit me with the same force. I fell to the floor, my clothes burning, and I rolled back and forth in a desperate attempt to put them out, no clear thought in my head except that I wanted to live, that I didn't want to die yet.

I pushed up to all fours, my clothes still smoking, and I crawled into Katrina's room. The walls and ceiling were aflame, and I was certain that they would collapse at any moment.

"Oma!" I called, or rather tried to call, because her name came out as a choking cough.

I tried to see through the smoke, ignoring my growing terror of being trapped in a burning room that might fall on me. I blindly moved toward the center of the room and bumped into the footboard of the bed.

The smoke eddied, and for a brief flash I saw Katrina's stockinged feet. She lay on the bed, perfectly still.

No, I thought, and ran around to the side of the bed so I could lift her. She was so small that it was nothing to carry her even when she was at her most robust, and her lack of interest in food these last few months made her lighter than any child.

Her body was still warm, and I thought she was still breathing but I couldn't stop to check. The headboard was on fire, and so were the pillows. She'd undone her braid so her long hair lay on the coverlet, and half of it was gone, consumed by flame.

I ran out of the room with her in my arms, her hair burning, thinking only of getting out of the house and worrying about anything else later. I didn't want to think that she might already be dead, that she'd suffocated on the smoke as she lay in that burning room.

I picked my way blindly down the stairs, terrified of tripping and falling and hurting Katrina. I'd only taken a few steps when I heard a tremendous crashing, and the building shook, and I knew that the bedroom we'd recently escaped had collapsed, along with almost every other room in that part of the house.

Just get down the stairs, just get out of the house, you're nearly there.

The smoke was so thick that I didn't realize I'd reached the bottom step, and I stumbled over nothing, my heart pounding as I held Katrina tight to me. The front door was only a few feet away, still open, and beyond the frame of the doorway I saw a larger crowd gathered, all of them staring at the spectacle of my family home burning to the ground.

I staggered onto the porch, and somehow I made it down the steps and to the drive. All of the people watched me with wide eyes, none of them moving to help me at all. What was wrong with them? What had happened to the idea of helping your neighbors? Why weren't they trying to put out the fire? Why weren't they trying to keep the fire from spreading to their crops?

I fell to my knees and released my grip on Katrina none too gently. She rolled onto the ground, her eyes fluttering, and I felt a surge of relief. She was alive. She was still alive. I could direct my attention to the gawkers.

"Your farms are going to burn if you don't go out and start dampening the ground," I said. "Get out of here! Stop staring! Go save your crops!"

Several of them stared at me with drowsy eyes, almost like they were half-asleep. I noticed, with a thrum of trepidation, that Henrik Janssen was one of them. He'd never moved away, and I'd encountered him more than once since the night he attacked me, but he'd never apologized nor shown any indication that he was even aware the incident occurred. He'd been under the influence of the woods, as I'd thought, but it didn't change the way I felt about him. I knew that deep down there was something inside him that should never come out.

"Get out of here!" I shouted, waving my arms in front of them. "If you aren't going to help us then leave!"

A few people started, and I saw awareness in their eyes that hadn't been there a moment before, a *what-am-I-doing?* knowledge.

These individuals started shouting, shaking their neighbors, indicating that they should be working to contain the fire before it affected their property. It was like watching them all wake from some shared dream. There was a sudden flurry of activity as they all ran toward their own homes.

Only Henrik Janssen remained, staring at me and at Katrina. There was something in his eyes that I hadn't seen since that terrible night, something I'd never wanted to see again. The edges of his mouth pulled wide, spreading into something like a smile but something far too big, something too full of teeth.

"Leave," I said. "You're not welcome here."

I wasn't a child anymore, and I was taller than Henrik Janssen. I wasn't afraid of him. I didn't have to be afraid, and I didn't have time for this. I needed to see to Katrina.

"Bente," he said, and there was a kind of slithering in the

way my name came out of his mouth, a sense that there was something underneath his skin that wasn't human. "I've missed you so."

My hands curled into fists. "Leave. Before I do something you'll regret."

"Soooo sssssweet," he said, his eyes dancing with malice. "So sweet the way you think that you're like Brom, that you can beat into submission anything that you don't like. But you're not Brom, little Bente. You're nothing but a delicate, delicious girl under those clothes."

I felt the knee-jerk response, the words bunching up in my throat. *I'm not a girl. I'm a man, and I'll prove it to you.*

"You can't make yourself something you're not, Bente. I know what you are, even if some of those fools don't. Nothing but a pale imitation of Brom Bones, always running after his ghost, always covered by his shadow."

I'm not. I'm not. I'm just as good as Brom.

"Don't listen to him, Ben," Katrina said.

She'd somehow pushed herself to her feet, and come to stand beside me. Her voice was weak and fluttery, and after a moment she leaned on my arm. But her eyes were just as fierce as they'd always been. She seemed more awake, more present, than she'd been in months.

"Don't listen to him," Katrina repeated. "It isn't true, and that isn't Henrik Janssen."

I swallowed hard. "I know. It's something from the woods."

"No." Katrina shook her head. "Not something from the woods. It came from somewhere but it didn't start in our woods, even if it did infect them, infect everything it touched. I don't know what it really is, but you shouldn't mistake it for human, though it pretended to be, for a while."

Henrik Janssen narrowed his eyes, and I saw that they were an unnatural red, almost sparking. "You always knew what I really was, Katrina Van Tassel, even if you never told Brom."

"Yes," Katrina said. "I always knew. You've done enough mischief today, Schuler. More than enough."

"Schuler?" I said, looking from Katrina to Henrik Janssen.

He laughed, a laugh that shredded nerve ends. "She's like Brom in at least one way. Too thick to see what's right in front of her eyes."

There was a sudden tang of rotting meat, of blood, and the sulfurous curl of a freshly struck match, and then I saw it. Saw what Schuler de Jaager had hidden all those years.

Henrik Janssen—or the thing inside his body—leaned close to me, and it took everything I had not to flinch away. I stared into those unnatural eyes and realized that whatever I thought I knew about Crane, about Brom, about Schuler, about the miasma in the woods, about anything at all, wasn't true. I didn't know what this creature was or what it wanted but it was evil, so entirely and completely evil that I felt my throat closing up, that it was choking me.

"I'll see you again soon, my delicious girl," he said.

Henrik Janssen's eyes rolled back in his head and he folded to the ground, unconscious. I didn't have time to worry about him as Katrina suddenly slumped against me, and a moment later she too was on the ground, all her strength drained away.

"Oma!" I knelt beside her, lifting her head into my lap. "Oma, you need to rest. You need water and food. I have to get you to a doctor."

She waved one hand weakly at me, her eyes shut. "No doctor."

"But—"

"No doctor. Doctor can't help. Don't want him to."

"Oma, you have to—"

"Schuler started the fire. I saw him, as Henrik, through the window, going around to the back of the house. I knew what he'd done the moment I smelled the smoke. I could have walked out the front door. But I didn't want to."

Her voice seemed to be fading away with each word, disappearing forever, and that scared me more than anything that had happened that day.

"I want to be with Brom," she said. "I want that so much."

"Oma," I said, and my tears fell onto her face.

"Don't cry, Ben," she said. "This is what I want. I'm sorry to leave you alone, but there's something you have to do. You're the only one left who knows. You're the only one left who can try."

"Schuler de Jaager."

She nodded, her eyes still closed. "You have to go into the woods. You have to find him, and root him out, or else Sleepy Hollow will be haunted by him—it—forever. Promise me. Promise me you'll do this."

I didn't want to promise. I didn't want to take on something so huge and terrible. I didn't want to do it alone.

Her hand gripped mine, and there was surprising strength there. "Promise."

I bowed my head. My voice was nothing but a whisper as I said, "I promise."

"You're not less than Brom," she said, her voice so low I had to bend close to hear her. "You're more than him, and me, and Bendix, and Fenna. You're all of us. Remember that. Remember we loved you."

I don't want to remember. I want you here, with me. I don't want to be alone, the last of the Van Tassels and the Van Brunts.

But it didn't matter what I wanted, didn't matter that I cried. The last breath sighed out of her, and she was gone, and I was all that was left of my family.

I sat there, weeping, with Katrina's cold hand in mine, and watched the house burn to the ground.

16

Ben.

I sat up in bed, where I hadn't been sleeping—sleep being hard to come by in the days since Katrina's funeral. My heart slammed against my ribs, trying to get out of its cage.

Had I heard him? Or was it just my imagination? Was it only a secret, shameful hope that he would appear again, that I would ride with him and all of my pain and fear and sadness would blow away into the wind and be gone forever?

Nobody can do that for you. Nobody can take the knot in your chest and unclench it for you, nobody can relieve your sadness and fear. Not even the Horseman.

I rose and went to the window, which overlooked the main street of Sleepy Hollow. Since the house burned down I'd stayed with Sander above the notary's office. His younger sister had married the previous summer, and his parents had decided to move with her to Ohio. It should have been a scandalous impropriety for me to live in the same household as Sander, except that nearly everyone in Sleepy Hollow thought I was a man, and those that knew different seemed to have forgotten that I'd ever been anything else.

This, too, was part of the magic of Sleepy Hollow, or maybe it was simply being a Van Brunt. In Sleepy Hollow you could decide to be a Headless Horseman if you were only Brom Bones, or could transform from a girl into a boy only on your say-so, and people accepted it, and it became part of the fabric of the town.

People *believed* in Sleepy Hollow. They were different from people in other places, or they used to be. I didn't know if Sleepy Hollow would stay that way. Sleepy Hollow wasn't even very sleepy any longer. It was thriving and bustling, the magic fading out of the air.

But not gone forever, I thought. Schuler de Jaager, or whatever he really was, for he was most certainly not human, was still out there. And Katrina had been right—as long as he was near, his poison could seep into the town, sicken its residents, make bad things happen that shouldn't be.

And yet I couldn't work up the energy to care, or do anything about him. Katrina was gone. Brom was gone. My childhood home was gone. My parents were long gone. There was nothing tethering me to Sleepy Hollow save a lingering affection for my best and only friend. Despite this, a weight seemed to press down on me every day. I barely slept at night, and yet all day I felt as though I was half-sleeping, my mind never in the same plane as my body. I barely spoke to Sander, who left me alone to wander in the apartment above his office, nothing but a half-spirit inside a husk.

He never asked questions, never wondered what I was going to do or when I would do it. He put food in front of me and I ate it. Mostly I sat at the window and watched all the people go by in the street below, people who hadn't lost all of their family, people who still had a life and a purpose.

You have a life and a purpose, too. You made a promise to Katrina and you have to keep it.

I stared down at the street, dark and empty, and hated myself because I couldn't make myself care about anything, couldn't make myself talk to Sander or act like a regular person. I was paralyzed by the pressure of grief, lost in memories of the past.

I'm a burden on Sander. I'm turning into Katrina, a ghost, always staring out the window looking for someone who isn't there.

Ben.

I froze, my head cocked to one side. I'd heard him that time. It wasn't my imagination. But he sounded far away, farther than he had ever been before.

"Where are you?" I whispered, my hands pressed against the window glass. "Are you here? Are you near me?"

Ben. Help.

My fingers curled into claws. *Help? How could I help him?* And underneath that thought, in the very tiny, petty, terrible part of me that blamed him for Brom's death—*Why should I help you when you didn't come for me? Why should I help when you're the reason I lost Brom?*

Ben. Help me.

He sounded weak, on the verge of death. But that couldn't be. The Horseman was immortal. He couldn't be in danger.

Could he?

I realized then that I'd heard him whispering sometimes over the last few weeks, heard him say those exact same words, but every time I'd shut him out, pushed away the tug of his voice, pretended I couldn't hear.

Ben.

He's dying. He needs me. He's been calling me and I ignored him, left him alone, and now he's dying.

"I'm coming," I said, all my lost purpose suddenly renewed. I couldn't leave him. I couldn't let him die. "Wait for me. Wait for me."

Ben.

"Wait," I said. "I'm sorry. I'm coming."

I didn't think about what might happen next, about how I could help him, about what could have occurred to put him in such a state. I felt wide awake for the first time in days, the weight that had pressed me down dissipating.

"Wait for me. Wait for me."

I dressed, but I didn't bother to take any supplies. The only weapon I had was Brom's knife, which I'd carried every single day since the day he killed Crane with it. The knife was strangely unblemished, though Brom's heart and my hand had been damaged by the touch of Crane's skin.

I paused in front of Sander's bedroom door, wondering if I should wake him, wondering if I should try to explain, but then decided to let him be. There wasn't time for me to help him understand.

I crept down the stairs to the back door. Halfway down I heard him.

"Ben?"

He stood at the top of the stairs in his nightclothes, holding a candle. His face was completely calm, no question in his eyes.

"You're going to the woods, aren't you?"

My breath caught in my throat, because I realized then that he understood so many things without my telling him, that he knew me better than anyone in the world, and that I'd never treated him as well as I should have. I should have been a better friend, should have given him more, should have pulled him closer instead of keeping an imaginary distance between us.

"Yes," I said.

"Of course," he said. "I won't see you again."

It wasn't a question, and it wasn't something I'd really considered as I dressed and prepared to rush out of the house, but it was true. Sander had realized it before I did.

"No," I said. "I don't belong in Sleepy Hollow anymore."

"Let me come with you," he said.

I shook my head. "I don't belong here, but you do."

He sighed, as if he'd expected that answer. "They were always more your woods than mine. You were a part of them, even when we were children."

I didn't know if that was true, but I'd always felt safe there, felt that no harm would come to me. At least, until the day we saw Cristoffel's body. Everything changed then. That was when, I realized, I started pushing Sander away, excluding him from my plans, keeping him at a distance. That was when I started thinking I could do everything on my own, that Sander would only get in my way.

"I'm sorry," I said, and the apology was for a lot of things, so many things, and it was entirely inadequate, but it was all I had.

"I'll miss you," he said, and then he turned away, and blew out the candle.

I stood for a moment, listening as he returned to his bedroom, heard the sound of the door closing.

Then I opened the door at the bottom of the stairs and went out into the night, out to the Horseman, out to whatever destiny waited for me in the woods.

I went on foot, not wanting to take gentle-souled Zacht with me into any potential danger. I walked through the silent village, the stars shining above me, the sliver of moon hidden behind a wisp of cloud. My breath showed in silvery puffs of air, though I didn't feel cold.

It was the beginning of autumn, season of change, like that day so many years ago when Sander and I played Sleepy Hollow Boys. I'd always felt most like myself in the autumn, when nature transformed from its summer glory into its winter cloak. Some people only saw death in autumn—the withering of plants, the falling of leaves—but I saw all the bounty and beauty that summer had wrought preserved for the next spring. Autumn was only a caterpillar in its chrysalis, sleeping until it was time to become a butterfly.

The expansion of Sleepy Hollow meant that the forest began much farther along the road than it used to. There were more buildings to pass, more houses that had never been there when I was a child, more trees cleared to make way for farmland. My ears were pricked for the sound of his voice, the call that had dragged me from my bed and my paralyzing grief into the night, but I didn't hear him again.

He wouldn't be in the part of the woods that was close to the road or the village in any case. He would be in the deepest part, the place still avoided by villagers.

Schuler de Jaager will be there, too.

My hand slid around the hilt of Brom's knife. I didn't know if I could kill Schuler, or if he could be killed at all. I didn't know if I could save the Horseman. I didn't know what kind of future I'd have when all of this was over, or if there would be a future for me at all.

Maybe I was the end of the Van Tassels and the Van Brunts, and when all of us were gone the world would move on, indifferent to our lives and deaths. We would be known only as a part of stories that people told in front of the fire on an autumn night, stories about a horseman without a head who rode through the darkness, stories about two men and the woman they both desired, but only one of them loved her.

And children would say it was only a story, that there was no Horseman and no Crane and no Katrina and no Brom, but they would pull their covers up tight to their chins anyway, and listen for the sound of galloping hooves.

I hadn't set foot in the woods in ten years, and I expected it to feel different, but the moment I was under the trees again something settled in me that I hadn't even recognized as restless. I belonged there. I belonged in the woods, a part of the air and the trees. I'd always been a child of nature and not of the village. This was where my heart had always been.

Sander was right, I thought ruefully. *Sander knew even when I didn't.*

For a while I strode easily, comforted by the familiarity of the trees, the sense of being welcomed back after a long absence. I avoided the road, which wouldn't take me where I wanted to go. The stars peeked through the branches, and I heard the sounds of night creatures all around me—little things scurrying in the brush, the far-off hoot of an owl, and once the too-close huffing of a bear hunting for a last meal before hibernation.

Then the trees seemed to press in closer, to hunch their shoulders and watch my passage with barely contained malice. The shadows became more substantial, took forms that darted closer and then away, visible only out of the corner of my eye. The scurrying of small things ceased, for all the small things knew better than to pass here, where there were large things with teeth that bit and claws that caught.

My steps slowed, and I tried to ignore the uneasy sickness growing in my chest, the feeling that I couldn't catch my breath, the feeling that something was just behind me, waiting for me to turn.

"Ben."

I pulled the knife from its sheath and spun toward the voice, which had come out of the darkness on my left. I almost dropped the knife when I saw who spoke, but I managed to keep my grip.

Cristoffel van den Berg stood there, impossibly whole, the same age he'd been when he died.

He's not real, I told myself. *He's only a product of your imagination, not a specter but an illusion.*

"What are you doing here in the woods, Ben?" Cristoffel said. There was a phosphorescent glow all around him, a soft blue light that emanated from his figure. "Boys shouldn't leave the path, you know. It's dangerous. Bad things can find you when you stray."

He stepped closer, and I backed away, holding the knife out before me.

"Stay away from me," I said.

"I don't mean you any harm. Though you never liked me, did you, Ben? Part of you always thought I'd gotten what I deserved when that monster found me."

"No," I said. "No, I never thought that. I was sorry for you."

His lip curled into a sneer. "Yes, sorry for me. Sorry that I was so poor, that all the good ladies of the Hollow would come with baskets full of food because my father drank away all of our money. Sorry that you lived in a huge house where people laughed and loved each other, while I lived in a tiny cottage with no candles, listening to the sound of my mother crying and my father shouting and the sound a fist makes when it hits flesh. Yes, you were sorry for me, all of you good folk of Sleepy Hollow, but nobody helped. Nobody took me away."

"They couldn't take you from your parents," I said.

"They weren't parents," Cristoffel said, and he seemed to grow a little, his child's-form swelling with anger. "Parents care about their children. My father cared only about himself and what he could find at the bottom of a glass, and my mother was too weak to leave him, even to save herself."

"I'm sorry," I said again, and it sounded horribly insufficient, but I didn't know what else to say or do. I couldn't fix it. I couldn't go back in time and make his parents better people, or make someone from the town—useless Sem Bakker, perhaps—take Cristoffel away and put him in a happier home. I couldn't stop him from going into the woods the day he died, couldn't stop Crane from killing him.

"Sorry. Is that all you have for me? Is that all the charity afforded me from the great Ben Van Brunt, who always thought he was better than the rest of us?"

"I never did," I said. "I never thought that."

But that wasn't true. Of course I thought I was better than everyone else. I was a Van Brunt, grandchild of the marvelous Brom Bones. Who wouldn't think themselves a cut above when they came from such a family? But I'd been a child then, foolish and arrogant, and I'd lost it all the day Brom died.

Sweat beaded at my hairline and rolled down my temple. I wasn't sure what to do. Should I try to run? Would Cristoffel chase me? What could he do to me, or I to him? Perhaps I should simply pretend he wasn't there and he would disappear altogether.

"Don't lie," Cristoffel said. "You did think you were better than me. You should have helped me instead of pretending that I wasn't there. You could have done something. You could have told the great Brom and maybe he would have taken me away from there and I could have lived in your great house with you."

I thought of the bullying little Cristoffel I'd known, a child I'd thought repugnant and mean, and my stomach turned at the thought of him inside my house.

My feelings must have shown on my face, because Cristoffel pointed at me, his expression twisted in anger.

"See? You do think I'm less than you, that I wouldn't have belonged there. But there's something you don't know, Ben Van Brunt. We're all the same, here in the woods. We all come to the same end."

His face changed. Then I realized it wasn't his face changing. His head tilted to one side, tilted crazily, impossibly, and a great gash opened wider and wider across his neck. Blood bubbled at his lips and nose and streamed from his eyes like tears.

"You're the same as me, Ben Van Brunt. There's only one fate at the end of this path."

He laughed, a wild sound that had no place in the world, and then the laugh stopped abruptly. He reached toward me, and there were no hands on the ends of his wrists, only bleeding stumps.

"Don't leave me here alone," he said, his head teetering on the edge of his neck. "Don't. I'm so afraid."

I ran, heedless of where I stepped, ran from the ache of loneliness in his child's voice, ran from the guilt that told me

I should have done more when he was alive and that being a child myself was no excuse.

After a while I slowed, my breath ragged, with no knowledge of where I was or how far I'd come. I glanced behind me, worried that Cristoffel would have followed, but there was only darkness.

The Horseman, I thought. *I can't be distracted by haunts in the woods. I have to find the Horseman. He's the reason I came here.*

Brom's knife was still in my right hand, and I didn't resheathe it. I felt better holding it, even if it couldn't protect me from a ghost.

"Little witch."

Again, the voice hissed out of the darkness, this time on my right. I spun toward the noise, already knowing who would be there.

Diederick Smit watched me, his eyes full of hatred. He looked just as solid as Cristoffel had, and was surrounded by the same phosphorescent glow.

"Damned little witch. You killed my Justus and then you killed me."

"No," I said. "I didn't hurt Justus. I didn't."

"But you killed me, didn't you? Didn't hesitate for a moment. Didn't think of anyone except yourself. You picked up a rock and beat me until all my breath was gone."

"You hurt me," I said, and I was bothered by the pleading

in my voice, my need for him to understand. "You kidnapped me. You were going to kill me first."

I sounded small, pathetic, defensive. His eyes narrowed. His hands curled into those terrible fists, the ones that had smashed into my face and made me bleed.

"You deserved everything you got. You thought you could hurt my Justus and get away with it, thought being a Van Brunt kept you safe. You were always lording it over the rest of us, you and your parents before you, and Brom and Katrina worst of all. Always acting like money let them do whatever they wanted, pretending to be the benevolent landowners, doing good works and looking out for the village. But I knew better. I knew that they didn't really care, that they only wanted to feel important. And you treated my Justus the same, treated him like he was mud on your shoes."

I shook my head. "I didn't. He was always cruel to me, and to Sander, and I only defended us from him, and avoided him if I could."

I didn't know why I was trying to explain to Diederick Smit, trying to make him understand. He was beyond understanding.

"My boy wasn't like that! He was high-spirited, to be sure, but only the way a boy is supposed to be. You're the one who was unnatural. Whoever heard of a girl pretending to be a boy, dressing like a boy, cutting her hair like a boy, running wild like a boy? And people believed you, believed that you were something you weren't. That wasn't right. I knew that there was wrong in you because of that, knew that you had witchcraft."

I'd been prepared to defend myself, to shout him down, to tell him that I wasn't what he thought I was, but his last words arrested me.

There was something wrong in you.

There was something wrong in me. It wasn't my desire to be a boy, though. There was nothing wrong in that.

It was a thing I'd turned away from the moment I'd found it existed, but there was something in me that shouldn't be there, something that came from the most unnatural creature imaginable.

Schuler de Jaager, or whatever creature he really was beneath the skin he used to disguise himself. He was my grandfather. His blood, however diluted, was in my veins. Had the power of that blood somehow hurt Justus? Perhaps Diederick was right and I was responsible.

Diederick took a step in my direction, his face contorting. "Everything that happened was your fault. Justus. Me. My line ended because of you. And you buried me in the woods like a dog, like I wasn't worth anything at all. You couldn't even put me in the ground next to my son."

His face changed, the skin seeming to bubble and stretch and break, blood bursting from the open wounds.

"You beat me with a rock," he said, holding his hands to his face. "Look what you did to me."

"No," I said, squeezing my eyes closed.

I didn't want to see his face again, for the moment I saw those wounds I could feel it, could feel the smoothness of the stone in my hand—and it had been smooth, smooth and perfect like a skipping stone—and then the way his flesh gave way beneath it.

"Look at what you did to me," Diederick said.

"No!"

"Look at what you did to me."

His voice came from everywhere, from the trees and the brush and the very earth, reverberated through my head and pressed behind my eyes.

"No!" I shouted, and ran again, blind this time, terrified to look at what I'd done to Diederick Smit.

I'd killed him. I'd killed him and I'd never really faced that, just buried it away in the deep dark secret part of my heart, where I hid all the things that brought me shame. And when that secret tried to push its way out in the night, when I was asleep, I'd wake with a pounding heart and push it down again, pretend it never happened, pretend I didn't remember.

It didn't matter that he was going to kill me first. It didn't matter what he'd intended for me at all. I should have run instead of hurting him. I should have stopped hitting him before he went completely still.

I killed a man, and Katrina helped me bury him in the woods and we'd never talked about it again.

I heard Diederick's voice shouting after me, but I pretended I couldn't hear him, and soon his voice faded away. He hadn't followed me.

The stars were gone, hidden by the deep shadow all around. I wandered blind, bumping into trees, tripping over rocks and roots. I didn't know if I walked in a straight line or in circles, but I was afraid. I was afraid of what the woods would show me next, for I knew it wasn't done with me yet.

"Ben."

I hesitated, for I'd known somehow that it would be him, that it could only be him. I wanted to see him more than anyone in the world and also least of all.

"Ben," he said again.

I had to look. I had to see. I had to know if he blamed me.

There he was, bigger than life or death, and for a moment I thought I would run to him and leap into his arms and he would swing me up into the air and laugh that great booming laugh. If he laughed, all the shadows and the specters would go away and I'd be safe again.

"Opa," I said, but he didn't smile that Brom Bones smile and he didn't open his arms. He looked stern, a thing that Brom had never been in life.

"Ben," he said. "What are you doing?"

I withered under his gaze. "I was . . . I was only trying to . . . Oma made me promise and . . ."

"What makes you think you can do anything at all about Schuler de Jaager? I told you to stay away from him. I told you so many times and you didn't listen."

"Opa, it's not just Schuler. The Horseman—"

"There is no Horseman, Ben. I told you the story. You know that. You know better."

"Not the Horseman that you were, a different Horseman." I felt scrambled, like I didn't know what I thought I knew a moment before. Brom never acted like this, never talked over me and made me flustered and defensive.

"There's no other Horseman. There was only me, playing a prank. Now stop this nonsense and go home where you belong, Bente."

I stilled, staring at him. "Bente. You never call me Bente. You never did, not even when I was very small. Katrina always complained about it, that to you I was always Ben."

"I told you to go home," Brom said.

"You're not Brom," I said. "You're not even a shadow of him, or a shade. You're nothing like Brom at all."

He did smile then, a smile that wasn't Brom's, a smile that went too wide, covered too much of his face. The illusion that was Brom faded away, but I was left feeling that the teeth were still there, floating in the air.

Ben. Hurry.

The Horseman. I'd half-forgotten him, forgotten why I'd come into the woods in the first place. I'd been distracted by haunts that were meant to throw me off my path, meant to keep me from finding him.

There was only one person who'd want to keep me from finding the Horseman, only one person who'd fear my presence in the woods.

Schuler de Jaager.

"I'm coming," I said, and I didn't know if I was telling the Horseman or my monster grandfather. "I'm coming."

17

It wasn't long until I began to hear the whispers.

They were very soft at first, soft enough to mistake for something else—a rustle of wind, the scrape of my boots. Gradually they grew louder, not loud enough to be counted as anything other than a whisper, but loud enough to distract, loud enough that I felt like something was buzzing against my ear, like a mosquito that kept flying too close. I waved my hand from side to side, trying to make it stop, but it didn't stop.

"Go away," I said, because the noise was making me angry, making me forget about everything except the whispers. The worst part was that I couldn't make out any individual words—only the mass of sound, continuously pulsing.

I remembered the moment, so many years ago, when Sander and I went to the end of the path through the woods, and I stepped off into the place that was forbidden. I'd heard the whispers then, too, and just a few moments of it had made me sick and scared. Dread rose in me, and no matter how hard I tried to push it down, to convince myself I wasn't frightened, it didn't work.

I *was* scared, and I didn't know how to make it stop, or how to find the Horseman, or if I could save him when I did. I didn't know anything. I was only Ben Van Brunt, the last of my family name, and I didn't have any special powers.

Yet there I was, trudging through the woods despite all my fear and doubt, because the Horseman had called me and I had to go to him. It had always been so, I realized—from the time I was very small, even before I knew he was calling.

He was the north of the compass, and the needle inside me pointed to him. That was why I'd always gone to the woods, why I'd always felt something pulling me there. When I was young I hadn't thought about it. I'd only followed it.

For a while I'd feared that call, feared what it meant for me. Then I'd longed for it, longed for it in a way I still didn't fully understand. I'd thought I loved him, but it was more than love. It was a desire for something only he could give, but I still didn't entirely comprehend what that "something" was. It wasn't love, though. It was something in the way we were tied together, the way the Horseman had only been a whisper of a thought when I first saw him as a tiny child, the vague coalescence of the villagers' nightmares. But he'd reached for me and I'd believed in him, and my belief made him more than shade, more than shadow.

The Horseman had sprung from me, from my longing for

something greater than the world I know, for my need for something beautiful long before I could define that feeling. He'd been a nightmare to the people of the Hollow, but to me he was a dream, a dream of flying and of freedom.

I noticed that the whispers had subsided. They weren't gone entirely, but they had receded to a distance that allowed me to think. As soon as I thought this, the volume rose again.

The Horseman. Think of the Horseman, and nothing else.

The whispers receded again.

I just had to think of him, keep him as my true north and let him pull me in his direction.

Ben. Ben.

Keep his voice in your mind and go to him. There's nothing else here. There are no whispering goblins, no ghosts of your past. There isn't even a cloak of darkness. These are all obstacles that Schuler de Jaager put in your path. He's trying to block you. He's trying to stop you from getting to the Horseman. Why is he trying to stop you from getting to the Horseman?

And the truth burst through me like the moon emerging from behind the clouds. *Because he's afraid.*

Schuler de Jaeger was afraid of the Horseman, and afraid of what might happen if I went to the Horseman.

That meant the Horseman and I could hurt Schuler.

We could hurt him if we were together. Perhaps we could even defeat him.

Hurry, hurry, and this time it was my own voice in my

head urging me to him. I had to reach the Horseman, because he was weak and hurt, and he needed me. I had to reach him in time. I had to. Schuler was trying to prevent me from doing that very thing, and whatever Schuler wanted couldn't be good for me or for the Hollow.

The path before me opened up suddenly into a large clearing. The night sky was visible above, the stars brighter than I'd ever seen them. They shone down on the dark form folded in the center of the clearing—a man, or something like a man, though I'd never imagined him alone and horseless. He was on his knees, his head bent, his back curved, like the weight of everything was on him.

"Horseman," I said, and ran to him.

He looked up at me, and he appeared more earthly than the last time I'd seen him—less powerful, more human.

"Ben," he said. He sounded exhausted and relieved, and reached his hand out to me.

Darkness pooled around him. I thought at first that it was his cloak, but as I got closer I realized the darkness was a cloud around him, and that it was dissipating. It was dripping away from him. That's when I realized he was injured. Whatever had happened, however it happened, he was hurt badly enough to bleed—or whatever passed for blood when you were a creature of magic.

I stretched out my hand to take his in mine, but a moment before our fingertips touched I bumped up against something else in the way. There was a crackling noise, a smell like lightning, and then I was thrown backward, away from the Horseman.

Someone laughed, low and long and vicious. I pushed up and saw Schuler de Jaager, or rather the thing that passed as Schuler de Jaager, emerging from the trees.

"You didn't think you'd be able to free him so easily, did you, little Bente?"

He appeared old and hunched and frail, but his voice was powerful and his eyes burned, just like they had when he was part of Henrik Janssen.

"My name is Ben," I said.

He smirked at me. "Ah yes, the little caterpillar who wishes to be a butterfly. But you'll never transform, no matter how long or hard you wish it so. You'll always be a girl instead of the boy you wanted, the granddaughter instead of the grandson Brom wanted."

"Don't you dare speak of Brom," I said, hate surging inside me. "You're the one who made Crane a monster. You're the reason Brom is dead."

Schuler shrugged. "Don't think I'd weep for the great oaf."

"Why?" I asked, rage bubbling under the surface of my skin. I didn't know what to do with it, where to put it. "Why hurt Brom? Or Bendix? Why let your own daughter die? Why change Crane? Why hurt *him*?"

I pointed at the Horseman, who was unnaturally still as

he watched us. The stuff pulling away from his body had continued unabated, and he appeared less substantial by the moment. I had to do something, free him from his prison, but I didn't know how.

Schuler de Jaager followed my gaze, and his smug expression made me want to leap on him, beat him senseless the way I'd done to Diederick Smit. Smit hadn't deserved my rage, but Schuler did. Schuler was the reason Smit had taken me in the first place.

"Why?" Schuler said. "'Why?' you ask? Because, sweet girl, it's in my nature."

I knew he was trying to bait me, make me snap and argue, use up my energy trying to convince him to call me by the name I'd chosen for myself. I couldn't allow myself to rise. I had to think about the Horseman, think about freeing him and getting away from Schuler de Jaager.

He'd waited for a moment, to see if I would respond, and when I didn't, I thought I saw a hint of disappointment in his eyes.

"Remember the day you came to visit me, so long ago?"

He made it sound as though I'd chosen to see him, that I'd tripped into the village to have tea by some prearranged plan.

"Of course," I said. *Let him talk. Let him talk while you determine how to help the Horseman.*

"I told you a story then, about a creature that came from the old country."

"The Kludde," I said, remembering.

"I said that it had attached itself to the people of the Hollow, and that it took a sacrifice in exchange for the well-being of the village."

I nodded, but I wasn't really listening. My brain was scrambling through possible solutions, each one more absurd than the last.

"You *believed* me," Schuler de Jaager said, and the laughter in his voice brought me back from inside my head. "You actually believed it. I could see it in your eyes. You went away with such a serious look, like you were going to solve all the problems of Sleepy Hollow. I could hardly believe how easy it was to convince you."

"You didn't convince me," I said, feeling foolish. "Nothing you said made sense. It didn't fit the facts. You only wanted me to stay away from the woods, to keep me from the Horseman."

Schuler glanced back at the Horseman, who'd managed to stand and was pressed up against the invisible barrier. I felt the Horseman's anguish and his fury at Schuler.

"The Horseman shouldn't exist at all, you know," Schuler said. "He was only a story that Brom made up, and then the people of the Hollow started to believe it. The people of the Hollow will believe anything, and their belief willed him into being."

"But he's not like Brom's story. He's not a headless Hessian."

"He was, for a time. But then you came along and changed him, changed everything. You didn't think he was a headless Horseman and therefore he wasn't. You thought he was your protector, and therefore he was. And you did it without even knowing what you were doing, without realizing you had the power to do it. That was my own fault. I should have realized what could happen with my blood in you. I was so certain Bendix would have a son, you see. All the Van Brunts had sons, always. Sometimes they had daughters as the third or fourth child, but never the first. I'd wanted a boy, needed a boy to mold. It seemed such a fine idea to root my blood in some tree, to see how it would manifest. But then my weak human wife made a daughter, a talentless little nothing like herself. Then there was you. I was sure you'd be like Fenna, so I didn't bother with you. That was my mistake. I should have known that blood will out, always."

Blood. Schuler's blood. Schuler's blood in my body. Of course. Of course. That's the answer. Blood is always the answer. I just need to get closer to the Horseman's prison.

I inched sideways, trying to make it look as though my movement was just natural repellence, that I was only moving away because I didn't want to be near him. I needed to keep him talking, keep him thinking about his wonderful plot so he wouldn't notice.

Once I free the Horseman we can rid the world of Schuler de Jaager, and then we can ride away together. That is where I

belong, where I've always belonged. I should have left with him
years ago. Brom might be alive if I had.

"I don't understand. Why did you do any of this? Why
change Crane into a monster? Why torment Brom? Why kill
my father, let your own daughter die? What is it that you want
from us?" I made the last line a plaintive wail, certain Schuler
would interpret it as weakness.

I am not weak. I'm a Van Brunt, and I can win. Van Brunts
always win. I won't let him *win.*

Schuler laughed again, and his eyes flared flame-red. "Want
from you? You overestimate your own importance. Yes, the
Van Brunts have been a special project of mine, but the whole
village has been my plaything from the start. It's in my nature,
as I said."

"I don't understand," I said. I was nearly there. In a few
moments I would be able to reach out and touch the barrier.

"There are many things you don't understand, and couldn't
begin to. The world doesn't always have reasons. Sometimes
terrible things happen without justification, or simply because
someone wants them to happen."

His form shifted as I watched, grew larger with each
passing moment. The skin of the old man fell away, and
something unfolded from inside it, something huge and
horned, something made of flame and darkness. Something I
could only call a demon. It was the only word that I had, the
only way my brain could make sense of what it was seeing.

Katrina had always tried to instill in me a sense of respect for the greater power of the universe, dragging me (and Brom, who no more wanted to be there than I did) to church services every Sunday, reminding me to say my prayers before bed. But I'd never really believed in God. In the Hollow it was easy to believe in ghosts and goblins, in haunted woods, in the Headless Horseman, but somehow a benevolent deity seemed impossible.

As I watched Schuler de Jaager reveal his true self at last, I had to face the possibility that Katrina and the earnest reverend might have been right. Surely such terrible things couldn't exist in the world without some counterpoint. Surely there had to be someone good watching over us. There had to be hope.

Hope, and a little bit of luck, I thought as I watched his wings unfurl. They seemed to cover the sky, to blot out the night with a darkness more complete than I'd ever imagined.

Don't think about what he is, or what he can do. Think of the Horseman. You're nearly there.

"You ask why all these things happened, looking for some motivation, some rhyme or reason to help you understand," Schuler said. His voice was deeper, louder, and the sound of it was painful, made my very bones tremble. "There is no reason, no rhyme. There is no explanation, no greater plan. There is only me, and what I am, and what I have done to amuse myself while I am here."

His words arrested me, though the Horseman was in

reach now, though my plan was only moments away from being fulfilled.

"You did all that, caused so much pain, just *because*? So you could laugh at our human frailty, so you could entertain yourself?"

"Don't sound so outraged, little Bente. I told you, I only did what was in my nature. The life of this world is long, much longer than you think, and I have been a part of it for eons."

"That doesn't give you the right to meddle, to ruin, to destroy," I said, fresh anger bubbling inside me. "That doesn't give you the right to toy with our lives, to crush our striving beneath your boot."

He laughed. I hated that laugh so much, wanted to stop up his mouth so I wouldn't have to hear it. "I can do whatever I please, little Bente, and you cannot stop me."

I drew Brom's knife from its sheath with my left hand, the one that was always gloved because of the mutilated fingers. Schuler snorted.

"Do you think you can harm me with that pathetic human blade?"

"Who said I was going to use it to harm you?" I said, and drew the blade over my right palm, slamming my bloodied hand on the barrier that imprisoned the Horseman. "And my *name* is *Ben*."

"No!" Schuler shouted, and for the first time I saw something like panic in his eyes.

I couldn't see the barrier but I felt it drop, felt the surge of anger from the Horseman. I felt a moment of triumph, was certain victory was in our grasp. I assumed he would charge at Schuler de Jaager, would fight the demon-form, but instead he swayed on the spot and fell forward. Without the barrier to hold him up the Horseman had no strength.

"No," I said, and ran to his side. I tried to put my arm around him, to help him, but there was nothing for me to hold on to. He was insubstantial as a ghost, fading away before my eyes.

"No," I said again. How could this be? How could the Horseman die? He was eternal, always riding beneath the stars. That was where I was supposed to be—with him, riding forever.

Schuler laughed again, laughed with the self-satisfied attitude of a man—a demon—who's not worried about getting what he wants. The Horseman was dying, and he knew it. Schuler had worried enough about the Horseman joining forces with me that the demon had hurt the Horseman, imprisoned him, hoped he would die before I arrived.

Now it seemed it didn't matter, that even my destruction of the barrier wouldn't free the Horseman. I was too late. I'd turned away from the Horseman for too long, pretended I couldn't hear him calling me. How long had he been inside the cage, hoping for my arrival? How long had he called my name in vain?

Ben, the Horseman said. ***He's weakened me too much.***

I was crying, and I was tired of crying, tired of watching everyone I loved die in front of me. The Horseman couldn't die. If the Horseman died then I was really and truly alone, alone in the woods with a demon whose blood ran in my veins.

"I'm sorry," I said. I was grieving for myself as much as him, grieving for Brom and Katrina and Bendix and Fenna, grieving for the farm that I'd sold, the house that burned down and the friend I'd left behind. There was nothing left for me, only a life of painful memories, memories of the ways I might have changed things, might have saved Brom, protected Katrina, reached the Horseman in time. "I'm sorry."

Ben. This was always meant to be.

His hand went around mine, more substantial than the rest of him.

Let me in.

I stared at the Horseman, not understanding. Schuler was talking again, but I wasn't listening, his words a mass of noise and triumph. He was celebrating the death of the Horseman, his rival, but the Horseman wasn't dead yet.

I looked into the Horseman's eyes.

Let me in.

And then I understood. The Horseman *couldn't* die. The Horseman couldn't die because the Horseman was immortal, the Horseman was life itself. Inside the Horseman was the part of me that I'd used to make him real, and that magic had become something greater and stronger than before. The Horseman had watched over me until I was grown. And now that I was grown we would always ride fierce and free and together under the stars, but not the way I'd imagined we would.

We would be so much more than I ever imagined.

"Yes," I said.

I thought it would be a rush of power, a sweeping hurricane force that surged through me. Instead it was quiet, like the first soft wind of autumn rustling the curtains—cold enough to chill but not to freeze, pulling a few fallen leaves in its wake.

It was as if I stood alone in a quiet forest, the scent of the earth and the trees and the sky filling up my lungs, coursing through my blood.

He was the forest and the wind and the sky, he was the stars and the earth and everything. He was coursing through my blood. He was part of me, the life inside my heart. I'd always wanted this, even when I didn't know what I wanted.

The Horseman became me and I became the Horseman. I was a butterfly unfurling its wings for the first time, a creature of earth tasting the air. Everything inside me that felt half-formed was renewed, was complete.

I was Ben Van Brunt, the last son of the line of Brom Bones and Katrina Van Tassel, and I was the Horseman of Sleepy Hollow, as I was always meant to be.

I stood before Schuler de Jaager, that nameless demon who'd wrought misery on Sleepy Hollow for so long. He screamed, howled fury that was meant to break me, summoned fire to frighten me.

His fury was only sound and air, had no power to injure me.

He could hurt the Horseman when the Horseman was only a single being. He could hurt me when I was only Ben. But any storm he sent now that we were one broke over us, broke and washed away without harm.

"You're nothing, nothing, nothing!" the demon shouted. "You're only a shadow of Brom, you have no power!"

It seemed he was only choosing things at random, trying to convince me that I had no value. If he could only convince me then I would submit, and he would win.

But I knew my own value. I'd gone into the woods to save the Horseman even when I didn't know how I would save him, had gone forward even when I was afraid. I'd always forged my own path—had felt safe to do so because Brom and Katrina had watched over me, had given me the great gift of their love.

Schuler de Jaager had never known love—not as a human, not as a demon. Love drove him away, made him small. I realized then why Schuler de Jaager had left the village after Brom died. I'd thought it was because he'd achieved something he wanted to achieve—Brom's death. But it wasn't. It was because Brom died for me, died to save me, and that kind of love and sacrifice is a shield that repels evil. It kept the demon away for ten years.

Brom's knife had fallen to the ground. I picked it up, and as I did I noticed that my broken fingers were whole again. I hefted the knife in my hand, saw my own blood on the blade.

Blood is its own kind of magic. It sustains life. It carries our history, all the blood that came before us. Brom's blood had spilled onto that knife when he died. It had mixed with Crane's blood—Crane, who'd taken Bendix's blood inside his own body, whose life and death had been so inexplicably intertwined with the Van Brunts. Crane, another victim of Schuler de Jaager's mischief.

I ran toward the great demon who'd tormented us for so long, who'd tried so hard to make me his victim. As I ran, I said their names.

"Fenna. Bendix. Crane. Katrina. Brom."

I thought Schuler would run, would fly away, would slash at me with his demon claws, would spit fire and venom. But each name I spoke was like a chain that bound him to earth, and he shrank as I said those names, until he was nothing but Schuler de Jaager again—a frail old man made of dust and spite.

The knife slid in between his ribs, pierced the withered muscle that used to be his heart.

He screamed, and grew and swelled again into the great demon. The knife in his chest looked comically small, the pathetic prick of a needle on a fingertip, but blood was its own kind of magic, and even Schuler de Jaager couldn't deny it.

The demon's body contorted. Light burst from the wound in his chest, followed by a torrent of darkness like buzzing insects pouring forth in a shifting cloud. His body folded in on itself, disappeared bit by bit as the insects gushed into the air. The insects spiraled up into the sky, and flew away into the night, off to a place that had nothing to do with Sleepy Hollow.

He might return one day. I knew that was possible. But he wouldn't find any purchase there again. The Horseman protected me so I could become the Horseman. I would protect the woods and the Hollow now, keep everyone's children safe from harm.

I didn't have to summon my horse. He was simply there, and then we were riding, riding, riding as I'd always dreamed, part of the wind and air and sky and stars, free to be the self I'd always dreamed of being.

I rode all the rest of the night, and just before dawn, when I felt the pull to return to the woods, I stopped under Sander's window.

"I'll keep you safe," I said. "I'll keep you safe, and your children, and your children's children. I'll always watch over you."

I'd turned away already when I heard the shutters opening.

"Ben?" Sander called.

I looked back, wondering if he could see me, but he squinted into the darkness, his gaze everywhere but on me. I smiled to myself, and sent a gust of wind to ruffle his hair.

"Ben," he said again, and this time there was wonder in his voice.

I rode into the night, and wondered if he heard the hoofbeats fading into the distance.

Once upon a time I was Ben Van Brunt, the only grandchild of Abraham Van Brunt and Katrina Van Tassel, the last child of the bloodline of legends.

Now I am the Horseman, and I ride every night through Sleepy Hollow, and keep watch there.

You might feel the wind as I pass, or hear the sound of a galloping horse, but there's no need to fear. I'm not coming for your head. That's a story some people told once, and a story is only a story.

A story is only a story, unless it comes true, and that did happen once in the Hollow. I heard the story of the Horseman when I was small, even when Katrina tried to keep it from my ears, and because Sleepy Hollow believed in him, the Horseman became real. Because I believed in him, he became something else entirely.

Now he's part of me, because this was the story ending I always wanted.

I ride through the night. I watch over your children, and keep them safe. I'll wait for the one who can hear me when I call, the one who wants to ride fierce and free under the stars, the one who believes.

Listen for me.

I am the legend of Sleepy Hollow.

I am the Horseman.

ABOUT THE AUTHOR

Christina Henry is a horror and dark fantasy author whose works include *Near the Bone, The Ghost Tree, Looking Glass, The Girl in Red, The Mermaid, Lost Boy, Alice,* and *Red Queen.*

She enjoys running long distances, reading anything she can get her hands on and watching movies with samurai, zombies and/or subtitles in her spare time. She lives in Chicago with her husband and son.

For more fantastic fiction, author events,
exclusive excerpts, competitions, limited editions and more

VISIT OUR WEBSITE
titanbooks.com

LIKE US ON FACEBOOK
facebook.com/titanbooks

FOLLOW US ON TWITTER AND INSTAGRAM
@TitanBooks

EMAIL US
readerfeedback@titanemail.com